CRESCENT CITY BLUES

Concho Book Four

A.W. Hart

WOLFPACK
PUBLISHING
— EST 2013 —

WOLFPACK PUBLISHING
— EST 2013 —

The characters and events portrayed in this book are fictitious. Any similarity to real persons, living or dead, is coincidental and not intended by the author.

Text copyright © 2021 A.W. Hart
Special thanks to Charles Gramlich for his contribution to this novel.

Published by Wolfpack Publishing
5130 S. Fort Apache Road, 215-380
Las Vegas, NV 89148

Paperback IBSN 978-1-63977-073-1
eBook ISBN 978-1-63977-072-4

CRESCENT CITY BLUES

CHAPTER 1

Bourbon Street. New Orleans.

Texas Ranger Concho Ten-Wolves stepped through the door of Lafitte's Blacksmith Shop Bar into a gumbo of smells. Beer. Sweet whiskey. People and their perfumes. It was a little after 8:30 PM in early December.

He'd been ten hours on the road, coming out of Eagle Pass, Texas, on US Highway 57 north, to I-35 north, to I-10 east, which he'd picked up in San Antonio. Six hundred and eighty-five miles. The last half mile had seen the heaviest traffic—the foot traffic on Bourbon as he'd made his way to Lafitte's through the crowds of tourists and locals.

It was a long way from the Kickapoo reservation outside Eagle Pass where he lived. He'd been to New Orleans before but only stopped briefly in the French Quarter. It was not his kind of scene. But a phone call from an acquaintance with whom he had a complicated history had promised information on an old and personal mystery he'd like to see solved.

The "information" was probably a dead end, just as other leads he'd followed in the past had been. But he was off work for a few more weeks as he recovered from a gunshot wound taken in the line of duty. And he'd started to get under the feet of Maria Morales, the woman he loved. She loved him too, but wasn't used to having his considerable attention 24/7.

Lafitte's was the oldest building used as a bar in the United States. It had been built sometime between 1722 and 1732. The Lafitte brothers, Jean and Pierre, were rumored to have used the building to vend the loot they obtained in the Gulf of Mexico through piracy and smuggling. Thus, the name.

Concho doubted any pirates hid here tonight among the crowd of twenty or so patrons. He couldn't rule out a serial killer or two. As he wove through the crowd toward a potential drink, he glimpsed two women loitering near a side exit to the building— one tall, exotic, and athletic-looking, the other a little shorter, platinum blonde and striking. Neither held a drink. Maybe they were too young. The taller girl looked it.

The taller one also seemed familiar, though not necessarily because he'd seen her before. She looked like someone he already knew. The woman's glance met his. She had green eyes against Spanish-dark skin, and dark hair nearly as long as his Texas-girlfriend's—Maria Morales—though this woman also had red highlights. A frown crossed her face, followed by a flash of recognition. Apparently, she knew *him*.

Concho relied often on his instincts. They told him this encounter was important. He made an abrupt left and started toward the two women. People milled about in his way. He sidestepped left and right. The taller woman saw his change of direction and muttered something to her companion, then slipped out the door at her back.

Ten-Wolves reached the same door a moment later. The blonde woman stood in his way. She stuck a palm against his chest as she smiled and offered a "Hey, Handsome!" He smiled back but didn't stop walking. His hands grasped her shoulders gently. He picked her up, took two steps out through the door, and set her down again to one side.

She gasped, with her eyes dilated as the Ranger walked around her. He could see no sign of the taller woman, though it had been no more than a few seconds since she'd gone out. A patio stood to the right of the door, with long tables and an open wrought iron gate. Concho peered through the gate. Half a dozen men and women lounged at the tables with booze in front of them. None were the woman he sought.

The lot next to Lafitte's held a beautiful wooden house painted yellow, with black shutters. A hedge wall of brilliant green isolated it from the street. Concho started along the sidewalk past the hedge.

The blonde called to him. "Wait!" He didn't respond. Instead, he broke into a trot along the sidewalk. Past the yellow house stood a building of dull, reddish-brown brick. Next to that ran a narrow alley, with a black gate pushed open. The address read 927 Bourbon Street.

Concho turned into the alley. It seemed the only place the woman could have gone to escape his view so quickly. A half dozen steps down the alley, a big dark man leaned against the wall. He straightened as he saw the Ranger. Something weapon-like, about two feet long, hung casually in his hand, a truncheon of some sort.

"Best go back the way you came," the man said. He smacked the truncheon into the palm of his other hand by way of a threat.

"Too late," Concho said.

"Too late for what?"

The Ranger smiled. "You let me get too close."

The man realized what Concho meant. His eyes flashed. He started to swing up the truncheon but the Ranger lunged forward, his left hand snapping down to lock on his opponent's wrist. His right hand grabbed the man's shirt collar, and he twisted him up against the wall on the right while he yanked the wrist behind him. The man cried out; his grip on the truncheon weakened and Concho took it away from him.

"Struggle and I break your arm," Concho said.

"You let 'im loose now!" a Cajun accented voice said from the mouth of the alley, "or I fillet you like a redfish."

Concho turned his head. A much smaller man loitered at the mouth of the alley. No more than 5'5" but built as wiry as a greyhound. A worn ball cap covered his head. Black rubber boots encased his feet. A straight bladed knife, at least ten inches long, glittered in his hand.

Concho pushed the big man toward the smaller one. Since he hadn't come here on official business, the Ranger wasn't wearing his badge, nor the twin Colt Double Eagle .45s he usually carried at his waist. He had a snub-nosed Smith & Wesson .38 tucked into an ankle holster but wasn't ready to take it that far yet.

Besides, this felt more personal than a bullet. He hefted the truncheon, which turned out to be a wooden nightstick with *Louisville Slugger* etched into the side of the shaft. He hadn't wanted any trouble but it looked like someone planned to provide him some. Sudden anger rode his shoulders and burned in his muscles; a snarl curled his lips.

"Bring it!" he snapped.

The small man blinked. The big man grabbed his arm, yanked him back toward the street. "Come on. Ain't worth it. Too late for him now, anyway."

The small man took a breath; he stepped back with his companion. The knife disappeared up a sleeve as if it had never been, and the two men faded toward the street and disappeared.

Concho took a few deep breaths and felt his muscles unknot. He looked down the alley, and sighed. The big man had been right. It was too late to catch the woman now. She was long gone, whoever she'd been.

CHAPTER 2

Concho returned to Lafitte's bar. As expected, the blonde woman who'd tried to block his way to her friend had disappeared, too. He puzzled over the oddness of this whole encounter. In his first moments in a bar where he'd never been, a woman, who looked familiar but whom he was sure he'd never seen, had fled after one good glimpse of him. Three other people had tried to cover for her. Nothing in the situation made sense.

A man standing at the bar ordering libations caught the Ranger's attention. Like Concho's own long hair, the man's black Kickapoo hair was held back by a leather band of rawhide. Other than that, the fellow was dressed very differently from Concho's jeans and long-sleeved t-shirt. His choices in clothing would have been exotic in most places but weren't overly remarkable in the French Quarter. He wore buckskin trousers decorated with fringe and an open vest of the same material over a sleeveless black silk shirt. A choker of polished bone encircled his neck.

The bartender handed the man his drinks. As the fellow turned with them in his hands, he saw Concho. A flicker of a smile crossed his features and he gave a little jerk of his chin as an invitation to join him. Concho followed out the front door and found the man seated at one of two wrought iron tables along the sidewalk just outside the bar. The Ranger sat as well, placing the confiscated Louisville Slugger nightstick he still carried on the table.

Bourbon Street teemed with Saturday evening traffic. Pedestrians only. No automobiles. Men and women of every variety wove past, some in casual outfits, others in suits and dresses. Many carried go-cups of beer; others sipped through straws from fluorescent green plastic containers with the bottom shaped like a hand grenade. Noise created a constant hubbub, a mixture of voices from the people of the street and party music from half a dozen nearby venues, including Lafitte's where a piano had started to jangle.

The fellow across from Concho set a plastic cup of yellowish beer down in front of the Ranger and gestured toward the nightstick. "For me?" he asked in English.

Though both men could speak Kickapoo, the native language would have called undue attention to itself in this setting. Concho replied in kind:

"Ran into the local welcoming committee a few minutes ago. They left it with me. You can have it if you want."

A low chuckle came back. "No need. But do you ever wonder why trouble follows you everywhere, Ten-Wolves?"

"Always figured it was just part of my skill set, but maybe you have another explanation?"

"Your spirit is too much at war with itself. The halves fight each other. The African half. The Kickapoo half. This attracts conflict from without as well."

"What about you? Two halves yourself. Kickapoo and Apache."

"They are not so different as yours. But it wouldn't matter anyway. I have reconciled them."

"Maybe you should write a book for the less fortunate."

The man shrugged. "Perhaps I will."

"All therapy aside," Concho said, "why'd you invite me here, Bull Knife? What is it you have to tell me about my mother?"

Other than the name, Concho knew very little about the young man sitting across from him. Some five months before, Bull Knife had shown up on the Ranger's Kickapoo reservation in Texas with two other young Kickapoo from the Oklahoma tribe. All three had been involved with the NATV Bloods, an Indian gang. Or so Concho had thought. Certainly, all three had been involved with a criminal named Jacob Drake, who'd been trying to corner the drug market on the Rez.

Bull Knife had even led Concho into a trap, although he'd also warned him of it at the last minute. And later, Bull Knife saved Concho's life when he shot a man who'd put a blade in his back and was about to finish him.

The last time Concho had seen Bull Knife was when the man visited him in the hospital and gave him the key to convicting Jacob Drake of the murder of Ben Deer-Run, who'd been the Ranger's friend. After that, Bull Knife had vanished—until a day ago when he'd called Concho with a request to meet him in New Orleans. Supposedly, the issue concerned the Ranger's mother, who'd disappeared when he was a baby.

According to Concho's grandmother, who'd raised him until she'd been murdered by the NATV Bloods, his mother was dead. She'd never told him anything else. Maybe she hadn't known. He'd always wondered how and where his mother had died. Over the years he'd searched haphazardly for clues. To no avail.

"Your mother," Bull Knife said in response to Concho. "Do you not wonder why *I* should know anything about *your* mother?"

"The question had occurred." Concho picked up the beer Bull Knife had given him. It smelled sour. After a sip, he made a face. "You pee in this cup?"

"If I had, it would taste better and be much stronger. It's why I am drinking water. But I know of your love for the white man's beer."

Concho hardly ever drank actually but felt no urge to share that with the present company. "Tell me," he said, putting down the cup, "why is it you *do* know something about my mother?"

Though the gene seemed to have skipped Concho, many Indians were born storytellers with a gift for drama. Bull Knife had the talent. And it could be irritating at moments like this.

The half-Kickapoo, half-Apache took a sip of water and cleared his throat. He gazed across the table to meet Concho's gaze, black agate eyes against dark brown-gold. He drew a deep breath.

Good thing I got the patience gene, Concho thought to himself. *Or I'd kill him right now.*

"Because," Bull Knife intoned, "she is *my* mother, too. We are brothers. Half brothers, at least." He straightened his shoulders as he took another deep breath, revealing the swell of young muscles in his arms and underneath his shirt. "My father was Apache!" he added, with a clear touch of pride.

Concho scarcely heard the last words. He was still in shock from the first ones. It seemed crazy, but as the shock drained away, certain events he'd questioned began to make sense.

"That's why you saved my life by shooting Cole Chase a few months back," he said. "Even though it wouldn't have been what your employer of the time, Jacob Drake, wanted?"

"Drake was never my employer. I thought I could work with him. I was wrong. More than I have ever been."

"You did give me the key to bringing him down," Concho admitted. "Are you still a member of the NATV Bloods? I've got no love for that bunch."

"I am only myself. Like my father, who raised me."

Concho nodded. "The Apache. Right. Well, Mister Half-Apache, my father came from a much larger tribe than yours."

"Oh, and what tribe is that?"

"Drug dealers."

Bull Knife smirked. "You joke because you don't know what to say."

"You're right," Concho agreed. He drew and exhaled a big breath. "It's quite a revelation. It'll take some getting used to. If it's true."

"It's true. And there's more."

CHAPTER 3

A man and a woman passing along Bourbon Street paused near the table where Concho and Bull Knife sat. Both had brownish hair and unremarkable features. The man wore a suit, with a tie askew. The woman had on a cotton print dress with no stockings and sensible black heels. She cursed as she rummaged through her purse.

"My cell phone!" she complained.

"Did you leave it at the hotel?" the man asked.

"I don't know. I didn't think so." She rummaged some more while the man checked his own pockets as if he might find the phone in one. A minute passed as traffic wove and muttered around the couple on either side.

"Oh, here it is," the woman said. "In one of the side pockets. Whew!"

She glanced up. Her gaze took in the two men sitting at the table in front of Lafitte's. She gave them each a blank smile.

Her husband-boyfriend-significant other took her arm. "Good. Let's go. We'll be late."

"Of course, dear."

The two moved along.

***

Concho's gaze followed the couple as they disappeared down the street. He glanced over at Bull Knife, who watched intently and suspiciously.

"Is that some of the 'more'?" the Ranger asked.

Bull Knife shrugged. "Perhaps. My inquiries *have* attracted interest."

"From?"

"Parties unknown. But maybe those were just tourists." He added, "There have been threats."

"Over this?"

Bull Knife nodded. "Someone does not wish me to continue along this path."

Concho frowned. "That makes no sense. Who would care about a Kickapoo woman long dead?"

"Tell me," Bull Knife said abruptly, "what do you know of our mother? Including her death?"

Concho considered what to say. He hardly knew Bull Knife. He couldn't be sure the fellow was telling the truth about them being brothers, though he also couldn't imagine why anyone would make up such a lie.

"My grandmother refused to speak much of her," he finally answered. "She ran off from the Rez. Took up with a man my grandmother didn't like. She came back with me about a year later. Left again to work. Without me. Supposedly in Las Vegas, I found out later. She sent money home for a while. Then the money stopped. Communication stopped. She disappeared. When I was about ten, grandmother told me she'd died."

"That can't be true."

A surge of anger swelled in Concho at hearing his grandmother called a liar. He fought it down. "Why?"

"I'm nine years younger than you. If our mother died when you were ten, I would have been only a year old. I would have no memories of her. But I do. She left my father when I was almost six. I know this because I have a birthday card she sent me on my sixth."

"I thought you were raised by your father?"

He nodded. "After the age of six. For most of my life. But she lived with us for those first five and a half years. Lived!"

A complex stew of emotions rose in Concho—sadness for Bull Knife's loss and his own, anger at a mother he didn't remember, even jealousy that Bull Knife had been granted a few years with that mother. It took him a minute to process it all, and to control it.

"So, what do *you* know about her?" he asked.

"Beautiful. Hair like a black flag of silk. Cheekbones sharp enough to cut the sky. At times she was still, at others only movement. Her eyes were like caverns, like an abyss. Sometimes warm. Often distant. My father called her 'Raven.' I never knew her real name until I began searching for her."

"Cakiwiiskenoohihkwee," Concho said. "Sparrow Woman. Though grandmother called her Wiskenoa."

"Yes."

"She left when you were about six? What happened to her?"

"My father said she went to California, to Los Angeles. After the birthday card for my sixth, I heard no more from her. Two years later my father, too, told me she'd died. In an automobile wreck."

"And what have you found since?"

"At twenty I went to Los Angeles. She had been there, I found out. She danced…" a look of pain flashed briefly across the young man's face before disappearing. "She danced in a gentlemen's club."

Concho huffed a breath. He'd expected as much, though he still hadn't wanted to hear it. All the rumors about his mother from his childhood claimed she was a druggie. And he knew from his years as a law officer where young female drug addicts often ended up—dancing in strip clubs or prostitution. Or both.

"And from there?" he asked.

Bull Knife shook his head. "She was only at that place a few weeks. Then she vanished again. No one seemed to be around who actually knew her."

"Not unusual. Those kinds of places have a high turnover rate."

"I did find a death report on a dancer named Raven Sweet. A car accident. The body had been cremated but it sounded like her."

"So, why are we here? In New Orleans? You could have told me this in Texas."

"Texas provided the key. It led me to Las Vegas."

"How?"

"I thought I had let my mother go. But in Texas. On the reservation. I met Donnell Blackthorne. Your father. Before he was murdered."

"I see."

"In my conversations with him, most about you, I found out *your* mother was my mother. And I heard about Las Vegas. I went there after I left your Rez. Five months ago. I found another dancer's name. Little Sparrow. I found another death certificate. Again, an auto accident and a cremation. Again, a woman who sounded like my Raven mother."

"Two deaths," Concho said.

"Which perhaps means…none. I don't believe our mother is dead. I believe she's here. In New Orleans or somewhere close by. I intend to find her. I thought you might want to help."

The emotions broke free in Concho again, like two storm fronts colliding, one cold, one hot. He took a swig of his horrible beer to give himself a chance to think. Finally, he asked in what he hoped was a calm voice, "What led you to New Orleans?"

"When…Wiskenoa and Donnell Blackthorne left Texas, they first came here. He had a sister near here. They stayed with her for a while. But they also spent time in the city. Our mother liked New Orleans, it seems. Claimed it felt like a home. He was the one who insisted on taking them to Las Vegas. She never wanted to leave. It's where you were born. In a place called Charity Hospital."

"Seems like *you* should have been the detective in the family. In a few months you've uncovered more than I ever have."

"I spoke to a man who was there. Donnell Blackthorne."

Ten-Wolves remembered months back being told that a murder victim found on the Rez had been identified as his long-missing father. He'd felt nothing. He'd never known the man or anything about him. But now, for the first time, a flash of regret crossed his thoughts.

"I wonder why he didn't approach me," he said. "I found out he was on the Rez for over a week before he was killed. But I never even saw him in that time."

"He talked about approaching you. He wanted to. But I think he was afraid."

Concho huffed a quick breath. "Probably with good reason. I'm not sure how I would have reacted to finding out he was my father."

"Perhaps you would have blamed him for our mother's death. You had no reason to believe she was not dead."

"No. No reason. All right, I'm in. I can give it a week. We start with the sister. Blackthorne's sister. You know how to find her?"

"No. But I believe you will be able to do so."

CHAPTER 4

Bull Knife had ridden into town on a bus and had a cheap room at the edge of the French Quarter. But while Concho had been on the road from Texas, he'd booked a room at the Hotel Monteleone on Royal Street in the Quarter. He headed there after agreeing to meet his new "half brother" in the morning to start their quest for Donnell Blackthorne's sister.

The Monteleone had valet parking but it was expensive. Concho had left his silver Ford F-150 in a different parking garage near the hotel. He stopped by now to pick up what little luggage he'd hauled along.

The garage reached six stories but he'd managed to find a parking space on the upper part of the second floor. He walked up, feeling the need to stretch his legs after all his time sitting this day. It was after 11:00 PM. The garage was lit like twilight on a rainy day. It felt cold, too, as if the tons of cement around him exuded refrigerated air.

In early December, many parts of the country fought with snow. Not New Orleans. The temperature hovered around sixty degrees Fahrenheit outside and was maybe a few degrees cooler in the garage. Concho's only concession to the chill was the long-sleeved black shirt he wore.

The click-click of his truck unlocking made a lonely sound in the vast building. The garage was partially open to the air and the moon spilled in a syrupy gold light to paint a little magic across the concrete. He felt a certain peace inside himself, despite, or perhaps because of, the pending search for final answers about his mother. That peace popped like a soap bubble when footsteps sounded up the ramp he'd just traversed.

Leaving his truck open and his suitcase in the vehicle's extended cab, the Ranger stepped to where he could see who was coming. Two men approached, both African American, both big. One was as tall as the Ranger himself, at least six-four, and probably carried an extra twenty pounds over and above Concho's two-sixty. The men stopped about five feet from Concho and stared.

"How nice of the garage to send me help for my luggage," Concho said, "but I can manage. I don't tip all that well anyway."

The men smirked. Neither moved. More footsteps came up the ramp and a short, Cajun-looking fellow strode up and stopped between them. He wore a ball cap and fisherman's rubber boots. Concho recognized him.

"Didn't we just meet a little while ago?" he asked the short man. "I believe you mistook me for a fish. Said something about 'gutting' me."

"You de funny fellow," the short guy replied. "But you ain't so smart. Mebbe you new to de city. We teach you a lesson on local manners."

"Just the three of you?"

"All it gonna take."

"Who sent you? The woman from Lafitte's?"

"No one sen' us," the man said, grinning. "I decide you wan' some lesson." He glanced at his two companions. "Boys!"

The two big men, the muscle-heavy enforcers for this operation, pulled expandable batons from their belts and flicked them out to a full length of about twenty-four inches. Concho smiled, and let it linger. He'd been told he looked like a shark when he smiled this way. He liked that thought, although the people he showed it to usually didn't.

Concho moved to place a big column of concrete behind him so his enemies couldn't encircle him. To his right was an open rectangular space between the floors, like a glassless window. He glanced out, saw an awning beneath them and the dirty concrete floor of an alley full of trash bins. Reaching behind his back he pulled out the Louisville Slugger baton he'd confiscated earlier.

"Look," he said. "I've got one, too. Maybe we could start a club. Get it? Club?"

The biggest of the two enforcers lunged forward, chopping his baton downward at Concho's skull. The Ranger parried with his own baton. The click-clack echoed in the garage.

At almost the same instant, the second enforcer rushed, thrusting his club toward Ten-Wolves' belly. Concho whipped his baton across, blocking this blow, too. He snapped the tip of his Slugger up, catching the man hard across the cheekbone. No doubt the blow hurt, but it did little real damage.

The first attacker came in again. Concho interposed his baton as the man rained blows down on it, trying by main strength to beat down the Ranger's defense. The second man spat blood and came to his companion's aid.

Concho's feet moved almost in a dance as he swayed and ducked. His Slugger whipped back and forth as he parried any blow that came his way. The night rang with clicks and clacks and grunts of effort.

"Might a well take you beatin'," the Cajun boss man shouted above the din. "Won't hurt as much in de end."

Concho didn't respond. He'd only been out of the hospital for a few weeks after being shot, but he'd worked intensely to regain his speed, strength and endurance. Most of it had come back, but could the same hold true for the two bully boys he faced? For the moment he could do nothing but defend and conserve his energy, but he doubted his foes had the stamina for a long-term battle.

Already, both men were breathing hard.

The biggest attacker poured sweat. It coated his face like a film and drenched his wife-beater t-shirt. His attack faltered. Concho whipped a quick sidearm blow at the second man, sent him skittering backward. Then the Ranger twisted toward the first man again. He plunged the tip of the Louisville slugger deep into the softening belly of the enforcer. The man gasped, doubled over. Yellow vomit sprayed across the concrete.

Concho snapped his baton up and back down in one swift movement. The blow cracked the fellow on the skull behind the ear. He cried out, stumbled forward and went to his knees in his own vomit.

The second enforcer lunged to protect his companion. At the same time, the Cajun cried out in rage and rushed to the attack, drawing the long fillet knife he'd already threatened the Ranger with.

The second enforcer was the closest threat. Concho met his charge, slid inside his reach. He partially blocked the swing of the man's nightstick with an elbow into the fellow's forearm. The nightstick thudded against Concho's side but had no strength behind it. Ten-Wolves whipped his own club into the fellow's knee. The joint gave out; the man dropped with a bellow of pain.

"Sum bitch!" the Cajun shouted.

The short man slashed at the Ranger with his knife. Concho blocked with his Slugger, then whipped the stick up for a strike into the face. Teeth cracked audibly in the man's mouth. Blood spumed as he threw his free hand to his lips. Concho brought his stick down like an ax into the Cajun's wrist. The bone snapped with the sound of a breaking twig; the knife went flying.

A high-pitched scream split the night. Concho bum-rushed the knifeman, forcing him back toward the open wall of the garage. The man fumbled at the pocket of his trousers with his good hand. The butt of a snub-nosed revolver appeared, but before he could finish drawing the weapon Concho latched onto his belt, levered him up, and thrust him out into the night.

The Cajun screamed again as he fell. He pinwheeled into the awning below, bounced off and out before slamming face-first into the concrete floor of the alley. He emitted a groan, showing he was still alive, but made no attempt to get up.

Concho turned. The second enforcer had pulled the first one to his feet. They'd dropped their clubs and limped away as swiftly as they could. Concho let them go. He picked up one of the expandable batons, folded it back into itself, and stuck it in his pocket. The Louisville Slugger, he deposited in his truck before pulling out his suitcase. Another glance into the alley showed the Cajun stumbling away holding his right arm close to his body.

"Good," Concho murmured to himself. "Didn't want to kill anyone on my first night in New Orleans."

As he turned away, his foot struck something that skittered across the concrete. The fillet knife the Cajun had carried. Concho put his boot on the blade. Covering his hand with the sleeve of his shirt to avoid leaving fingerprints, he grasped the knife handle. He bent it upward until the weapon snapped. After kicking it against the wall, he plucked up his suitcase and headed for his hotel.

Time to put a period on an eventful day and night.

CHAPTER 5

Concho's cell phone rang as he entered the quiet lobby of the Hotel Monteleone. He answered as soon as he saw the caller ID.

"Maria!" he said warmly. "Glad you called. Figured you'd be in bed by now, though."

"Figured you wouldn't. Not with all the excitement of the French Quarter at your fingertips."

"It *has* been a full evening."

"Uh-huh? Not with any of those New Orleans' ladies, I trust."

Concho had been dating Maria Morales pretty seriously for the past five months. He'd saved her from a Neo-Nazi terrorist. She'd nursed him through a knife to the back and a gunshot wound. They'd made love, and argued, and made love some more. When not making love or arguing, they'd eaten dinners both romantic and otherwise. They'd watched movies and taken walks. He'd read her poetry.

He'd seen Maria angry and in the throes of passion. He'd groaned at her puns and laughed at her dirty jokes. He'd talked her through sad moments and just tried to hang on when she got excited about some new thing in her world. But he'd never heard her sound jealous before. He wasn't quite sure how to respond.

"The only woman I even *tried* to speak to tonight took off running at first sight of me," he joked.

"Better make sure they all do. If you know what's good for you."

"I know you're good for me. No way I'll mess that up."

Maria sighed. "Sorry. I'm just missing you and being silly. I didn't think you left on the best of notes."

"We'd been together nearly non-stop for weeks. Inevitable that we'd have to stretch the ties that bind just a bit. I'll be back in another week, and you know what they say about absence."

Maria laughed, sounding completely like her own self again. "It makes the heart grow hornier."

Concho grinned. "Yep!"

"All right, I'll see you soon. Call me every couple of days to let me hear you're OK."

"I will. Love you."

"Love you too."

Maria hung up before Concho could remark that this was the first time she'd said "I love you" on the phone. It was probably for the best. Maria did not like to be pushed on the romance front. He'd learned the hard way.

Making his way beneath the lobby's four chandeliers and past a grandfather clock, the Ranger checked in at the front desk and picked up his key. His room was on the fifth floor. He opened the door and stepped inside. Something was wrong.

***

After leaving Ten-Wolves, Bull Knife strode down the street. Only when he reached the end of Bourbon Street where it met Esplanade Avenue did he pause. He was being followed. He'd gotten glimpses of his tail, but they were good. And they were in their own element, the narrow, tight streets of the city.

Quickly, he crossed Esplanade into the Faubourg Marigny. The Marigny had had its ups and downs. Parts of it had been built in the 19th century to house the mistresses of prominent local Creoles. In the 20th century it had been home to jazz musicians and music venues appreciated by locals but unknown in the broader New Orleans area. At times it had been a haven for criminals, or for immigrants who couldn't afford the real estate of the nearby French Quarter.

Not far inside the Marigny lay Washington Square Park. It wasn't a big place, but there were trees, mostly large oaks and a few palms mixed in with grass and tall ferns like the palmetto. It smelled like living things, like life. The city might be the element for those who followed Bull Knife. But nature and the night belonged to him.

***

Stepping into the dark as he entered his hotel room, Concho smelled perfume, an intense jasmine and lilac smell. It was too strong and immediate to have been left by a cleaning lady. Someone wearing that scent had to have been in the room in the last few minutes, or *was there now.*

Concho bent down and drew the Smith & Wesson snub .38 from his ankle holster. As he straightened, he flipped on the lights. Brightness stabbed. Concho found himself in a short hallway of no more than three paces. A gasp came from the main room where a woman sat up suddenly in the bed, squinting against the light.

"Who are you?" Concho demanded.

"I...I...I"

To Concho's left lay the bathroom. It was open, with the shower curtain pulled back. The room was empty. The only other place to hide was the closet. Concho strode quickly past the bed and yanked back the folding door of the closet. It, too, was empty, except for half a dozen bare hangers waiting for cargo.

The Ranger spun back toward the woman in the bed. She'd pushed herself up against the headboard and tugged the sheet up to her chin. She was of Asian descent, lovely and waifish. Long black hair cascaded down past her shoulders. She stared with fright at the gun in his hand.

Not wanting her to see where he kept the Smith holstered, he stuck the short-barreled weapon in his pocket temporarily. "I'm not going to hurt you," he said. "But I still need to know who you are?"

"Holly!"

"Holly. Good. Now tell me why you're in my room."

"You…you're Concho Ten-Wolves, aren't you?"

Concho frowned. "Yes. So what?"

"I was…sent for you."

"Sent by who? And for what?"

The woman's sigh came softly. She looked about eighteen or nineteen but could have been a few years older. She slowly pushed the sheet down from her chin. Beneath the sheet, a white satin corset shaped her body into everything most men could desire.

Concho understood. "That's not gonna happen. You should get dressed."

Holly sighed again. She swung her legs out from under the sheet and stood up. Sheer white stockings encased her from feet to thighs. On the bedside table lay a neatly folded black skirt and black satin top. She slipped the skirt on with her back to him and zipped it up adroitly, then pulled on the shirt as she turned toward him and began buttoning it.

Concho didn't want to stare, but he didn't want to 'pretend' to look away either. He kept his gaze focused on the woman's face.

"I want to know who sent you?" he asked.

Holly left the top three buttons open on the shirt. She shrugged, giving the Ranger a return glimpse of what he'd just asked her to cover up.

"I don't know," she answered. "A man gave me an envelope with money and a note saying who you were and where to find you."

"Was it a short fellow with a Cajun accent?"

"No. Tall and thinnish. A white guy in a suit."

"Doesn't sound familiar," Concho said.

"He probably wasn't the one who provided the money, though."

"No, I'm sure you're right. What about the note? You still have it?"

Holly shook her head. "I…burned it as soon as I'd memorized it."

"How did you get in my room?"

"I know someone who works at the hotel. I've…been here before."

"Right. Were you just supposed to seduce me? Or was there more?"

Holly shook her head, then lowered her gaze. "Just…the sex. I wouldn't have agreed to anything else."

"Not my place to lecture you on your choices," Concho said. "But if you ever want out, contact me. I normally live in Texas. The name's not hard to remember."

Holly nodded. "The money," she started. Her hands smoothed down her skirt. "It's…already been paid. Six hundred dollars!"

"Keep it," Concho said. "As far as anyone is concerned, you did what you agreed to do. In any sense, you earned it."

Again, the woman nodded. She picked up her purse from the floor and started walking toward the door. She turned for an instant.

"I'm sorry," she said.

"For what?"

"There…there was one other thing. A message to deliver. After we…."

"What message?"

Holly straightened. "Just four words. Go home or die!"

A quick, sad smile melted across her lips and she slipped away.

CHAPTER 6

Concho locked the door behind Holly. He searched the room for any listening devices the woman might have installed, though he didn't expect to find any. He didn't. Unzipping his suitcase on the bed, he took out his two Colt Double Eagle .45s. One he slid under the pillowcase, the other he carried with him to the bathroom and lay it on the counter before he climbed into the shower.

While hot water sluiced away the day's dirt and sweat, Concho considered many things. The surprise of having an unknown half brother had begun to fade. More surprising was the idea that his mother might still be alive. He doubted it, but if there was any chance, he wanted to know. It would start with identifying Donnell Blackthorne's sister. He didn't even have her name but there were ways to find out.

The other mystery on his mind was the woman in Lafitte's who'd looked familiar to him. She'd recognized him, too—he felt sure of it—and had fled because of that recognition. His attempt to follow her had set a series of odd encounters in motion.

The Cajun threatening him made some sense. The woman he'd tried to follow probably had bodyguards, or at least the money to pay for protection. It meant she wasn't your typical New Orleans lady. However, Ten-Wolves had the feeling his garage encounter with the Cajun and his two enforcers had been more about the short man's pride than about the woman.

But what about Holly? Who had pointed *her* in his direction? It seemed unlikely she'd been sent by the same person or persons who'd sicced the Cajun on him. One wanted to beat his head in; the other wanted to get inside his head as well as his bed.

Holly made no sense in several ways. She'd been waiting for him in *his* hotel room, a room he'd only reserved this morning. And he hadn't even known what room number he'd get until he walked into the lobby of the Monteleone.

He'd told Bull Knife about the Monteleone, but only a couple of hours ago. He'd told Maria Morales barely half an hour ago. And he'd told neither of them his room number because he hadn't known it.

Someone had learned of his coming to New Orleans, had learned what hotel he'd be staying at, and had gotten his room number from a hotel employee when even the Ranger himself couldn't have given it. And all this had to have been planned before he'd walked into Lafitte's and seen a woman's face with something familiar about it.

Bull Knife was the only vaguely reasonable suspect as an informant behind these events, but that just didn't seem right to Concho. He held no illusions that Bull Knife was telling him everything about his motivations, but the story about being Concho's half brother and the search for their mother did not seem like a ruse. If so, it was certainly needlessly complicated.

Concho shut off the shower and dried himself. He wiped condensation off his .45 with a fresh towel and returned to the main room. His cell phone lay on the bed and as he picked it up he saw he'd gotten a text from a restricted number. He swiped to read it. The mystery deepened.

***

One man slipped past the black metal pole fence into Washington Square Park in the Faubourg Marigny. He was non-descript in every way, from the clothes and coat he wore to the disheveled hair on a hatless head. Medium height, medium weight, medium build.

He stopped by a green metal trash can holder near the park's entrance, peered around as if searching the shadows for potential muggers. Streetlamps glowed around the park but couldn't dispel all darkness.

The man eased forward along the concrete walkway into the park. His hackles rose. The target he'd been following had vanished but had to have cut through here. Where had he gone? How had he disappeared so suddenly? The man took a few more steps ahead. No one else was around.

He stopped beneath a wide-spreading oak from which the gray tendrils of Spanish Moss trailed like monkish beards. A breeze brushed him. He tugged the collar of his coat closer around his neck. As a native New Orleanian, the night felt cold to him even though the temperature still hovered in the sixties.

"Where are you?" he muttered to himself.

"Right here," a voice answered from behind.

He started to turn but froze as an arm whipped around his head and something cold and sharp pressed into his neck.

"Keep still!" a rough voice ordered.

"Look!" the man said. "I don't have much money but you're welcome to it. My wallet's in my front right pocket."

"So, since you are a thief, you think I am as well?"

"No, no. I mean, I just…. OK, you're holding a knife at my neck in an empty park."

"You were following me!"

"Oh!"

"Yes, oh!"

The man blinked sweat out of his left eye. "It was just a job," he said. "I wouldn't have hurt you. I'm a private eye."

The arm around his head went away but the knife remained at his throat. A hand snaked into his pocket and pulled out his wallet. He heard the leather squeak as it opened. His PI license sat right up front.

"Porter House," the voice behind him read. "You expect me to believe that's your real name?"

"Afraid it is. My dad. George House. He hated his own name. Said it was lame. Forgettable. Claimed he wanted me to have a memorable moniker, something folks wouldn't easily forget. And he was a big fan of the porterhouse steak."

"I certainly won't forget it. Who hired you?"

"Don't know. Everything was contracted over the phone. The money.... They dropped it off. I didn't see who left it."

"Man or woman's voice on the phone?"

"Man. Sounded like a local." Porter shrugged. "That's all I've got."

"How were you supposed to report to him?"

"He said he'd call me every day at 6:00 in the evening."

"No emergency number to get in touch with him?"

Porter shook his head very slowly. "No, nothing."

The wallet went back into Porter's pocket; the knife slid away from his throat.

"Walk on straight through the park. Don't look back. Don't take any more money and don't follow me again."

"Sure thing," the PI said, but he had a feeling he was speaking to the air. The ghost behind him had already dematerialized.

***

Concho read the mysterious text on his phone: *Take Bull Knife and go home. There's nothing for you in Orleans save pain and heartbreak.*

No use trying to text back. And probably no use trying to trace the number. It was likely from a burner phone, one bought prepaid and meant to be thrown away after a single use.

He saved the text, then punched in another phone number from memory. It was almost 1:00 in the morning but the man he called seldom went to bed before dawn. A voice answered, alert and full of curiosity.

"Old friend," the voice said. "You hardly call anymore. Why's that?"

"I'm calling now," the Ranger said.

"True. What kind of favor do you need?"

Concho told him.

CHAPTER 7

Two of the many things Concho had learned in the army were, eat when you can and sleep when you can. Even after all the stress and strangeness of the day, when he closed his eyes he quickly fell into slumber. He woke again at 6:07 AM. He'd overslept by seven minutes.

He did some stretches, then set up his laptop and checked his email. Maria Morales had sent him a funny gif and he sent her back a smiley face emoji. Not for the first time, he thought of what a profoundly silly world modern humanity lived in. Yet, it was certainly nice to be able to momentarily cross a physical gulf of hundreds of miles to share a chuckle with the woman he loved.

His stomach began to growl. A check outside showed him a cool day with lightly clouded skies and a breeze. He pulled on a jacket and tucked one of his Double Eagles into a shoulder holster rig. Locking his other weapons and laptop in his suitcase, he sought food.

One thing Concho hadn't particularly liked about the French Quarter when he'd been here before was the smell—a mélange of fruity drinks, liquors, and spoiled sugar, of strange perfumes worn by a thousand strangers, of hints of human sweat and urine that permeated the buildings and streets. But that time he'd visited in the evening. Today, in the morning, with a breeze blowing off the river, the heaviest scents were muted and mostly he seemed to get the odors of cooking. Or perhaps it was just because he was hungry.

On Iberville Street, just around the corner from his hotel, he stumbled on a Cuban-Mexican place called *Country Flame.* The restaurant sign said they didn't open until 10:30 but the doors stood wide and a few folks who looked like locals dined inside. Concho stepped through the door and asked in Spanish if they were serving. Half a dozen people greeted him like a relative they were actually fond of. So, he had seasoned beef tacos for breakfast instead of bacon and eggs, and drank a big glass of milk and another of orange juice.

He'd agreed to meet Bull Knife outside Lafitte's at 9:00, so he headed down Bourbon as soon as he finished his meal. The sun had warmed the day and winter seemed to have forgotten the French Quarter. He arrived at the bar a couple of minutes early but found Bull Knife already lounging at the same outside table they'd used the night before. Concho sat down across from his recently discovered half brother. The bartender came outside and looked at them with exasperation.

"If you're gonna sit here, you're gonna have to buy a drink," the man said.

"You have coffee?" Concho asked.

"We've got soda."

Ten-Wolves pulled a five out of his billfold and handed it to the man. "I'll have a soda. Coca-Cola. And whatever my colleague here wants. Keep the change."

"Water!" Bull Knife said.

The bartender took the five and looked a little less irritated as he returned inside.

"I was followed after we left here," Bull Knife said. "A man named Porter House. He had a private investigator's license."

How Concho wished he could arch an eyebrow at the name of the PI. "Really? Was Porter working with Bud Weiser? Maybe in the employ of Jack Daniels?"

Bull Knife smirked. "For that, you do not deserve to hear the story he told me about acquiring his name. A fascinating tale."

Concho grinned. "I'm sorry. Please, do tell me the story."

Bull Knife waved his hand around dismissively. "Too late, now. The moment has passed."

"I guess I'll survive. Somehow. Did Porter tell you why he followed you?"

"Hired by someone he only spoke to on the phone. If he is to be believed."

"Do you believe him?"

The bartender returned with their drinks and Bull Knife sipped his water until the man left. "I do," he said. "He did not seem adept at deception. Which makes me wonder about his future in his chosen profession."

Concho sipped his own drink. "I was followed, too. In fact, I got to meet three of New Orleans' finest citizens up close and personal in a parking garage. I'd already had a run-in with the leader right here around Lafitte's before you arrived last night."

"I suppose the bruises don't show," the half-Apache said, giving Concho the once over.

"Bet they did when the three of 'em got up this morning."

"We seem to have attracted undue interest in a very short time."

"Yep," Concho said, as he added the piece about Holly the prostitute, her message to him, and the later text message he'd gotten concerning the two of them.

"There can be only one reason why we've gotten certain people so upset."

Concho sipped his soda again. "You're gonna say it's because someone's afraid we'll find out the truth about our mother."

"And because we're getting close."

"Could be other reasons. But it's enough to make me wonder.

I've asked someone for a favor. If he can do it, we should hear back soon."

"To identify Donnell Blackthorne's sister!"

"An insight worthy of no less of a detective than the great Porter House," Concho said.

***

The two half brothers separated again after sharing their information. Bull Knife went off to find food while Concho sought adventure. Adventure meant a visit to a local bookstore he'd heard much about—Faulkner House Books over on Pirate's Alley. William Faulkner himself had lived in the house where the store was located, though only for about six months back in 1925.

As he stepped into the building, the lawman's nose welcomed the pleasant scent of books both old and new. He took his sweet time perusing the crowded shelves and was delighted to find an excellent copy of *In Battle for Peace: The Story of my 83rd Birthday*, by W.E.B. Du Bois. William Edward Burghardt Du Bois had lived from near the middle of the 19th Century to past the middle of the 20th. He'd been a sociologist by profession and a social and civil rights activist by necessity.

Du Bois's famous collection of essays, *The Souls of Black Folk*, had been required reading at Haskell Indian Nations University where Ten-Wolves had gone to college. While in the army, he'd discovered a ratty old copy of Du Bois's *In Battle for Peace*, but had only been a third of the way through it when it was stolen. He was happy to finally replace it, even though the price was steep at nearly a hundred dollars. A cheaper copy might have been found online but few things could beat the thrill of capturing a long-desired book in the wild.

As he stepped out of the bookstore with his prized new possession in a plastic bag, a young girl on the sidewalk spoke to him. "Sir, could you help me please?"

Concho glanced down. The child who'd asked for help barely

reached up to his waist. Maybe seven or eight, she had skin the color of milk mixed with a touch of chocolate syrup. Her curly auburn hair had been cut in a short bob around her face. Beautiful large green eyes stared questioningly at him.

"How can I help you, ma'am?" Concho asked.

"I'm no ma'am. I'm just a little girl."

"Ah, my mistake. If you'll give me your name, I'll just call you by it. Then we won't have any confusion."

"I'm Hannah!"

"Well, Hannah, I'm Concho. How can I help you?"

"I don't want my mother to be hurt."

Concho dropped down into a squat, bringing his face closer to the girl's. "Who is going to hurt your mother?"

"You are!"

Concho frowned. He shook his head so she could see. "That's not true, Hannah. I don't even know your mother. I don't want to hurt anyone."

"If you don't leave her alone, she says she'll get beat up," Hannah shouted loudly. She spun and ran down the street.

Concho leaped to his feet. Onlookers who'd heard the last part of the exchange glared at him with disapproving faces. He ignored them. For an instant he considered pursuing the girl. But even in a place as given to unusual sights as the New Orleans French Quarter, a big dark-skinned man chasing a mostly white little girl down the street would attract attention—and a riot's worth of police.

CHAPTER 8

Being taller than most people around him, Concho could see over their heads as the little girl, Hannah, raced away, weaving in and out of the crowd. Many noticed. No one came to her aid or tried to stop or question her.

The girl had not found him and said what she'd said without coaching. An adult had put her up to it, and someone surely watched to make sure she was all right. Concho checked faces, checked doorways to clubs and bars, checked balconies. He saw no one who showed any particular interest in Hannah. Or in him. And then the girl was gone, lost to the human river of Bourbon Street.

Anger clenched the Ranger's fists. Adults might have issues but he didn't like it when they used children as proxies to deal with their problems. Little Hannah should not have been put in this position, to approach a man she didn't know, a man who might be dangerous, to tell him something that could make him angry.

The mother had to be the woman he'd found so familiar in Lafitte's just the night before. Her skin was darker than Hannah's but the green eyes were the same. What was she hiding and who was she hiding it from? Was she to blame for sending her daughter into potential danger? Or could it be someone else?

Concho shook his head. Perhaps the girl knew more than he gave her credit for. Children might be innocent but they weren't stupid. Even children could have someone they loved and wanted to protect. A memory came, of a different place and time, but of a girl who wasn't much different from Hannah.

Afghanistan, 2011.

"You will help us?" the young girl asked in Dari. She *couldn't have been more than thirteen. Her dark eyes shone with fear. The pink scarf she wore over her hair shook as she trembled.*

Concho Ten-Wolves translated the girl's words for his Army Ranger commander, Russ Adelaide. They stood in the protective shadows of a huge boulder, near battlefields both ancient and modern.

"Help her with what?" Adelaide asked.

Concho spoke again to the girl.

"My brother," she said. She nodded her head toward a rough hut about thirty yards away. It was the only sign of civilization in this small, rocky valley in the hills of Afghanistan. "He is... injured," the girl continued. "He needs..." She used an English word. "Med...ical."

"Her brother is hurt. In the hut," Concho told Adelaide.

"All right," Adelaide said. "We'll check it out. But carefully."

Adelaide glanced at the rest of his Ranger detachment— twelve men in all, in what was called an ODA, Operational Detachment Alpha. They'd been on routine patrol when they'd spotted smoke rising from a valley ahead. An investigation led them to this single hut set amid a field of rocks. A young girl stood outside, wearing a dark linen dress with a brocaded top. She'd walked slowly toward them with hands in the air, though each step she took seemed to bleed the strength out of her and ramp up her terror.

"Stay in cover but keep an eye on everything," Adelaide ordered the remainder of the ODA.

He lifted his palm to the girl and waved it toward the hut. The girl shook some more but led the way. Only a ragged blanket covered the opening into the hut. Concho lifted it back with his left hand, keeping his right index finger near the trigger of his M4A1 carbine.

The girl flicked Ten-Wolves a brief, perfunctory smile, then ducked slightly and entered the hut. Concho followed her in, tense. Adelaide came in a second after and stepped to one side, his hands holding a Colt .45.

The weapons weren't needed. The room sat almost empty. An iron stove with a pipe leading up through the roof ticked as it cooled. Both soldiers smelled the residue of a recent fire. This must have been the source of the smoke that led them here.

The only furniture in the room was one rickety chair and a cot. A man lay on the cot, covered with blankets. Concho studied the covers for any outline of a weapon beneath them. He couldn't see anything.

"Please," the girl begged.

Ten-Wolves moved cautiously over to the cot and bent down. The man in it glared ferociously at him. His face was flushed, his eyes shining with fever. He said nothing as Concho pulled the blankets back. The only dangerous thing under the covers was a badly swollen left leg with streamers of red and white running from the point of a wound about four inches above the knee.

Concho studied the wound, then pulled the blankets back over the man. "Who are you?" he asked in Dari.

"Just a farmer," the man answered in the same tongue.

"And your name?"

"Abdul."

Concho repressed a chuckle. Abdul was second only to Mohammed as the most common male name in these hills. Maybe this moniker was real, maybe not. It wouldn't help them much to identify this "farmer," though.

"What happened?"

Abdul gritted his teeth, as if he were going to refuse to answer.

The girl answered for him. "A stray bullet. We were hiding from…rebels. My brother was protecting me and a bullet hit him."

Concho nodded. He studied the girl, studied the room, studied Abdul. He nodded for Adelaide to join him outside.

"What do you think?" Adelaide asked when they were out under the brazen sun.

Concho sighed. "Hard to be sure but it looks like the wound was made by one of ours. Pretty sure the guy's Taliban. Probably left behind when his group retreated from this area."

"What about the girl?"

"Left to care for her brother. I imagine she set the fire to send up the smoke. She wanted us to find them. Probably because she thinks we can help. You saw the leg. Is it gonna have to come off?"

Adelaide shook his head. "It's badly swollen. Infected. It could certainly kill him in a few days. But if the infection is drained and he's given antibiotics he should be OK."

"About what I figured, too."

The girl came out of the hut and crossed the dirt ground to the men. She glanced from Adelaide to Concho. Her voice murmured quietly. "If you help him, I will give you information you need. I will help you. If you help him. But you must not tell him I did so."

Concho translated for Adelaide and his commander nodded. "Tell her we'll do all we can."

Concho explained to the girl that they'd have to drain the infection from her brother's leg and give him medicine, and that he should live, though there were no guarantees.

"And you will let us go after you…treat him?" the girl asked.

"Yes," Concho agreed.

The girl nodded. "Then I will tell you. Please start to help him now."

Concho translated for Adelaide, who called over two other members of the ODA—Petry and Simmons. Simmons had medical training.

"*See about the man in the hut,*" Adelaide ordered. "*I want him to live.*"

The men nodded. Simmons unslung his pack and took out his medical kit as the two entered the hovel.

"*All right,*" Concho said to the girl. "*They'll do what they can.*"

The girl nodded. She began to speak quickly. Concho asked her to pause while he took a pad and pencil from his pack, then gestured for her to continue. He jotted down notes about Taliban locations, troop strengths, and supplies. Eventually the girl ran dry.

"*That is all I know,*" she said.

"*Thank you,*" Concho said. "*What is your name, by the way?*"

"*Hameeda.*"

"*Thank you, Hameeda. You can go to your brother.*"

The girl nodded and retreated into the hut.

Concho glanced at his commander. "*What now?*"

"*Simmons treats him. We leave. Radio in everything we've got and let the high rankers make the decision on what to do.*"

"*He's one of them,*" Concho said. "*He'll likely be carrying a gun for them again as soon as he's healed.*"

"*A deal with the Devil,*" Adelaide said. "*Sometimes it's the only deal available. If he goes back, gets in our way, he dies.*"

"*The girl's no devil. She's as innocent as a thirteen-year-old can be in a war zone. If her brother goes back to the Taliban, she'll follow. If he dies, she'll likely die with him.*"

"*No one ever said a Devil's bargain was fair,*" Adelaide replied.

Concho's mind spun away from Afghanistan, returned to the here and now in New Orleans, Louisiana. Hameeda and Hannah—both caught in the middle of something bigger than themselves, both trying to protect someone they loved, both willing to make a deal with the Devil.

Such deals seldom worked out. Six months after Concho had met Hameeda, he'd seen her and her brother again, on a battlefield far away from that lonely hut amid the boulders. The brother and sister had been hit by mortar fire. They were dead.

Only Hameeda's face had been left untouched by shrapnel. Her eyes were open and staring, not with accusation, but with betrayal. Concho hoped the same would not happen to Hannah and her mother.

CHAPTER 9

After dropping off his new book at the hotel, Concho phoned Bull Knife with an update on the event with Hannah. Feeling peckish afterward, he returned to Country Flame for an enchilada and dark beer lunch. His phone rang when he was about halfway through. It was the friend he'd asked for a favor.

"Hope you have good news for me," Concho said into the phone, making sure not to refer to the man by name over an open line.

Chris Doolan was CIA. Concho had worked with him on occasion in Afghanistan. In fact, he'd hauled Chris's wounded ass out of a mission meltdown that should have killed them both. Mostly by luck, Concho had to admit. But Chris had not forgotten. And he made a loyal friend.

"Have I ever let you down?" Chris asked.

"Nary a time."

"I've got the info you wanted. Took longer than expected. Had to work through several levels of security."

"That's why I called the best."

"And she wasn't available so you called me."

Concho chuckled. "Nobody better than you, and you know it."

"Modesty precludes. But anyway, Abigail Blackthorne,

daughter to Hamilton Blackthorne and younger sister to Donnell, married Nolen Carmichael III, who often refers to himself as 'the third'."

"Old money?" Concho asked.

"Older anyway. The Carmichael's are not worth as much as the newer money of Abigail's father, but respectable. Nolen became a musician and something of a disappointment to his family, however, which is apparently why he lives quietly and relatively modestly in Louisiana rather than at the family estate in New York."

"Where exactly in Louisiana?"

"That was the most difficult piece to find. The address is for Covington, Louisiana. A fairly small town north of New Orleans. Considered upscale, though. You have to cross a very large lake called Pontchartrain."

"I know the general area," Concho said. "Read something about the longest bridge in the US crossing that lake."

"Twenty-four miles of it," Chris explained. "And more to Covington. The actual address is 121 North Florida Street. Last house on the street. A big one. Sits right near the bank of the, uhm, *Bogue Falaya*, which is apparently a small river."

"Ah. I recognize those words. Choctaw. I knew they were native to this area. *Bogue* means stream and *falaya* is long."

"Trust the language major. You need me to text you the address?"

"Nope. Got it. I appreciate you always coming through."

"It's nothing. We won't be even until I save your life. And since it looks like you've got at least a dozen, I'm sure I'll get my chance."

"I've used up a couple here recently."

"Don't use 'em all. And if you get up to Washington drop by and see me."

"No one sees the invisible man," Concho said.

"Except a ghost ranger," Chris replied. "Take care." He hung up.

Time to take a quick trip across a long bridge, Concho thought.

***

With Concho piloting his silver Ford F-150, the two half brothers hopped on the I-10 West toward Baton Rouge, exited on North Causeway Boulevard, and took the Twenty-Four Mile Bridge across Lake Pontchartrain. Neither man spoke but remained alone with their thoughts.

The lake was massive, like an inland sea crossed by lonely twin spans of concrete. Under a partially clouded sky, the water glistened a steel gray. Pelicans glided on a stiff breeze, which stirred whitecaps that looked like the manes of swimming horses. At 1:30 in the afternoon, traffic was light.

The bridge merged into US Highway 190, which took them to an oddly planned zig-zag to get on Business 190 into Covington itself. Never having been one to use GPS, Concho had picked up a local map at the hotel and studied it before leaving. Still, he drove past his North Florida Street target once before having to backtrack.

Covington was a small town, almost quaint. Concho noted only one large grocery store—the oddly named Acquistapace's—but a variety of other businesses and restaurants seemed to be doing brisk business, including a small coffeehouse along Main street where several customers lounged outside under a warming sun.

On his second pass through town, Concho found North Florida Street and turned along it. Half a mile brought them to the end, where asphalt faded to dirt and a barrier of cypress trees prevented anyone from driving into the meadow beyond. The Ranger pulled to the side and parked.

The truck's windows were down. Birdsong filtered in and only a distant hum of traffic floated to them. The meadow ahead still had some green grass even in December, and beyond it, Concho glimpsed sheening flashes of the Bogue Falaya River through a bordering of trees and brush. He could smell the water, or at least some combination of wet muck and growing things.

Bull Knife climbed out and Concho joined him. 121 North Florida was indeed the last house on the road. It sat to their right behind a six-foot wall of yellow brick that formed a street-side shield for the owners. A black iron gate provided ingress through the wall but was closed and locked when they approached.

Concho studied the house. Two stories, built of wood. Big but not ostentatious. No mansion. Any wealth revealed here was understated. Oaks and cypress trees surrounded and shaded the home. The oaks still held some brown leaves, though many had fallen. The needles of the cypress trees had turned a bright orange.

A call box attached to one pole of the gate caught the Ranger's attention. He pressed the button, heard a faint buzzing. A beat later, he pressed it again. A woman's voice responded.

"If you're selling something, we're not interested."

"Not selling anything," Concho replied. "We're looking for Abigail Blackthorne Carmichael."

"This is she. Who are you?"

"I'm your nephew."

"Nephew! I don't…. What are you talking about?"

"Donnell Blackthorne. I'm his boy, Concho Ten-Wolves."

A gasp came over the air, followed by silence. Concho began to think Abigail Carmichael had written them off when she spoke again.

"So, you are Donnell's son?"

"Biologically at least."

"Donnell is dead. I have nothing to say about him."

"I didn't come to talk about him. I wanted to talk to someone who knew my mother."

"Sparrow Woman! But she's dead, too."

The half brothers crossed glances. "All the more reason why I'd want to talk to someone who knew her," Concho responded. "I've come a long way. It won't take much of your time."

The silence this time was not so long. The gate buzzed and the lawman pushed it open. He and Bull Knife strode up a red-brick walkway to the house. Any vehicles must have been parked around the back. The front door stood open when the two reached it. Abigail Blackthorne Carmichael awaited.

Abigail had been Donnell's younger sister. Concho reckoned her age at a little over fifty. She was pencil thin, with a stern face that did not go with the messy bun in which she'd tied up her curly hair. She wore no makeup and had on black pants and an old gray sweater. Again, no wealth on display here.

"Who is this?" Abigail demanded, gesturing toward Bull Knife.

"My brother. Half brother. Sparrow Woman was his mother as well."

Abigail's light brown eyes studied them both before she took a deep breath and let it out.

"I can give you thirty minutes," she said. "No more."

"Should be plenty of time," Concho said.

"Good. Because my husband will be back from his runabout then and he won't like having you here. Bad things happen to people when he doesn't like them."

CHAPTER 10

Abigail Carmichael led her visitors down a hallway lined with bookshelves holding subduedly jacketed volumes on history and politics. The shelves and books had been freshly dusted with some lemon-scented cleaning agent.

Beyond the hall, they entered a living room done up all in white—white plush sofa, overstuffed white chairs, white walls, and a white carpet, even a white piano. Other than the people, only a low, rectangular table of black lacquered wood with a glass top relieved the domination of the pale.

Abigail perched very precisely on the edge of the couch, leaving Concho and Bull Knife to chairs across from her. Bull Knife usually seemed at equilibrium, but in this place he looked distinctly uncomfortable and didn't say a word. Concho had been in plenty of rich folks' homes, and the chair he'd been directed to was even big and sturdy enough for his heavy frame. He took the lead with a question.

"You and your brother, Donnell. Did you two get along?"

The woman tugged the bottom of her sweater down at her waist. "That's none of your business," she said primly. "You wanted to know about your mother. I'll answer a few questions about *her*. *If* I find them appropriate."

"The reason I asked what I asked," Concho replied, "is because, when he left Texas with my mother, he came here rather than going to northern California to stay with his father."

"Our father would not have approved of Donnell's choice in... women. Nor would he have been happy with a pregnancy outside of marriage. Besides, Donnell always thought he could overawe his younger sister."

"I take it that was not the case?"

A thin smile did little to lessen the sternness of Abigail's face. "My brother always had an inflated opinion of his talent to impress. However, he brought your mother here primarily because he knew I'd be open-minded enough to accept her."

"I know they eventually traveled to Las Vegas. Can you tell me how long they stayed with you before they moved?"

"These questions don't really seem to be about your mother."

"Sorry," Concho said. "We're trying to backtrack her after she left Texas. More than thirty years later. I'm not really sure what might be helpful."

Abigail seemed to soften a touch. She responded. "She and Donnell lived in this house only a month. My husband did not care for the arrangement. Nor did your mother. Donnell found them a cheap apartment near the French Quarter in New Orleans. I did visit them there on occasion, and they came here for holidays. I believe they were in Louisiana for about a year. That would have been until almost six months after you were born."

"Why didn't my mother like it here? At your place? Didn't you two get along? Or was it just your husband?"

"Neither of those really. She and I actually got on quite well. I would not say we became close friends but we accommodated to each other nicely. I was happy to see she kept Donnell clean."

"You mean she kept him from using drugs?"

"And alcohol. At least to excess."

"So, she wasn't using either?"

"As far as I saw she didn't touch any kind of drug while pregnant with you. She even quit smoking."

Concho found himself surprised. His whole life he'd heard that his mother was a drug addict, unable to control her cravings for heroin, cocaine, nicotine, alcohol, and anything else she might find to mix in her system. If that wasn't true, then it raised more questions than it answered.

"Why didn't she like it here?" he asked.

Another thin smile rewarded his question. "Have you driven through Covington?"

"Yes. Seems like a nice town."

"A *boring* town," Abigail replied. "Donnell took after our father. They both liked the nightlife, the bright lights. Your mother was much like Donnell in this. She wanted music, shows, crowds, dancing. I prefer the sounds of birds myself."

"New Orleans must have been perfect for her. I understand she liked it. Why did they leave to go to Las Vegas?"

For the first time, Abigail fidgeted. She looked down. "I'm sure most of it was Donnell," she eventually said. "He and one of his schemes. But, well, your sparrow mother. She liked to dance. And she was good. She began dancing…in the Quarter. After she lost her baby weight.

"Donnell told me she wanted to go to Las Vegas to get into one of the casinos there as a dancer. That perhaps she could become a star. I was not…seeing her then. I suppose I did not approve of her new lifestyle. And she with a small baby. I told Donnell to discourage her, that her chances of being discovered dancing in a casino were virtually nonexistent. I don't even know if he spoke to her about it. They went anyway. But first, she took you home to Texas."

"She turned me over to my grandparents," Concho said.

"I'm sorry."

Concho shook his head. "I'm not."

"She loved you," Abigail said abruptly. "I saw her with you. As a baby. She loved you."

The words were surprisingly hard for Concho to hear. It felt like someone had poked him through the belly with a sharp stick and kept twisting his guts around on it like spaghetti on a fork. He'd always known his grandmother and grandfather loved him. He'd considered his mother's love many times but imagined her to be more concerned with her own world and vices than with him. The evidence had seemed to support that, but Abigail's words now put a crack in his thinking.

"Very old history now," Concho said, aware of a faint thickness in his voice that had not been there before. "I'm...we're," he gestured toward Bull Knife, "more concerned with modern history."

Abigail shook her head. "There is no modern history for your mother. She's dead. Certainly, a tragedy."

"That's just it. We have reason to believe Wiskenoa, Sparrow Woman, may still be alive. And perhaps living in Louisiana again."

Abigail frowned, then slowly shook her head. "That's not possible. Her body was positively identified. She's dead, and cremated."

"Who identified her? Donnell?"

"No. Well, I mean, he did too. But—"

"I did," a voice said from the hallway behind them.

***

Both Concho and Bull Knife turned swiftly in their chairs. A tall, black man loomed behind them in the entrance to the living room. He stood over six feet, muscular in a thin white t-shirt and black nylon jogging shorts. Sweat beaded his face and arms and trickled down his legs, which bulged with muscle.

Concho had expected Nolen Carmichael III to be a few years older than his wife, or somewhere in his early sixties, but this man looked more than ten years younger. Given that he apparently lived a healthy lifestyle and stayed in shape, he might have been able to hold on to a more youthful appearance, but he still should be at least in his early fifties.

When Concho had heard from Chris Doolan that Carmichael

often referred to himself as "the third," he'd imagined a very different man than this one. It was a good lesson in not assuming things about people you haven't met.

Abigail had said about her husband, "Bad things happen to people when he doesn't like them." Concho had imagined that to be an exaggeration, or maybe to mean he used his money to hire knee-cappers for people who crossed him. This Nolen didn't look like he needed such help.

The most surprising thing was how silently the fellow moved. To have come in the house and walk up behind a Texas Ranger and a half-Apache would have taken some doing. Neither Concho nor Bull Knife was easy to sneak up on.

"Honey, would you get me a towel?" Nolen asked his wife.

Abigail popped up from the couch immediately with an "of course, Dear," and left the room.

Nolen walked around to stand in front of his visitors. In a voice neither friendly nor cold, he asked, "Who are you and why are you here?"

Concho introduced them and told the man the same thing he'd told Abigail, that they were looking for any information they could get on their mother.

"Then I'm sorry to be the purveyor of bad news, but Sparrow Woman is certainly dead. I saw the body myself. I watched her be cremated."

"In Las Vegas?" Concho asked.

"Yes."

"Can I ask why you were the one who went out to identify the body?"

Abigail returned with a large, fluffy purple towel and handed it to Nolen before sinking silently back onto the couch.

"Thank you," Nolen said to his wife as he began to towel himself dry of sweat. He showed no self-consciousness about that act in front of two strangers.

"The Las Vegas police called Abigail first, of course," Nolen answered. "But she was indisposed at the time. I was able to fly out and give Donnell some needed support, as well as identify the body."

"The police were involved? I thought it was supposed to be a car accident?"

"Alcohol and drugs were found at the scene so naturally there were police."

"I see. And there's no doubt? You could see her face clearly?"

"I was told her neck had been broken. Otherwise, she was relatively undamaged."

"And when was this? What year?"

Nolen draped the towel over his shoulder but still didn't sit down. He didn't answer immediately either. Instead, he walked over to the coffee table in front of where his wife sat. A whiskey shot glass on the table held a dozen wooden toothpicks. Nolen plucked up one and stuck it between his teeth. It was a sign, Concho had found, of someone who'd once been a smoker and still occasionally had the urge.

"1991," Nolen said, answering the lawman's question. He switched the toothpick from one side of his mouth to the other as he added, "April, I believe."

Concho sighed—he hoped not too dramatically. He rose and slapped his hands on his thighs. "Guess that settles it."

Bull Knife stood, too, and seemed about to say something. Concho placed a hand on his shoulder. The half-Apache shut his mouth.

"I'll show you out," Abigail said.

"No need," Concho replied. He offered his gentlest smile. "We appreciate your time and candor."

Shortly, the two were in Concho's truck and cruising back up North Florida Street.

"We know he's lying!" Bull Knife snapped. "If she'd really died in 1991, I would not have been born."

Concho tapped his fingers on the steering wheel. "I doubt Nolen missed that little nugget. Not with you sitting right there. He said what he said for a reason."

"What reason?"

"Maybe to discredit your claim that we're half brothers. To cast doubts between the two of us."

Bull Knife blinked in surprise. "I...did not think of that." His gaze studied Concho. "So, now you doubt me?"

"I don't doubt your sincerity. But it is possible you missed something along the way. I need to double-check your evidence."

"I missed nothing," Bull Knife said angrily.

"It won't hurt to go over the evidence again, so the next time we see Nolen Carmichael III we'll be able to confront him with our unified knowledge."

"You're confusing me. Do you believe me or not?"

"What I believe is, Nolen is lying. Just like you said. But we have to be careful how we call him on it."

"Why?"

"Because Nolen Carmichael is likely a very dangerous man."

CHAPTER 11

By the time the two half brothers got back across the Causeway to Concho's hotel, the day had grown late. This morning's thin clouds had gotten thicker over the city. The sky finally looked like a winter sky and the temperature had dropped into the forties.

After the incident with the three men in the parking garage, Concho had moved his truck to a new lot, an outside one. He and Bull Knife had to walk through a faint drizzle straight into a chill breeze blowing from the east. Most of the locals had fled indoors to avoid the cold and the streets were only sparsely populated.

They ordered room service, a dish called "blackened redfish," which was new to both of them but tasted very fine. Bull Knife could barely sit still to eat, however, and popped up and down from his chair repeatedly to pace a few feet back and forth across the room.

"Us Indians are supposed to be patient types," Concho said, interrupting Bull Knife's pacing.

The other man gave him a glare, then flopped down in his chair. "We should have confronted the Carmichaels immediately with their lies," he snapped. "What use is it to have them think they've fooled us?"

"I don't know that Abigail was trying to fool us. And Nolen probably doesn't *believe* he fooled us. He wanted to get under our skin, and possibly pit us against each other. We can't let him succeed in either of those."

A sharp retort seemed to rise up to Bull Knife's tongue but he bit it off without speaking it. "You're right," he said. "I am not behaving correctly. I let myself become like the gah, like the rabbit who dashes this way and that when danger threatens." He took a deep breath. "I would prefer to face things head-on."

"I would, too, but it can't always be done."

"So, what do we do? Sit here eating the white man's food and sleeping in the white man's soft bed?"

Concho forked up the last bite of his redfish and stuck it in his mouth. He chewed, swallowed, gave an exaggerated sigh of pleasure. "If this is white man's food then count me in. As for a soft bed, there'll come a time when you'll appreciate one yourself. However, if you're staying in my room tonight you're sleeping on the floor."

Bull Knife shook his head but also offered a faint smile. "You have not answered my question. What do we do? You are the trained one in this sort of endeavor."

Concho let his fork drop into his plate. "We started getting warnings before we'd even discovered anything. And whoever is trying to stop us knows what we *want* to know. Some of it at least. If we keep pushing, they'll come at us again. Harder this time. We'll have to be ready to take advantage of any break we get."

"Didn't I already suggest confronting Nolen Carmichael? Is that not 'pushing' as you say?"

"Maybe, but I think he's the wrong man to push right now. We need to be more subtle."

"How?"

"We pay a little visit to a certain private investigator of your acquaintance."

"Porter House? But it didn't seem like he knew anything to

help us."

"He might know more than he thinks he does. But he doesn't have to know anything to be useful. The people who are watching us just have to believe we might learn something from him."

"I see," Bull Knife said.

"You have a gun?" Concho asked.

The half-Apache slid his hand inside the vest he wore and pulled out a long, bone-handled hunting blade. "I have this."

"Steel is good. But gunpowder is usually better." He pulled up the leg of his jeans and took off the ankle holster holding his snub-nosed .38. "Take this. "I've got a couple of Colts. And I intend to wear them and my badge for our visit with Porter. He may tell a law officer something he wouldn't reveal to an Apache in the park."

***

Being a working private detective, Porter House had an official office, which Concho located via the internet. It sat on Magazine Street, off the CBD, the Central Business District of New Orleans. The two half brothers showed up at the house at 10:00 on Monday morning. They didn't call ahead, not wanting to give the PI any warning.

Last night's clouds and cold had given way to bluer skies and slightly mellower temperatures. The site of House's office was a refurbished two-story home, painted a bright green with blue shutters. According to the large wooden sign out front, Porter shared the house with a divorce lawyer. Probably not a bad location for a private investigator.

"Benedict Cooper," Concho said to Bull Knife, reading the lawyer's name off the sign. "Whatta you bet he's nicknamed 'Eggs Benedict?' You know, like steak and eggs."

Bull Knife made a face. "Are you under the impression that you're humorous?"

"It's no impression. If this Texas Ranger thing ever falls

through, I'll take my standup routine on the road. I foresee sold-out shows nationwide."

"Your 'foreseeing' needs glasses."

Concho grinned as he opened the door to the green house and stepped inside. To the left and right were closed interior doors with big square windows in them. The window on the left was dark, with white lettering at the top reading "records." Light and the sound of a clicking keyboard came through the window on the right. The lawyer's name was written there.

A short hallway between the rooms led to stairs. Concho proceeded up them, with Bull Knife a step behind. A door at the top stood pegged open and the two went through into a waiting area.

The second floor of the house was smaller than the first but still had ample space. The waiting area was large, with a dozen empty wooden chairs sitting around, their seats upholstered in faux blue leather. A low central table held some badly out of date magazines, but the place was dust free, neat, and smelled fresh. Whatever service the lawyer paid to clean downstairs probably also did the upstairs.

Two other rooms extended off the waiting area. One sat closed and dark. The other had an open door through which the Ranger glimpsed a stretch of brown carpet and the corner of a wooden desk. The PI's office, no doubt.

Porter House must have heard their footsteps from the office. He called out, "Yes, can I help someone?"

Concho started forward. Porter appeared in the doorway with a big smile on his face. The smile disappeared like free food at a church social as the PI caught sight of his visitors.

After staring at Bull Knife, Porter's gaze shifted to Concho. The Ranger could see the man examining the Texas Ranger badge pinned to his blue work shirt, as well as the two Colts holstered at his hips.

"I, uh…" Porter started, "I was expecting a client. I'm afraid you'll both have to come back later."

"It's OK," Concho said. "I have a feeling your client has canceled without telling you. But we're here to talk some business. We won't take up much of your time."

Porter was younger than Concho had imagined, probably in his mid-twenties. He wore khakis and a light blue shirt. Both were rumpled, as was his collar-length light brown hair.

"Look," the PI said, jerking his chin toward Bull Knife, "as I told your friend there, I don't know anything about the people who hired me to follow him. I never saw any of them. They called last evening just as they said they would, and I told them I was off the case and would happily refund their money."

"And how did they respond?"

The young man hesitated. He chewed his lower lip.

"Let me guess," Concho said. "They told you the job was still on and you better earn the money they gave you."

Porter huffed a short breath but didn't answer.

"Let's talk in your office," Concho said, pushing past the PI.

Porter hesitated but was now sandwiched between the Ranger and Bull Knife with nowhere to go. He turned on the heels of his cowboy boots and walked around behind his desk to sit down.

The desk butted up against the office wall to one side. It held a laptop computer and a large day planner/calendar. Only one other chair rested in the room, directly across from the PI. It was big but looked rickety. Concho motioned Bull Knife to sit and remained standing at the side of the detective's desk where he blocked any exit and could see out the closed window behind Porter's right shoulder.

Rows of bookshelves lined both the front and left walls of the room. They were of real wood rather than particleboard. Some had glass doors on them, and locks. Other than a few stacks of manila folders, they were all empty. Concho figured the bookshelves had been left by the previous occupant of these premises, who—given the size of the waiting area—had most likely been a doctor of some kind. The closed off room had probably served for examinations.

"How did you know?" Porter asked.

"That you'd been ordered to stay on the case?"

"Yeah!"

Concho tapped his badge. "Folks who try to work a private investigator the way these worked on you are criminals. With something to hide. I've had ample experience with their sort. I'm surprised you haven't. In your line of work."

Porter shook his head. "I've only been a PI for six months. And business has not been good. They offered me eight hundred bucks up front. In cash. I needed it."

"The problem is, once you're in with that kind you can't get out again. They'll make sure they get their eight hundred bucks worth out of you."

"I'm starting to realize it."

"Then let me tell you two important things. First, they're gonna know we were here and they're not gonna like it. If they believe you've told us things, they may decide to quit worrying about getting their money's worth."

Porter blanched. "I…I was afraid of that."

"Second," Concho continued, "the best way to protect yourself is get someone on your side and *tell them* everything."

"Someone like a Texas Ranger?"

Concho flashed a smile. "Exactly."

"But I don't know *anything*!"

"Let's just see. I'll ask questions and you answer. Keep to the truth and everything should go OK."

CHAPTER 12

Nolen Carmichael III sat across the breakfast table from his wife, Abigail. He'd made them fragrant omelets with peppers, feta cheese, diced ham and mushrooms but Abby barely picked at his offering. He finally placed his fork down on his monogrammed cloth napkin and spoke:

"You've been awfully quiet since our visitors yesterday evening. I hope they didn't disturb you too much."

"It's all right," Abby said. "It's just…they brought up old memories. Things I thought I'd long forgotten."

"And sadness at the loss of your brother?"

Abigail nodded. "That, too. He wasn't much but he was blood." She placed her own fork on the table and sighed. Her gaze found her husband's. "You lied to them when you said she was…'undamaged.'"

Nolen smiled faintly. "A small lie. A necessary one. In Vegas, I merely corroborated what Donnell had already told the police. The body was Sparrow's. But to tell these men that the body had been badly burned would have only kept them coming around with questions."

"Aren't their questions natural? She *was* their mother."

"Ten-Wolves' mother. She could not possibly be the other's.

He's far too young. Surely you realize that?"

Abigail gasped. "I...I hadn't...thought."

Nolen reached across the table to pat Abigail's hand. "Of course. You were distracted. Upset. But it brings their motive into question. I don't suspect it was a 'natural' one at all."

"What else could it be?"

Nolen smiled again, a much thinner smile. "Dear, how can you have been born the daughter of a wealthy man and not understand the motive of money?"

"But they seemed sincere!"

"All conmen do."

Abigail took a deep breath. "What do we do now? If they come back? If they won't leave us alone?"

Nolen picked up his fork and cut off a healthy slice of omelet. "Don't worry. If need be, I'll take care of it." He tucked the bite into his mouth and chewed with pleasure.

***

Concho leaned against one of Porter's unused book-shelves as he began to grill the private investigator. He hoped to find some lead on where to go next with the mystery of Wiskenoa—Sparrow Woman.

"Exactly when did you get the first call to retain your services?" he asked.

Porter's fingers tapped on his desk while he considered. "Let me check my phone. I use it for business, too." He pulled out his cell and swiped through it, held up a screen for Concho to see.

"Saturday, 5:37 PM," the PI said. "There's a number with it but it must have been a burner phone. I couldn't trace it."

"What did they say? As precisely as you can remember."

Porter scratched his head before replying, "'We want to hire you to follow someone.' I remember they opened with that. They described *him*." He nodded his head toward Bull Knife. "Said he was an Indian." He made a face at the word. "Not my choice of terms. Theirs. Said he had long black hair. Said he went by the name Bull Knife."

"'Went by?'" Concho asked.

"That's what they claimed."

Concho glanced at Bull Knife, who stared back impassively, then turned back to Porter. "Go on."

"They wanted to know about everyone he talked to. If he made any phone calls. Mailed any letters. Oh, and uh, they told me I could find him at Lafitte's Bar. They told me they'd call every day at 6:00 PM to get my report."

"What about the money?"

"Right. They offered me eight hundred dollars cash. I already told you I needed it. I accepted."

"How were you supposed to receive the money?"

Porter frowned. "That was a weird thing. They said if I went outside to my car, I'd find the money in an envelope on the front seat."

"*Inside* your car?"

"Yes. And I found it right where they said."

"Do you leave your car unlocked?"

"No. Never. It creeped me out. It felt sort of like they were leaving me a message."

"A message saying they could get to you whenever they wanted."

"Yeah."

"Did they mention anything about me?"

"Only that Bull Knife might be meeting a Texas Ranger at Lafitte's and they wanted a report on what was discussed. I saw you when you came in the bar but didn't recognize you. You weren't wearing your badge."

Concho nodded. "Walk us through your observations that night."

"Excuse me," Porter said. He reached for the center drawer on his desk and pulled it back. Glancing up, he saw Concho's hand hovering over the butt of one of his Colts and blanched again. "Just getting my notes," he murmured, as he slowly lifted a small writing pad out of the drawer.

"Fine."

Porter flipped the pad open and read: "8:52 PM. Bull Knife enters Lafitte's, purchases beer. 9:02. He's joined at a table outside by big black man. Not sure if he's the Texas Ranger I'm supposed to watch for. 9:04—"

"Let me see the notepad," Concho said impatiently, holding out his hand.

Porter first looked discombobulated, then irritated, but eventually slapped the pad into the Ranger's big mitt. Concho scanned the first entries, then began flipping through. He found three pages of notes just like the ones the investigator had read to them already."

"You're thorough. I'll give you that. No mention here of Bull Knife catching you by surprise and telling you to back off, though."

"Once you've had a knife at your throat, you don't need to write down the experience," the PI replied dryly.

Concho closed the notepad and tossed it back to its owner. "Guess so. Tell me what was said when they called last night for your report?"

Porter sighed. "I told them Bull Knife put a blade to my throat and I hadn't signed up for that. Told them I was off the case and would fully refund their money."

"And?" Concho asked.

"The guy laughed. He said, 'It doesn't work that way. You need to earn your money. And now you know how careful you have to be. We'll call tomorrow at the same time.'"

"And?"

"And nothing. He didn't even wait for me to respond. Just hung up."

Concho made a small snicking sound with his teeth. His gaze found Bull Knife. "Guess we're done here."

Bull Knife rose from his chair as Concho moved toward the door.

"Wait! Wait!" Porter said, jumping to his own feet. "What am I supposed to do?"

"What do you mean?"

"I mean I can't quit on them. And I can't follow you now you know everything. What am I supposed to tell them when they call?"

"I suppose you could travel a bit."

"Travel?" Porter's voice grew shriller. "I can't travel. These people live here. I'd never be able to come home."

"California might be your best bet to relocate," Concho said. "Nicer weather than here. Stay out of Texas, though. On the bright side," he patted one of the empty bookshelves, "you don't have any books to pack. A big timesaver."

"I can't just run away. I've got…roots here. You've gotta help me."

"Hmm," Concho said. "I feel for you. I really do." He paused a few beats. "Tell you what. Be at my room in the Monteleone at 5:45 this afternoon. We'll take their call together and I'll get you off the hook."

"How?"

"Don't know yet, but I'll think of something."

Porter rubbed his forehead and moaned, "I'm gonna get killed."

"Not if you show up at 5:45."

"OK, OK. What room are you in?"

"You're the detective," Concho replied. He and Bull Knife left the man standing in the middle of his office.

***

"What did Porter mean when he said you 'went by the name Bull Knife'?" Concho asked once they were in the truck and headed back toward the Quarter.

"I was born in a white man's hospital. The name on the birth certificate is not Bull Knife. But the name recorded on the Apache tribal rolls is. Bull Knife is the name bestowed on me by my father and my tribe."

"What *is* on the birth certificate? Maxwell, or Marcel, or something like that?"

"I'm not going to tell you."

"I can always look it up."

"Do so," Bull Knife snapped.

Concho grinned, and changed the subject. "I think you're right about Porter House. He's not the deceptive type. The biggest question remains, how did our stalkers know you were in town, that I was *coming* to town, and we'd meet at Lafitte's?"

"Maybe they knew about me coming to New Orleans because I asked a lot of questions in Las Vegas about our mother. And the death certificate I found there listed New Orleans as the previous residence. I started asking questions about that as well."

"Asking who?"

Bull Knife shrugged. "Anyone and everyone. The clubs where she danced. The police. The coroner's office. The coroner who ruled on the case is dead, by the way."

"Convenient."

"Yes."

"So, if the word of your coming originated in Las Vegas, it means someone there is still keeping an eye out for any questions arising regarding the faked death."

"That makes sense to me."

"But what about *my* coming to New Orleans. And our meeting at Lafitte's?"

"I'm wondering if there is some way they listened in on my phone conversation with you," Bull Knife said.

"Where did you make the call from?"

"From a balcony. I was not thinking."

Concho flicked his teeth with his tongue. "If they were expecting you here, and watching you, they could have heard the conversation with a directional microphone."

"That must be it."

"When did you get into town?"

"Friday morning. Early."

"But you didn't notice anyone following you until Saturday night's incident with Porter."

"No."

"Which means at least two different groups are tracking us."

Bull Knife frowned. "Why do you say that?"

"Two reasons. First, if someone was following you and doing a good enough job to stay hidden and be able to catch your phone conversation, then they wouldn't have needed to hire a PI. Second, the messages I got. Different tones. One said to 'Go home, or die.' A threat for sure. The other read, 'Take Bull Knife and go home. There's nothing for you in Orleans save pain and heartbreak.' That's not a threat. It's a warning. It sounds almost like a gesture of concern."

"Our mother must have sent it. She knows we're here and is reaching out."

"That's a long step beyond any evidence we have."

"Who else would care? It must have been her."

Concho frowned. "If it was, it means she doesn't want us here. She doesn't want to be found."

"Because of a danger. To her. To us. Perhaps all three. She needs us. We can't abandon her."

"You're not being rational. *If* our mother is alive, she disappeared for a reason and she's never tried to contact us. I can't imagine she's been held against her will for so many years. She clearly doesn't want to be found!"

Bull Knife shook his head and offered a sly smile. "Are you going to be rational now? Are you going home when we are so close? Tell me!"

"Not on my life," Concho said.

CHAPTER 13

At 5:43 PM, private detective Porter House arrived at Concho's room in the Hotel Monteleone. Concho let him in. Porter wore the same rumpled clothes he'd worn that morning and it didn't look like he'd combed his hair. He paced back and forth with nerves.

"What are you going to do to get these people off my back?" he asked.

"You'll know soon enough."

Porter spun toward Concho. He straightened his shoulders. "Not good enough!" he snapped. "My life is at stake here."

Concho glanced at Bull Knife.

"He seems adamant," Bull Knife said. "You want me to throw him out the window?"

"He does seem adamant, doesn't he," Concho said. "But let's give him a little leeway." He turned back to Porter. "We want these people to come after us. Not after you. I'm going to piss them off! Get their focus on us. That good enough for you?"

Porter blinked. "That…doesn't seem smart."

"Not your problem," Concho said.

Porter seemed about to say something else when the phone in his pocket began chiming. He jumped, glanced at Concho with his eyes wide. "They're early!"

"All the better," Concho said. He held out his hand.

Porter pulled out his phone as it kept signaling the call. He placed it in Concho's palm. The Ranger swiped to answer, then put it on speakerphone so they could all hear.

"Hello. You've reached Concho Ten-Wolves. Porter House is not available to take your call. I'm his new answering service. Talk to me."

"Ten-Wolves! What? Where is House?"

"We've removed him from the equation. Wait, that sounds bad. We haven't killed him. At least not yet." Concho winked at the investigator. "But we've made sure he won't follow us anymore. And we've confiscated the eight hundred bucks you gave him. You want to know about us. We want to know about you. Let's cut out the middleman."

"You're making a bad mistake, Ten-Wolves! This is not how business is done."

"Guess I missed that class in college. But I met a lot of chicken shits just like you, would-be rough boys who hide in the background while others do their dirty work."

Everyone listening could hear the anger snapping in the caller's next words. "All right! The gloves are off. You sang down the lightning now, boy! You'll learn."

"Yeah, yeah, reap what you sow. I've heard it before. Just remember it goes both ways."

He swiped the end call button and tossed the phone back to its owner, who caught it in both hands. "OK, get outta here," he told House. "Stay away from us and everything else to do with this case."

"Th...thanks," Porter said. He started toward the door, then looked back once as if to say something more.

"Remember you owe me one," Concho said.

Porter nodded, and went.

"That should do it," Bull Knife said. "You've kicked the

bumblebee nest."

"I positively stomped on it," Concho said. "Now, let's get out of here before they arrive with guns and rocket launchers. No sense in being sitting ducks."

***

Concho didn't check out of his room just yet, though. He wanted whoever might come to visit him with ill intent to think he was still home. He and Bull Knife took the elevator to the ground floor and exited through the hotel garage. The Ranger left Bull Knife on surveillance duty in the garage where he could watch that entrance.

"Probably don't have to tell you this," he said, "but keep your phone on vibrate. Text me if you see anything. The most likely ingress for our enemies is through here. I don't want to start a shooting war in the heart of the city but you've got the snub-nose .38 I gave you if you have to use it. It doesn't have much range; you'll need to be close. It can't be traced back to me so don't be afraid to dump it."

"Understood. What about you?"

Concho hoisted the gray gym bag in his left hand. It contained his laptop and what few other items he'd taken into the hotel. "Gonna stick this in the truck and move it. Then I'll float. There's a glorified alley behind the hotel called Exchange Place. Not heavily used and with lots of places to disappear into the walls. It's got a view of the garage entrance. There's also construction on Royal Street. I'll be able to keep an eye out for any suspicious folks coming in. I'll text you what I see."

Bull Knife nodded. He looked around at the garage, which was decently lit but still had plenty of shadowy places to hide. "Don't like this concrete around me. How could a soul find the sky? Not a good place to die."

"So don't die," Concho said. He slapped Bull Knife on the shoulder and headed for the street.

**

Concho couldn't be sure if his enemies knew where he'd
left his Ford or not but moved it just in case. He drove it back to
the first garage where he'd parked, this time finding a slot on the
fifth floor.

Returning to the Quarter in December's early dark, he headed
down Exchange Place. It had at one time been a narrow street
where commerce was "exchanged" but was now little more than a
wide alley through which people occasionally walked.

The part of the Exchange directly behind the Monteleone was
being worked on. A short wall of black nylon stretching between
metal poles closed off nearly half of it. Concho found the wall a
convenient place to hide as he kept an eye along Bienville Street,
where he could see the entrance to the garage.

Cars came and went. People disembarked as they handed their
vehicles over to the valet staff and headed into the hotel. One
heavyset man came walking along the sidewalk and turned into
the garage. He didn't look like anyone set on violence but Concho
texted Bull Knife to watch for him.

Several young men walked past in the alley, chattering about
women in unpleasant language. A drunk staggered along, fell
down, got up again, and brushed off his torn pants before weaving onward. A tall young woman strode purposefully past, looking
neither left nor right. None of them noticed the Texas Ranger
crouched where he blended with the shadows.

During a lull in the traffic coming through the alley, a young
man of medium height and build stopped and leaned against
the wall not ten feet from Concho. He wore a tan linen jacket
and a hat pulled down over his face—a fedora of all things.
The man lit a cigarette using a real match. The flash of light
revealed his features.

"Pretty sure you can hear me, Ten-Wolves," the man said.
"Saw you come into this alley."

Concho straightened, his right hand resting on the butt of a Colt .45. "Detective Porter House. You look ridiculous. And I thought I told you to stay away from us. You got a comprehension problem?"

CHAPTER 14

"Like you said, I owe you," Porter replied to Concho's question. "There's only two of you. I can help watch for anyone who might be coming to try and hurt you."

"You got a gun?" Concho asked.

"No. I mean, not with me."

"You any good in a fight?"

Porter acted nervous but seemed to have found a little backbone. He shrugged as he drew on his cigarette and let the smoke out. "Not really."

"Then if we get visitors, you better run."

"I'll be happy to."

Concho gave Porter his cell phone number. "You can watch the front of the hotel on Royal. Text me if you get a hit. Or think you get one."

"All right," Porter said. He dropped his cigarette, toed it out.

"Be still!" Concho whispered fiercely as he shrank back into the shadows.

Porter froze. Two men stepped free of Exchange alley across Bienville from Concho and the detective. They paused, looking around. One saw Porter across the street and pointed him out to the other. Neither could see Concho.

Porter held onto the wall beside him and leaned over to give a convincing portrayal of a drunk with the dry heaves. The two men studied him, then turned away down Bienville toward the Monteleone. Both were dressed like tourists, in t-shirts, light jackets, and jeans. A camera hung at one man's neck. Both had fanny packs around their waists, rather large ones.

"Good acting job!" Concho whispered to the PI. He grabbed his phone and sent Bull Knife a text reading, "2 men. Dressed as tourists. Watch fanny packs." He hopped over the nylon wall and snapped to Porter, "Better get going!"

"Wait!" Porter said. "I recognize one of those men."

The Ranger was about to follow the two but stopped and spun back toward the PI. "Tell me!"

"Jason Kulick. He works for the local mob, but always with a partner and it's not the guy he's with. It's a fellow named Kage LeBlanc. They call him 'Skull.'"

"You're saying there's a third one beside these two?"

Porter nodded. "Probably!"

Concho yanked his phone back out of his pocket and sent another text to Bull Knife warning of a possible third killer. He still hadn't gotten a response to his first one. He should have.

Concho huffed a hard breath. "OK, get going. I'm headed in."

He rushed to the corner of the Monteleone and peered around it. The two men were out of sight, meaning they must have gone into the garage.

"Watch yourself, Bull Knife," the Ranger muttered to himself as he hurried forward.

***

Bull Knife read Concho's text. He started to respond but the two men the text described came walking in. The half-Apache tucked his phone away again. He stood between a concrete pillar and a parked car where the light did not find its way.

It was dank and he did not like the smell of this place, but he could easily see the entrance from the garage into the Monteleone. The two "tourists" stood there. They were silent, not a common characteristic of visitors to the Crescent City.

The two stepped into the hotel and Bull Knife lost sight of them. A vibration in his pocket signaled a new text coming in, but he didn't dare fall too far behind the men he wanted to follow. He darted into the hotel himself but went to the stairs rather than the elevator. Slipping into the stairwell, he raced up to the fifth floor.

Silently, he drew the stairwell door back a few inches and peered out. The two men stood about thirty feet away in the hallway outside the elevators. They appeared to be reading room numbers, looking for a particular one—a very good sign they weren't paying customers with beds in the hotel.

In the next moment, the two must have figured out the floorplan. They started along the hall toward Concho's room. Bull Knife slipped free of the stairwell and eased the door closed behind him. The ice room stood on his left. He darted into it and peered around the corner.

The two men reached Concho's door. They looked at each other, then looked around as if to check for observers. Bull Knife ducked back swiftly to avoid being seen. He waited for a count of ten before taking another glance. The men had unzipped their fanny packs. They drew out black semi-automatics with extended magazines stuffed into the handles.

One took something else from his pack, a small square of material. The man inserted this into the electronic key slot in Concho's door. A faint click sounded as the door unlocked.

The man on the right shoved back the door and leaped inside, his gun rising. The second man followed. No sound of shooting came. Bull Knife straightened, drew the snub-nosed .38 Concho had given him. He started to step out from his hiding place but heard the whisper of the stairwell door opening again behind him.

He spun. A big man with a pockmarked face stood there holding a sawed-off pump-action shotgun. The weapon pointed directly at Bull Knife's belly. At this range it would cut him in two.

The fellow smiled. All his teeth were yellowed except for a silver one in the middle carved into the shape of a skull.

The blue eyes of the man with the shotgun were cold as glacial ice. "One dead Injun," he said, as he hefted the weapon slightly in his arms.

Bull Knife's heart galloped like a runaway horse. He prepared to move, to throw himself toward the gunman in a desperate gambit to avoid sure death. Seemingly from nowhere, a figure appeared at the shotgunner's shoulder. A sharp voice spoke.

"Don't think so," the voice said. Concho Ten-Wolves pressed the tip of his Colt .45 to the shotgunner's skull just behind the ear. He added a few more words to those he'd already spoken. "Not unless you want a complete brainectomy."

"How..." the gunman started. His pupils were dilated, filling his irises. "How you get up those stairs without me hearin'?"

"Maybe I'm a ghost," Concho replied. "This hotel is supposed to be haunted. But be very sure this gun is real. And the bullet will slaughter you."

The man took a slow breath, lowered the butt of the shotgun to indicate his acceptance of the sudden reversal in fortunes. Bull Knife grasped the barrel of the sawed-off weapon. He drew it out of the man's hands and met no resistance.

"Thanks," he said to Concho.

"What are big brothers for? How long have the other two been in my room?"

"No more than two minutes," Bull Knife replied.

"They'll be out in less." The Ranger nodded quickly toward the shotgun. "That'll hold 'em at the elevator. Meanwhile..." He pulled the now disarmed gunman around and handcuffed him with his back to the steel balustrade of the stairwell, then stepped through into the hotel hall and shut the door.

"The ice room," Bull Knife said.

Concho nodded and they slipped into the small room. Immediately from down the hall came the sound of a door opening and closing. Footsteps padded on the carpet, traveling toward them.

Bull Knife glanced at his brother, looking for a signal. Concho held up a finger, counted silently to five with his lips moving. A click came from the hall, the sound of a finger poking an elevator button.

Concho raised a hand to Bull Knife. They stepped out of the ice room together. The two men who'd entered Concho's room stood in front of the elevator. They looked irritated but their hands were empty. No doubt the guns had been tucked back into their resting places inside the fanny packs.

"Gentlemen!" Concho said loudly.

Startled, the two men spun toward the voice, their hands dropping instinctively to their packs. But the big Texas Ranger in front of them had two black semiautomatics in his hands, and Bull Knife made sure they could see the huge bore of the sawed-off shotgun he carried.

"You boys need to find a new profession," Concho said to the two would-be assassins. "Or maybe it's just not a good night for killing Indians."

CHAPTER 15

Concho studied the three men in his room. They were bound back to back to back on the floor. Bull Knife leaned against the wall nearby, the sawed-off shotgun hanging loosely in his hands. He was trying to look mean and doing a fair job.

"The first one who tells me what I want to hear gets to walk," Concho said.

"I tell you go screw youself," the pockmarked shotgun man said.

Concho stopped next to him, looking down. "You'll be Kage LeBlanc. The one folks call 'Skull.'"

"I be you worse nightmare is what I be."

"I take it that means you aren't going to talk. At least not in something approximating decent English."

The Ranger moved over to a second man, the tallest of the three, with wheat-colored hair he was obviously proud enough of to have professionally styled.

"And I'm guessing you're Jason Kulick," the Ranger said to him. "You look a lot smarter than Kage here. Smart enough to tell me a few things."

"Don't know any Jason Kulick," the man replied. "Nor any Kage whatchamacallhim, for that matter. But seeing as how you kidnapped us standing innocently in front of the elevator, you ought to let us go before the FBI comes down on you."

"Guess I'm gonna have to revise my estimate of your smarts downward," Concho said. "Kage carried a shotgun and stated his intention to kill my brother there." He nodded toward Bull Knife. "You other two broke into my room carrying semiautomatics with illegal magazines in them hidden in your fanny packs. The police are going to be very interested in why you attempted to murder a visiting Texas Ranger."

"Made no such attempt," Kulick said. "And we've both got permits for the pistols."

Concho glanced at the third man. He was shorter than the others, a little heavyset with reddened nose and cheeks suggesting high blood pressure.

"How about you?"

The man looked down and shook his head.

"Let me skin one of them in front of the others," Bull Knife said. "I bet the others will talk then."

"It may come to that," Concho said.

Kulick laughed. "You're a lawman. You aren't going to do anything to us except try to have us arrested. And you won't do that if you know what's good for you."

Concho smiled at Kulick. "You're right, I'm a lawman. But my brother isn't. He's an Apache. Ever read any history? The Apaches understood some things about inflicting pain." He glanced at Bull Knife. "They've got fire ants here. Maybe we can take them somewhere and find a mound."

"I know I'd like to hang his pretty scalp on my teepee wall," Bull Knife said, with his face impassive as he got into the spirit of the game.

Kulick looked a little less sure of himself as he said, "Bullshit!"

Concho shrugged. He hadn't expected any of the three to talk but figured he'd give it a try. He pulled his phone out and headed for the door. "Keep an eye on them while I call the police," he told

Bull Knife. "And no scalping."

"I'll try to abstain."

Concho stepped into the hall. He did intend to call the police but first wanted to check the text message he'd gotten a moment before when he'd felt the phone vibrating in his pocket. It was from Porter House.

Hope you're OK. I know who they work for. We can meet and I'll tell you."

OK. Tomorrow. I'll text later. Consider the details.

A "thumbs up" emoji came through a few seconds later.

Concho deleted all the texts from the last hour, then punched in 911.

***

On the testimony of Texas Ranger Concho Ten-Wolves, officers of the New Orleans Police Department hauled Jason Kulick, Kage LeBlanc, and their unidentified partner off to jail. All three were charged with the attempted murder of a lawman. It didn't happen without a lot of questions from the NOPD.

Concho spent over an hour explaining why he was in New Orleans. He told the truth. Most of it. He explained that, on his own time, he was investigating a cold case involving the disappearance and possible kidnapping of a woman who might conceivably be his mother. He didn't mention her name or her relationship to the Blackthorne family.

He described the threats he'd gotten and showed them the text from an unknown source saying: *Take Bull Knife and go home...* He mentioned the prostitute named Holly and her message to him, but left out Porter House's name. He also left out the green-eyed woman from Lafitte's and the little girl named Hannah, who might or might not have been the woman's daughter.

An NOPD homicide detective came in just as Concho finished his tale and he had to repeat the story. The man gave his name as Solly Burstein. Burstein was a painfully thin fellow who looked to be in his sixties and maybe close to retirement. Despite that, he exuded the energy of a much younger man. Pairing youthful energy with the acumen of the experienced, Solly seemed a formidable detective. The Ranger immediately liked him.

"What aren't you telling me?" Solly asked as Concho finished saying his piece.

"I don't like to lie," Concho said.

"Then don't!"

"How long will you be able to hold those three reprobates?" Concho asked, changing the subject.

Solly surely noticed the change in topic but didn't remark on it. "Probably no more than a few hours. Kulick and LeBlanc. They've got a good lawyer."

"Figures."

"Let me give you my cell number," Solly said. "I answer at just about any hour."

Concho listened, programmed it in.

Solly glanced around the room while Concho input the number. The other officers had left. Bull Knife had gone to the bathroom.

"I know you aren't telling me everything," Solly said softly to the Ranger. "Guess you've got your reasons. I get a good feeling from you. I'll let you have a little slack. Don't abuse my kindness, though."

"Promise," Concho said, though he thought that might not be a complete truth either.

***

As soon as the police left, Concho checked out of the Monteleone, and he and Bull Knife climbed in his Ford and hit the I-10. They got off on the Causeway Boulevard exit they'd taken once before and made several random turns and loops to make sure they weren't followed. Eventually, they found an out-of-the-way motel along a highway called Airline. The sputtering neon sign in the courtyard stained the night a garish red, even with the room's curtains drawn.

Bull Knife took a walk to find them food. Concho texted Porter House: *Tomorrow. When, where?* He then called Maria Morales to tell her he was doing OK. They talked a few minutes, though he didn't mention the attempt on his life. The motel room felt a lot lonelier when he hung up. They always did when you were away from home and loved ones.

Bull Knife returned with sodas and service station burgers far too thick with onions. They ate in silence, without even the TV. A text came in from Porter. *11:00 AM. Treasure Chest Casino. Lakeside end of Williams Blvd. I'll show you what you're up against. It ain't pretty.*

Concho texted back, *Fine.*

They'd gotten a room with twin beds. Concho took the one closest to the door. He hooked his phone to his charger and slid a Colt under the pillow as he lay down. He thought about all the times he'd had to sleep with a weapon close to hand. Far more than he could count or wanted to.

The neon light pulsed through the curtains like a crimson heartbeat, but once in a while it buzzed and sputtered. If it was a heart, the patient didn't seem to be doing too well. Concho tried not to take that image as a prophecy as he worked his way toward sleep.

CHAPTER 16

Williams Boulevard ran from Airline Highway to the shore of Lake Pontchartrain, crossing under the I-10. At the lakeshore end it rose slightly, passing through a concrete floodwall into something called Laketown, which consisted of a boat dock, a small park, and the casino complex.

From what the Texas Ranger had read, when the casino was put in, only offshore gambling was allowed in Louisiana. Thus, the Treasure Chest had been built into a riverboat and anchored a few feet off the lake's bank. Parking facilities and support buildings had been constructed on shore and a closed-in plank bridge connected the two.

Although valet parking was available, Concho found his own space near the back of the lot where it was nearly empty. The sky was cloudy. A cool breeze would explain the windbreaker he pulled on to hide his Colt.

As soon as he strode onto the boat he experienced a jolt of nostalgia melded with a faint tinge of homesickness. A little of it was the smell, the mix of body odors and disinfectants and hot metal from working machines, but mostly it was the sound, the jingle-jangle-ring-chime of slot machines doing their thing. The same sound filled every casino, including the Lucky Eagle on the reservation back outside Eagle Pass, Texas.

The Ranger stepped into the main gambling room and moved back against the wall, out of the way of people surging to and fro on various quests and errands. He'd left Bull Knife at the motel, partly because the two of them together were as conspicuous as salt and pepper at a hot sauce convention, and partly because he wasn't completely sure he trusted Porter House yet.

Concho checked his phone. 11:03 AM. No texts. But he didn't see Porter anywhere. To avoid standing out, he exchanged some bills for quarters and began sampling the slot machines, playing where he could keep an eye on the entrance. He lost steadily. He'd never been lucky at games of chance. He had always figured he used too much of his luck just staying alive.

It wasn't long before the PI arrived. He'd doffed his fedora for a short-brimmed white straw Panama hat. He wore a yellow linen jacket today over white trousers and a white shirt. It was the nattiest outfit Concho had seen the man wear. It might even have been ironed.

The investigator barely made eye contact, though. Instead, he got a small silver bucket loaded with his own quarters. He played toward the Ranger. Ten-Wolves followed his lead. Eventually they were on the same row of machines with only one seat between them. The remainder of the row sat empty.

"Sorry, I'm late," Porter said. "Traffic."

"Not a problem."

"Reason I had you meet me here, Kulick and LeBlanc work for a man named Roman Boudreaux. His name's not on the deed for the Treasure Chest but he's got a 'hidden' interest in the place."

An elderly couple passed along the narrow walkway behind them and Porter waited until they were gone before continuing.

"Boudreaux is a crime boss. Can't describe him any other way. Local rather than nationwide, though. He's got three sons. Christoph, Nicholas, Samuel. Or Sammy. The middle boy, Nicholas, is a session musician now and also plays in a blues band. He used to be better known. He goes by Nick Barron, that being his middle name. The other two work in their father's business. In fact, since Roman is pushing eighty, Chris mostly runs the business."

"All right," Concho said.

Porter won a small jackpot and laughed in surprise as the quarters clink-clinked into the machine's silver dispensing tray. As he scooped these up and dropped them into his bucket, he added,

"The father is old-time Cajun. Short, stout, something of an accent. Though it's mellowed over time. He's smart but not educated. Chris went to Loyola and got a law degree. You'd never know the two were related if you saw them together."

"Appreciate it, but I'm still waiting for why we met *here*."

"Figured you might want a look at Roman. He has a dedicated table upstairs at the buffet. He's there most days of the week. Works from there. Chris Boudreaux often joins him. Sometimes Sammy. Other prominent local criminals."

"The scales fall from my eyes."

Porter responded with a crooked grin. "I'm not going up. It's quite possible someone in his group will recognize me. They may recognize you, too, but I doubt there'll be any trouble in the buffet. Still, you better be cautious. You heeled?"

"Heeled? At least you have the PI lingo down."

Porter blushed. "Sorry. Noticed you're not wearing your badge. Just wondered if you had a gun."

Concho had his badge in his jeans pocket but didn't reveal that. He wore civilian clothes—jeans and a black t-shirt. But he'd put on a blue windbreaker against the outside chill. Under it nestled a shoulder holster and one of his Double Eagles.

"Don't worry," he said with a small smile. "I'm definitely carrying heat."

***

Concho headed upstairs to the riverboat's second deck and found his way to the Treasure Island Buffet. He hadn't felt hungry but the smell of food changed that and his stomach began to growl. He paid his fee and loaded a plate with steak, shrimp, frog legs and a baked potato. He poured himself some sweet tea and dished up a bowl of Louisiana gumbo.

Across the room from the service line, next to a row of tall windows, rested a large table with three men seated at it. Two other men stood beside the table; they were clearly muscle but Concho gave them a careful once over in case he had to go up against them.

The power in the room rested with the three seated men. Concho had seen their general types before. Roman Boudreaux stood barely five-eight but probably weighed a good two-seventy. His features were heavy and coarse, with a large fleshy nose and at least three rounded chins.

He had to be in his late seventies but still had a full head of dark hair, although it had surely been dyed. He'd dressed today in a blue-striped linen suit with a loud, moiré-patterned silk shirt. A ruby just a little smaller than Concho's baked potato gleamed on the middle finger of his left hand.

The man liked to "hold court." His hands were constantly in motion, emphasizing whatever tale he was telling. He chewed and talked at the same time, and did both expansively, sometimes spewing masticated fragments of his meal across his place setting.

To Roman's right sat a very thin, pale fellow in a tailored black suit with a matching hat who never remained still. The man gave Concho the impression of a small, nervous dog. He looked like an undertaker but the Ranger bet he was some kind of glorified personal assistant.

To Roman's right had to be Christoph Boudreaux, Roman's oldest son. The son was at least three inches taller than the father, with lighter skin and lighter hair and at least a hundred pounds slimmer. He must have taken after his mother physically; his features were handsome, his nose straight and thin over a generous mouth and a sharp chin. He wore a restrained gray business suit with a white shirt and yellow tie.

Concho sat where he could watch the Boudreaux table. He made no secret of it. The crime boss soon noticed. It irked him. He glanced toward the Ranger several times before turning his head to speak to one of his bodyguards. Concho smiled to himself as Boudreaux jerked his triple chins in the lawman's direction and the bodyguard nodded.

Before the guard could act, though, Christoph said something quickly and rose. As a dutiful son, he must have been aware of his father's distracted attention. He'd turned his head several times to check out the cause and now strode directly to Concho's table.

"Excuse me," he said to the Ranger, "but can I help you with something?" His voice was modulated, educated, without any hint of an accent.

"I forgot to get bacon," Concho said, gesturing toward his plate. "Maybe you could bring me half a dozen strips."

Christoph's smile was thin. "You've been staring at our table. It's starting to irritate my father and I don't think that's a good idea for you. Not really a good idea for any of us."

"Sorry. I thought he was a celebrity. Wasn't he in *The Godfather Part III*?"

This time Christoph chuckled. "Deliberately trying to provoke. I'm wondering why. What do you get out of it? Mind if I sit, by the way?"

He didn't wait for Concho to say 'yeah or nay' but pulled out the chair across the table and settled into it.

"You seem to know my father," Christoph continued. "But he doesn't know you. I don't know you. Which tells me you're some kind of lawman with a chip on his shoulder."

"That why you stopped old Roman from sending his goon over to beat me up?"

Christoph cleared his throat before answering. "I stopped him from sending a man over because violence in public is not good for business. I wasn't sure you were a lawman until I got close enough."

"I thought you were gonna finish that sentence with 'close

enough to smell you.'"

"Random insults seem more your sort of thing."

"Touché! Looks like I underestimated you."

Again came the thin smile. "So we come back to my original question, can I help you with something?"

Concho took a big bite of baked potato, chewed and swallowed. "You can tell me why your father is so concerned I'm in town that he first hired someone to follow me, then hired some gunmen to whack me."

"That's ridiculous."

"Jason Kulick and Kage LeBlanc."

Christoph's shoulders stiffened. The movement was subtle, and gone in an instant, but Concho had been watching for it.

"So, you recognize those names," he said.

"I've heard them somewhere. Now, who are you?"

"I figured you'd surely googled Concho Ten-Wolves. Maybe studied a picture."

Christoph's eyebrows flashed. He clearly recognized the name but all he said was, "I still don't know who you are."

"Now you're just lying. Maybe I didn't underestimate you after all."

Christoph hesitated. "This is not a place to have this conversation."

"Anyplace is fine with me. Tell me where?"

"Outside. Down the hall to the right. There's a conference room with a frosted glass door. Meet me there in five minutes."

"Roman and his goons coming along?"

Christoph took a deep breath. "Not sure. But let's hope not. The sight of blood always makes me queasy after I've eaten." He rose and walked back toward his father's table.

Concho finished his last frog leg, licked his fingers, then carried his tray to the discard table and exited the Treasure Island Buffet.

"Pretty good last meal if it comes to it," he murmured to himself. "And reasonably priced!"

CHAPTER 17

Concho found the conference room easily enough. He texted Bull Knife and Porter to let them know he was still alive. He waited. Christoph Boudreaux joined him six minutes later, sans father and goons, and unlocked the door. The Ranger let the other man go in ahead of him but the room lay empty and quiet when he entered himself. The silence suggested very good soundproofing.

Christoph gestured toward the dozen comfortable-looking cloth chairs surrounding an oval table in the center of the room. Concho remained standing. Christoph shrugged and sat.

"Unload your weapon," Boudreaux said.

Concho didn't argue. He shucked his Colt, released the magazine into his hand, and ejected the bullet already in the chamber. The pistol went back into his holster, the bullets into his pocket.

"Thanks. This room is swept regularly for bugs so we'll be able to talk freely here. We don't have a lot of time, though. My father will be joining us in about ten minutes. Can I assume you're not wired?"

Concho pulled up his t-shirt to reveal his lack of microphones, then thrust it down again. "You've probably got an audio jammer on this room anyway. But it sounds like you intend to talk about things you don't want your father to hear."

Christoph didn't directly answer. He leaned back in his chair and linked his hands across his flat belly. "You were right about what you said earlier. I did lie to some extent when I said I didn't know who you were. But it was a small lie. I recognized your name. I'd heard it before. But I didn't know anything about you, really. So, I *did* google you. I already knew you were a Texas Ranger, but I learned you're something of a hero down there. Which means you aren't here to kill my father. And I'm sure you realize this isn't Texas. It's Boudreaux-land. My father's land."

"And your land," Concho added.

Christoph nodded.

Moving slowly, Concho walked around the table. He didn't sit but leaned against the outside wall where he could keep an eye on the door. "I'm only passing through. But I have a reason for being here and I'm not going to be run off."

"I'm not trying to run you off, and neither is my father," Christoph replied. He looked unsure of himself for a moment. "At least I don't think he is. He denied it when I asked him about it. I believe him."

"Yet, Kulick and LeBlanc work for him?"

"My father employs them from time to time." He smiled. "Strictly for legal matters, of course. In this case, I don't believe he's the one who hired them."

"So who?"

Christoph rubbed his chin with one hand. The fingers of the other stroked at the table in front of him. "I've got two brothers. You probably know that."

"Nick and Sammy!"

Christoph nodded. "And there are other people—"

He broke off as the door opened and Roman Boudreaux walked in with his two goons in tow.

The goons took up positions to either side of their boss. Both had their arms crossed, which brought their hands within reach of the concealed weapons ruining the hang of their suit coats.

Roman glanced at his son, who nodded back. Concho assumed the nod indicated he was safe to be in the room with.

Roman seated himself heavily in the biggest chair at the head of the table. When he spoke, Concho could hear the Cajun in his voice, but the words were mostly all there and mostly standard English.

"So, you are the great Ten-Wolves. You don' look like so much to me."

"Opinions vary," Concho replied.

"What is this nonsense my son says you believe? I am trying to kill you? I don' try such things. If they become necessary, I do them."

"As I told your son, Jason Kulick and Kage LeBlanc came after me. I assumed a man like yourself would know everything his employees were doing. Perhaps I made a mistake."

The skin tightened around Boudreaux's glittering brown eyes. "I am already finding out about this. I will have answers soon."

"Dare I imagine you'll share those when you get them?"

Boudreaux smiled. It was a small and ugly expression, reminding Concho of the look on the face of a feral hog eating a snake carcass.

"I only keep my *employees* in my confidence," the man said. "Of course," he gestured expansively, "I could possibly find a place for a Texas Ranger on my payroll."

"Thanks," the Ranger said, "but I already have trouble spending all the money I make."

Boudreaux shrugged. "Your loss."

"If *you* didn't order me taken out, who in your organization did?" Concho asked.

Christoph interspersed a statement before his father had a chance to respond. "Before we answer any more of your questions, we need you to answer one of ours."

"What?"

"You claimed you had a 'reason for being here.' I'd like to

know what it is?"

Concho had been expecting a lot more blowback than he'd gotten from confronting the Boudreaux family. Christoph, at least, seemed genuinely confused about the situation. So, things weren't as simple as "him against them." Maybe he had to give a little to get a little.

"Fair enough," he said. "I was told a long time ago that my mother was dead. Recently, it was suggested she's still alive and living in the New Orleans area. It seemed a simple enough investigation to find out. But before I even started asking questions, people started warning me off and threatening me. When I insulted one of the folks making the threats, he sent three killers after me. People who work for you."

Christoph glanced at his father and got an almost imperceptible nod before looking back at the Ranger. "The person you insulted," the son said. "What did they sound like?"

"A man's voice. New Orleans accent. But not heavy. They used the phrase 'not how business is done.' The oddest thing they said was "You sang down the lightning now, boy!'"

Christoph frowned.

"Sound familiar?" Concho asked.

"Not particularly. Colorful at least." Christoph took a deep breath. "The scenario you've described makes no sense. At least, it seems like an overreaction regarding someone who doesn't want to be found."

A light knock on the door derailed any response Concho might have made. One of the goons opened the door and in came the thin man in the black suit who'd been sitting at the Boudreaux table earlier. The man looked even more like the stereotype of an undertaker up close. His cheekbones were high, his cheeks hollow, his lips too red for a wan face that seemed to reject the light.

The man's gaze passed very quickly over Concho before returning to his boss. Even here he could not be still. He fidgeted. "I have the information you wanted," he said. His voice sounded like it was being piped through a vibrato effects pedal.

"Tell, tell," Roman Boudreaux replied.

The man glanced once more toward Concho. A quick frown pruned his mouth but he did as he was told.

"Jason Kulick and Kage LeBlanc were arrested by the New Orleans police yesterday evening. Along with a third man named Devin Casper."

"Who is?" Roman demanded, his eyes narrowing.

"Unknown at present, sir. But I'll keep looking. All three were bailed out early this morning."

"By who?" Roman snapped.

"A-1 Bonding Agency. No specific name given. I've left a message for the head of A-1 to call me back."

The crime boss tapped his fingers on the table. He wore some heavy scent that smelled like perfume covering up rot. When he glanced at Concho, his piggish eyes were red-rimmed. Maybe from lack of sleep or dissipation. Who could tell?

Roman gestured at the faux undertaker. "This here is my… administrative assistant. As they say today. He speaks for me when I need him to."

The man turned toward Concho. His eyes gleamed a pallid gray. He took off his hat and offered Concho a half nod, half bow in greeting. "Piotr Morozov. At your service."

Concho understood just enough Russian to recognize that Morozov meant "Frost," but he didn't think *this* Morozov was actually from Russia. The man had very little accent but his language was subtly off. Ten-Wolves thought he might be Polish.

Roman Boudreaux pushed to his feet, his breathing coming heavy. "Tell him what we discuss," he said to Morozov. Without a glance at his son or elsewhere, he warped himself out of the room surrounded by his bodyguards.

Concho glanced at Morozov expectantly.

CHAPTER 18

Nolen Carmichael III moved quickly through his office, throwing a few items into an expensive brown leather gym bag. His wife, Abigail, stepped into the room and gave a small gasp.

"Is everything…OK?" she asked.

Nolen smiled at his wife, walked across and kissed her on the forehead. "Of course, Abby. I got a call about some work across the lake. I intended to come find you in just a minute."

"What kind of work?"

Nolen frowned. "Not sure yet. The client didn't want to chat about it over the phone. He wants a personal meeting."

Abigail nodded. "When will you be home?"

"I won't really know until I hear about the job. I'll call and let you know but I rather doubt I'll be home for dinner. Eat when you're hungry."

"All right."

Nolen turned away, tightened the leather straps holding the gym bag closed and hefted it.

"You don't think it has anything to do with our recent visitors, do you?" Abigail asked.

Nolen paused. "You mean the Texas Ranger and his trusty Indian sidekick?"

"I think they're both…Native Americans. But yeah."

A stern look crossed Nolen's face. "I really don't know. But you understand I don't like to talk business around the house anyway, my dear?"

"Yes. I'm sorry."

Nolen smiled. He kissed his wife again, lightly on the lips this time. "No harm, no foul. But I have to go.

He stepped past her and walked out; she watched him leave with dread in her heart.

***

Piotr Morozov, Roman Boudreaux's assistant, waited until his boss was gone and the door closed behind him before speaking.

"It is important for you to know," he said to Concho, enunciating very formally, "that Mr. Boudreaux had nothing to do with the attempt to harm you. In fact, he is quite furious about it. If he finds out someone within his…business retained the services of Misters LeBlanc and Kulick, they will be severely reprimanded for acting in such a reckless and independent manner."

"The main problem being they acted without orders from him," Concho interpreted.

Morozov continued as if the Ranger hadn't spoken. "If he finds out Misters LeBlanc and Kulick took such an outside commission, they will never work for Mr. Boudreaux again. I trust this is to your satisfaction?"

Concho chuckled. "Not even a little bit. But I don't imagine I'm going to get any more. What I'm hearing, though, is that no one will interfere any further in my search for my mother."

"It is Mr. Boudreaux's opinion, as it is mine, that the incident we're discussing here had nothing to do with your mother. No doubt when everything is diagrammed out, we'll find some old personal conflict at the heart of the matter. However, it is not acceptable to use business assets to settle such issues. Now, if you'll excuse me. I have work to do."

Concho waved. Morozov gave his half nod, half bow, then left the room.

Concho looked over at Christoph, whose jaws worked as if he were chewing gum. He had to be chewing thoughts instead.

"You mentioned your brothers," Concho said. "Nick and Sammy. You think one of *them* might have sent Kulick and LeBlanc after me?"

"I don't know enough yet to have an opinion on it. But I'll find out. And I was about to tell you that *others* in the organization could be involved when my father came in."

"You're being rather forthcoming," Concho said. "Unless you're lying to throw me off."

"I'm a very good liar, Mister Ten-Wolves. When I want to be. But…all I want right now is for this nonsense to go away. And the best way to do that, and assure nothing else like it happens in the future, is to identify whoever is responsible."

"Could it have anything to do with my mother?"

"I'll check out that angle, though I doubt it's the instigating event you think it is. Give me your cell number and I'll be in touch."

Concho did so and got Christoph's in return. Both men rose from their seats.

"Have to confess," the Ranger said. "I wasn't expecting cooperation from anyone on the Boudreaux team on this matter. It's a pleasant surprise."

Christoph smiled. "Folks in our line of business don't make a habit of fighting wars with the law. It's almost always a losing proposition for our side."

"I'm not exactly the law here."

"Close enough.

The two men stepped out of the quietened conference room into the hallway. Sound returned, tripled it seemed from having been gone. Neither man offered to shake hands before they went their separate ways.

***

Concho took a spin through the gaming room to see if Porter House was still around. No sign of him. He headed out to his truck. A beat-up old Ford Taurus had parked along the driver's side of the Ranger's F-150. The Taurus might once have been green but its paint had weathered to a dull gray.

Someone sat in the car, which didn't make Concho comfortable. He'd deliberately chosen the emptiest section of the parking lot, and it was still empty except for his truck and this one other vehicle. He approached cautiously until he identified Porter. The PI signaled the Ranger to join him. He opened the passenger side door and slid in. A tight fit.

"This isn't a good idea," Concho said. "Not if you want to maintain your anonymity."

"Too late. They made me in the casino. Made it clear they knew we were together."

"And yet you're still alive."

"I think you're my only protection now. As long as they know I'm hanging out with a Texas Ranger they're not likely to murder me."

"They tried to murder an actual Texas Ranger. Me! I'm not sure I'm providing protection. Besides, I'll have to go home sometime."

"Maybe I'll go with you."

Concho scratched at the shadow of whiskers he wished he'd taken the time to shave away this morning. "You may be safe anyway." He explained what he'd learned, and that maybe the people who'd hired the PI were working on the sly and were about to get called on it.

"Hope so. If someone in their organization has gone rogue, my money is on Sammy Boudreaux."

"Christoph mentioned Sammy as a possibility, too. Any idea where he lives?"

"He lives at the Boudreaux compound, which is a Fort Knox to get into. But he doesn't stay there much. I know where he hangs out."

"Do tell?"

"The Rivershack Tavern. Over on River Road."

"In New Orleans?"

"The official address is Jefferson Parish. Outside Orleans."

"Think he might be there now?"

"No idea."

"All right, let me swing by and pick up Bull Knife. You follow me there. Then I'll follow you to the Rivershack."

"Only one heads-up I'll give you."

"Which is?"

"They sometimes cater to a rough crowd. The kind of crowd that might not like certain folks who look like you do."

Concho grinned. "You mean because I'm way too handsome?"

"Yeah, that," Porter replied.

CHAPTER 19

Concho turned off River Road into the graveled lot of the Rivershack Tavern. He was lucky to find a parking space. Someone must have just left. A dozen vehicles and a few motorcycles filled most of the spaces in front and alongside the tavern.

Concho killed his Ford and got out. Bull Knife joined him. Porter House pulled in a moment later but had to park across a side road and walk over. Concho had strongly suggested to Porter that he show them the Rivershack and describe Sammy Boudreaux, but then stay out of it. The young man insisted he wanted to "do his part." It seemed dangerous but Porter was full-grown and could make his own decisions.

The Rivershack was built of wood and painted green. Its tin roof had rusted in places. Two signs reading "Jax Beer" and "Dixie Beer" hung from poles in the parking area. Other painted signs and words adorned the building itself, including a phrase that read, "Home of the tacky ashtray." Whatever that meant.

Concho checked his surroundings. A white canopy had been erected to the left side of the building. He could see a band staging area and long, rough wooden tables with no people sitting at them.

Despite various industrial buildings and a few small houses stretching along the road to the left and right, the area felt lonely.

Part of it was the late afternoon light dimmed by scudding gray clouds. Part of it was the rising bulk of the levee, which started just on the opposite side of the road from the tavern.

A line of nearly barren trees marked the top of the levee. You couldn't see the winding Mississippi beyond, which was a good thing because along much of this area the water level was actually higher than the surrounding land. A flood was always an imminent threat in southern Louisiana.

Concho started toward the bar. His companions followed. They stepped through a door into a single large room. A music stage marked one end but was currently unoccupied. An odd mix of Country and Cajun tunes played from the jukebox. A single pool table stood surrounded by half a dozen men. Another dozen patrons sat at the bar itself or at tables spread around.

The inside smelled like any drinking establishment and was warm, almost uncomfortably so. None of the ceiling fans seemed to be working. Mardi Gras decorations and booze signs hung on every wall. Elvis stared down with painted eyes on all who entered. Behind the bar rose a wall of assorted booze. Bottles full of russet and red and translucent liquids gleamed in the diffuse light.

In front of the scuffed brown wood of the bar sat the strangest bar stools Concho had ever seen. Their rounded tops rested on carved legs—human-looking legs that appeared to have been cut off just above the knee. The legs weren't painted. They were "clothed," in jeans, skirts, pajama bottoms and other such articles, with footwear ranging from high heels to muck boots. Concho chose a khaki-and-muck-boot stool and tried to make himself comfortable on its too-small frame. Bull Knife and Porter House joined him to either side.

"What can I get you?" the bartender asked.

"You have Shiner Bock?" Concho inquired.

"Sure do."

"I'll have one. And whatever my friends want."

"Miller Lite," Porter said.

"Water," Bull Knife said.

Concho glanced at his companions. "Let's hope they don't mix your drinks up. You'll never be able to tell them apart by the taste."

Bull Knife's expression didn't change. Porter smirked. "Ha!"

The bartender returned with their drinks, picked up the twenty Concho placed down with "keep the change," then nodded and moved down the way to speak to another customer.

A loud voice from one of the men at the pool table called attention to itself. "Hey, Barney! Better put on Elvis's *In the Ghetto* to make our new guests feel at home."

Apparently, Barney was the bartender's name. It seemed appropriate. He glanced toward the pool table with a disapproving look but only shook his head and returned to his conversation.

"Or maybe Cher's *Half-Breed*," the same voice called out before breaking into wild laughter. A few other voices joined the laughter, though most sounded strained.

"Any sign of Sammy Boudreaux?" Concho asked Porter.

The PI shook his head as he sipped his Miller Lite. "No. Might be a little early for him. If he comes."

"We'll wait a bit," Concho replied, taking a long swallow of his Shiner Bock, which tasted cold and good against the heat of the room.

"Or, hey," the loudmouth called again. "That song *Cherokee People* might be approp...appropriate." Again came the laughter.

Barney gave up his conversation and came back down the bar. He called toward the pool table, "Timbo, man. Cut that crap out." The man called Timbo must have flipped Barney off because the bartender returned the gesture. Then he glanced at Concho and the others. "Sorry about that nonsense. He's just a drunk asshole."

"He needs to watch his mouth," Bull Knife said.

"Yeah." Barney shrugged. "Let me know if you need a refill."

Concho nodded. "Say, I met a dude who claimed to hang out here sometimes. Said his name was Sammy...Sammy something. Local name. You know who I'm talking about?"

Barney studied the Ranger and seemed to find him acceptable to respond to. "Sammy Boudreaux?" he asked.

Concho snapped his fingers. "Yeah, Boudreaux! He said I should drop by sometime for a beer. He been around?"

Barney frowned. "Generally don't talk about my customers to folks I don't know."

Concho nodded again. "Good practice. The only reason I asked is because he was talking about maybe having some work for me. I could use it." He gestured at his companions. "We all could."

Barney considered. "Haven't seen him in a few days. But he's usually only here irregularly. Give me your name and number and I'll make sure he gets it if I see him."

"Sounds fair," Concho said. He recited his number for Barney, who wrote it down on a clipboard pad from under the bar. He added, "People usually call me Ten-Wolves."

Barney added the name to his pad. "All right," he said.

From the direction of the pool table, the drunken Timbo began doing his rendition of a supposed Indian chant. "Haya haya, haya haya."

Bull Knife swiveled around on this stool and said loudly and clearly. "You need to shut your mouth!"

***

Nolen Carmichael III pulled his yellow Lexus LC 500 into one of the parking lots near the Laketown Fishing Pier. He got out and stretched his back and shoulders after the hour and a half drive across the Causeway bridge.

Off to his right, he could see the pearl-white gleam of the Treasure Chest Casino. Two parking spaces away on his left sat a limo with the logo of the casino on the side. He took the toothpick out of his mouth and stuck it in his shirt pocket, then walked across and got in the back seat of the limo.

Piotr Morozov sat writing on a tablet computer but put it face down in his lap as Nolen climbed in. He did not smile but said,

"Good afternoon. I trust you are well."

"Better than most," Nolen said.

Morozov offered a small smile at Nolen's words but it was unclear if he'd really processed them or not. "I have two names for you."

"Concho Ten-Wolves and a man named Bull Knife."

Morozov arched an almost invisible eyebrow. "You seem to be ahead of me."

"They visited my wife a couple of days ago. I spoke to them. Ten-Wolves is pretty smart. Had a feeling they might work their way around to a Boudreaux."

"About what did you speak with them on, may I ask?"

"They're searching for their mother."

"Ah," Morozov said, nodding. "That is apparently the common story they are using. *And* why Ten-Wolves showed up at the casino earlier today and nearly started a war with Roman Boudreaux."

"He gets around."

"I found him quite off-putting. One would not imagine a dead woman could cause so much trouble."

Nolen chuckled. "If you say so."

Morozov gave Nolen a sharp glance. "Is there a problem?"

"Not for me. But Ten-Wolves is my wife's nephew. Not that she's ever seen or spoken to him before two days ago."

"That is…disturbing."

"It's just another variable to be considered."

"For how long?"

"What is Nicholas's stance on all this?"

"I am generally trying not to burden him with the problem. He does not always know what is best for him and the family anyway."

"You're right about that," Nolen agreed. "I've been taking care of his troubles for him since the days we toured together."

"A response is needed quickly," Morozov said. "Ten-Wolves has already overstayed his welcome."

Nolen flashed the other man a smile. "I'm going into the casino and getting a bite to eat. I'll let you know after that what level of response I can provide."

Morozov nodded. "There's another name. A bonus if you'd like."

"Now that name I can't guess."

"A private investigator named Porter House."

Nolen laughed. "It's just dumb enough to be real. I wouldn't have thought *you'd* be stupid enough to hire a PI, though."

"I didn't. Someone else did without consulting me."

"I see. You're just cleaning up the mess?"

"Correction. I called you to clean it up. All I do is point it out."

CHAPTER 20

As Bull Knife told the man named Timbo to shut his mouth, Concho turned on his stool to take in the scene. Beside him, Porter House tried to melt into the bar. Except for the jukebox playing a raucous zydeco tune, the tavern had fallen silent.

Four men stood around the pool table, mostly grinning as they watched the antics of a fifth. The fifth man wore an open gray work shirt with the name Timbo embroidered in white over the pocket. A mostly-white wife-beater t-shirt underneath the man's workwear revealed the blocky muscles of someone who toils with heavy things.

Timbo was bald; his pate shone with sweat. He might have been in his early forties. He probably didn't stand quite six feet but looked nearly as wide as he was tall. His friends were all younger but wore the same type of shirt and had to be from the same crew. Most were also drunk, though not as sotted as Timbo.

Timbo stared at Bull Knife. His eyes were small, brown, and nasty. "What the hell did you say to me, boy?" he demanded.

"I said, shut your mouth!"

A scowl remolded Timbo's face to make it even uglier than before. He flushed and clenched his fists as he took the first steps toward Bull Knife, who prepared to meet him.

"Hold it!" Concho said loudly. "This doesn't need to happen."
Timbo paused, his gaze drawn to the Ranger's face. One of his
friends stood rooted to the floor on the far side of the pool table
and looked sick. The other three had come around to back their
buddy up. He seemed to be aware of it and draw courage from it.

"You've had your jokes," Concho said directly to Timbo. "It's
not worth fighting about. But enough is enough. You cool off and
we'll cool off. And everyone goes home tonight intact."

Timbo wasn't sober enough to be reasonable. He lifted both his
big hands and stuck up the middle fingers.

"Screw you!" he snarled.

Bull Knife charged the man; he ducked under Timbo's arms
and hooked him around the waist, picking up his not inconsid-
erable bulk and carrying him back six steps to smash against the
pool table. The table shuddered; pool balls rattled. Timbo bellowed like a castrated bull.

Two of Timbo's friends leaped forward to drag Bull Knife away.
Concho intervened. He shoved one man hard, sent him reeling
into an empty barroom table that collapsed under his weight.

The second man slung a punch. Concho blocked with his left
arm and smashed a straight right jab into the fellow's face. The
man stumbled back but was too drunk to realize he'd lost a tooth
and was gushing blood from a cut lip. He rushed forward again
just as the third man among Timbo's cronies grabbed a pool stick
and whipped the thin end at the Ranger's head.

Concho ducked away from the pool cue and swept his right leg
out across the path of the charging man. The fellow tripped, went
face-first into the floor with his hands out. Still in a crouch, Concho twisted around. The man with the pool cue snapped it down
hard toward his face. The Ranger threw both arms up to block
and the stick cracked across his forearms with numbing force.

Concho hadn't been angry. Now he was. The blow hurt. He
powered to his feet; a standing front kick slammed into the man's
stomach before he could raise his stick again. The blow flung him

back against the table and Concho followed, fists up to strike.

With his senses shifted into overdrive, Concho could see and hear everything. Bull Knife and Timbo had wound up on the floor in a wild punch fest. Porter faced off with the one man on Timbo's crew who didn't seem to want to fight. The two danced back and forth, feinting at each other without making contact. People in the tavern screamed but the only words Concho could make out were the bartender's shouts to "stop it or I'll call the cops."

Already here, Concho thought. *And not stopping it.*

Two punches to the jaw put Concho's opponent out on his feet. As the fellow wilted, Concho twisted around. The man he'd flung into a table charged him, his head bent low. The Ranger snapped his knee up, connecting with the man's chin. The fellow's eyes rolled up in his head as he blacked out and went sprawling.

The man who'd gone face-first into the floor tried getting up but then sagged back with a groan. It seemed the pain of his injuries had finally cut through the liquor haze dulling his brain. He flung a hand over his busted mouth but blood still seeped through the fingers.

Concho turned toward Bull Knife. His half brother was straddling Timbo and punching down while Timbo had his arms up desperately to protect his face as he yelled, "OK, OK, stop, OK."

"Enough," Concho said to Bull Knife. The half-Apache seemed oblivious.

"Enough!" Concho shouted.

Bull Knife heard him this time. He took a deep breath and lowered his arms. Abruptly he stood up. Timbo didn't move except to shake his head back and forth on the floor as crimson flowed from his nose and mouth and from a cut above his eye.

Porter and the last of Timbo's friends had stopped dancing. A glare from Concho sent the other fellow running for the door. Porter met the Ranger's gaze, dropped his hands and shrugged. Concho slapped him lightly on the shoulder.

Barney the bartender had come around his bar. He held a

nightstick he'd pulled from somewhere but clearly had no intention of using it.

"Look at this! Look at this!" he kept saying.

Concho looked. The pool table had been shifted from its position. One patron table had collapsed. Bodies dotted the floor,
some unconscious but none of them dead. The blood could be
mopped up.

"I've seen worse," Concho said. He pulled four twenties out of
his billfold and offered them to Barney. "This ought to cover it."

Barney blinked. He took the money, then hmmed without any
real words coming out.

Ten-Wolves walked back to the bar, picked up his bottle of
Shiner Bock and drained it. "Gentlemen," he said to his companions as he set the bottle down. "It looks like our work here is done."

As the three headed out the door, Concho glanced back at a
forlorn-looking Barney. "Don't forget to give Sammy Boudreaux
my number," he called.

***

After picking up some debris from the fight and doctoring
a few cuts, Barney ushered Timbo and his crew out of the Rivershack. Most of the rest of the patrons had cleared out already,
though a couple of die-hard drinkers hung on.

Barney went back behind the bar, stuck his unused nightstick
under the counter, then refilled whatever drinks his two remaining
customers wanted. He swept the empty Shiner Bock bottle off the
bar and started to toss it, then thought better of it. Using his bar
rag, he wiped his own fingerprints from the neck of the bottle,
then slid it into a plastic sack for storage.

Pulling out a cell phone, he swiped a number for one of his
contacts. The phone rang. A man answered.

"You're gonna want to hear this," Barney said.

CHAPTER 21

Nighttime was sliding into home base in the world out-side the Rivershack as Concho and his two companions stood next to the Ranger's pickup. Bull Knife's left cheek was swelling but other than that he seemed uninjured. Porter had neither been hit nor done any hitting himself.

"Sorry," the PI said as Concho glanced at him. "Told you I wasn't much of a fighter."

The Ranger grinned. "You kept the other fellow occupied. That's doing your part."

Porter shook his head but didn't say anything else.

"What now?" Bull Knife asked. "I can't see where the road goes from here."

"Don't know about you," Concho said, "but I'm going back to the motel and read a while. Then sleep on it. Fill my belly some-where in between those two. You reckon the motel we're staying at has room service?"

Bull Knife smirked. "The gas station next door is probably still serving its cuisine."

Concho made a face. "Good thing I had a big lunch."

Porter sighed and turned toward his car. "Talk to you fellows tomorrow."

"Night," Concho replied. He watched the younger man walk away and could see the depression working in him. He wasn't sure what to say. He'd begun to like Porter, though maybe the fellow wasn't suited for the private eye biz. "Try to get in a good sleep," he called after the man. The only response was a backward wave.

***

Porter House parked on a quiet side street off Magazine near his office. The lawyer he shared the building with, Benedict Cooper, who was also his uncle, had gone for the day. The windows were dark and the front door locked. Porter let himself in with his key and tramped heavily upstairs to the three-room suite where he both lived and worked.

Dropping the Wendy's bag he carried on his desk, he stripped off his linen jacket and hung it on the coat rack by the window. With a heavy sigh, he slid into his chair and opened the bottom drawer on his desk to pull out a paper plate and a hand towel.

The Wendy's Single and fries went on the plate. Porter opened the burger and scrapped off the onions. He took his first bite and chewed. It tasted like paste. The bread clung to the roof of his mouth. He tried a fry. It felt like a cold and stiffened worm between his fingers and didn't taste much better.

Normally, he liked Wendy's. But today, tonight, he was unhappy with himself, with his world, and so with his food. He sighed again and leaned back in his chair. He'd failed at everything, he told himself. He was in debt past his eyebrows. His car was fifteen years old with an odometer that didn't work. If his uncle hadn't let him slide on his rent he wouldn't have this office or a bed to sleep in. Not without going home to his parents with his tail tucked.

Maybe it was time to give up his dream of being a private investigator. He'd had it in his head since he was fifteen when his mother, Benedict Cooper's sister, had introduced him to Raymond Chandler's *The Lady in the Lake*. After that, he'd read everything Chandler had written, as well as everything by Dashiell Hammett,

Chester Himes, John D. MacDonald, and the New Orleans-based PI series by James Sallis about a character named Lew Griffin. He still had all those books, though his parents kept them for him. He didn't think they'd look professional displayed in his office.

He'd also known better than to accept fiction for real life. He'd taken courses, read forensic books, watched forensic how-to videos. He'd undergone both police and weapons training. Despite such, he hadn't even been able to follow Bull Knife without giving himself away. And earlier tonight he'd proven how inept he was at anything resembling a physical confrontation. He'd proven it in front of a Texas Ranger no less.

Porter ate another French fry and made a face. He finally took the bun off his burger and just ate the meat. He half wanted a drink and considered lacing his Coca Cola with some whiskey from the bottle he kept in his desk. He decided against it. Truth be, he didn't really like the taste of whiskey.

Yeah, he smirked to himself, *you're a real he-man*.

With a final sigh, he scraped the remains of his meal into the trash. Tying off the bag, he carried it downstairs and out to the curb for tomorrow's pick-up. Returning upstairs, he opened the closed off room next to his office. It had once been an exam room for the pediatrician who'd rented this same space before him. One wall still held cabinets with leftover bandages and other medical accoutrements inside. The room also had a sink and a toilet, though, and Porter had moved in a single bed.

Stripping to his underwear and flinging himself down on the bed, Porter tried for sleep. He tossed and turned for nearly an hour before slumber claimed him. It was past midnight when he awoke. Someone stood in the room with him, a tall, shadowy figure.

Porter sat up. He'd left his gun in his desk in the other room. "Who...who are you?" he demanded. "What do you want?"

"Shhh!" the figure responded.

***

Concho knew that dreams arose from one's own mind,
from daytime thoughts and worries, and from the books and games
and movies you fed it. But sometimes the origins were hard to trace.
So it was with the dream that troubled him on Wednesday morning.

He was a child standing in a winter-killed pasture of brown
grass and the long stems of blackened flowers. Patches of dirty
snow clung to shadows wherever they could be found. A tornado—far out of season—churned across the field toward him,
kicking up dark columns of dirt and the shrapnel of dead leaves
and stems. He was excited and afraid at the same time, but unable to run.

The funnel of the tornado looked like none he'd ever seen.
Despite the dust it raised, it was pure white, the color of crystal-
line snow. That was not the strangest thing about it. At its base, it
flowed in a twisted knot around and around upon itself. The cone
above stretched in a curve high into a gray-clouded sky where
winks of strange light constantly detonated.

Other people roamed the field between Concho and the tornado. They seemed oblivious to their danger. Or perhaps they were
in no danger. They, too, were knotted, with crooked limbs twisted
around their bodies.

Sleet thrown off by the approaching tornado began to strike
Concho like shotgun pellets. He cried out but no sound came
from his lips. He tried to force his legs to move. He tried and
tried, and could not.

Someone began to sing behind him. There were no words, only
a melody that rose and fell, swept and swooped. Concho could not
turn his head to see the singer but he didn't need to. The image
burned itself into his head as if cast there by sorcery.

An angel stood just at his shoulder. Not one of the beautiful
angels of renaissance paintings, but one of the dread beings of the
Bible. Its legs were columns of glittering dust. Its torso consisted of
sticks twisted into knots. It smelled of fire and tigers.

The being had only two wings, one black and one white, with

the feathers coiled upon themselves like melted jacks. In the center of a face of many bubbling eyes, a round mouth lay open. It bled a threnody both beautiful and terrible.

The angel reached out. Concho sensed it. It touched his shoulder with a hand that both burned and frosted. He snapped awake, breathing hard. When he checked the time on his phone it read 5:57, three minutes before he would normally have awakened. Bull Knife slept quietly in the other bed.

Concho wiped his hand across his mouth. Not all dreams had meaning but this one…. It was unusual, even for him. He couldn't make any sense of it, at least not yet. His phone rang, making him jump.

Bull Knife exploded up from his own sleep, his hand clutching the bone-handled hunting knife he'd hidden beneath his pillow. Concho signaled him for calm, then swiped to answer the call.

"Ten-Wolves!" a voice said.

Concho recognized it—Solly Burstein, the NOPD homicide detective who'd said he'd cut Concho a little "slack" after the attempt on his life by Jason Kulick and Kage LeBlanc. It didn't sound like Solly was about to cut him slack right now.

"What's wrong?" Concho asked.

"I need you to come in. You and your brother. This morning. Right now!"

"Why?"

"I believe you know a man named Porter House."

A chill flashed up Concho's spine. "What happened?"

"Just meet me at police headquarters. District 8. At 334 Royal Street.

"All right. We'll be there. Probably half an hour."

"If it's much longer, I'll have to issue a warrant." Solly hung up.

CHAPTER 22

Concho and Bull Knife had to park half a mile from Dis-trict 8 Police Headquarters and walk quickly the rest of the way. The building stood right on Royal Street, set off from the sidewalk by one of the black, wrought iron fences ubiquitous in New Orleans. It was a two-story complex, a faux Greek structure painted in faded peach with white Doric columns supporting the roof.

It was cool enough for a coat to conceal it but Concho left his shoulder holster and Colt .45 behind, knowing they'd have to pass through a metal detector to get into the station. Bull Knife reluctantly left his knife.

Ten-Wolves asked for Solly Burstein at the front desk and was directed up the stairs to the second floor. A babble of voices assaulted them; a hundred odors vied for their attention. They passed offices and wove through desks staffed with policemen who paid them no mind, eventually discovering Solly at a small, crowded desk against the back wall.

He was on the phone when they approached, looked up with relief and motioned them to the two chairs across from him while he finished his call and hung up. He'd aged in the last couple of days. His face was drawn thinner than before. His starched white shirt had lost much of its starch and his red tie hung crooked.

"What's happened to Porter House?" Concho demanded.

Solly didn't respond immediately. Concho chafed. A cigarette encased in Lucite sat on the detective's desk. He looked at it with momentary longing, then picked up the mug by his right hand and took a loud sip. Concho smelled coffee with chicory, a biting if not particularly appealing scent. As Solly drank, his gaze searched Concho and Bull Knife. He took a deep breath as he put down the cup.

"I'm going to ask you that same question. And since I'm the cop working this case, I get to hear an answer first."

"If there's a *case*," Concho said, "it means he's dead, hurt, or missing. Tell me which one, and I'll tell you everything I know."

Solly scratched his nose but his brown eyes never left Concho's. "At least two of the three," he finally said. "Blood was found in his apartment. Quite a bit. Type O, which is his type. But no body."

Ten-Wolves sighed. "When?"

Solly shook his head. "Not how this works. Tell me how you know him."

Concho nodded. "All right." He told Solly about Porter following Bull Knife, about their visit to the PI's office to seek information, about calling out the man who'd hired Porter over the phone, and about Porter identifying two of Concho's attackers and linking them to Roman Boudreaux, and last about meeting the private investigator at the Treasure Chest and checking out the Rivershack Tavern to see if Sammy Boudreaux might show up.

"He left us around 8:00 last night," Concho concluded. "We were supposed to touch base today."

"Why?"

"Good question. I tried to get Porter to stay out of it but he kept wanting to help. And he knew the city and the underbelly of it better than I did. I should have kicked him to the curb. I knew he was putting himself at risk."

"Why didn't you tell me this the other night at the Monteleone?"

"Like I said, I was trying to get the man to stay clear. Besides, I kind of liked him."

"Didn't work out," Solly said. "You shouldn't lie to a fellow lawman."

"A lie of omission. But you're right, it didn't work out. And now a good man is in trouble. Or dead. Was there enough blood loss to kill him?"

Solly considered. "The coroner is not sure. The blood had soaked into the carpet. Maybe some had been absorbed by his clothing. Hard to tell exactly how much spilled. However, I'm thinking he's dead. Though I don't know why the killer took the body. Either of you have an alibi between about 10:00 last night and 3:00 this morning?"

"Only each other," Concho said. "But if you're not arresting us, you have some reason to believe we weren't involved. What is it? And is that how you found out we knew him?"

"I'm not inclined to share anything further with you."

Concho shook his head. He leaned forward, his gaze focusing intently on the homicide detective. "Come on, Solly! Porter might still be alive and we can't waste time if he is. By now you've done your research on me. You know who I am and that I didn't come to New Orleans to kill some barely dry-behind-the-ears private detective. You've got something that clears us. What?"

"It doesn't clear you. But a note was left that sows a little extra confusion."

"Oh?"

Solly stared at the Ranger for a moment longer, then opened a thin manila folder on the desk in front of him and took out a photocopied sheet of paper. He slid this across the desk to Concho, who picked it up. Bull Knife leaned in to study it as well.

"That's a copy of it," Burstein said. "The original was on an index card from Porter's desk. Done with one of Porter's pens. And before you ask, we didn't get any fingerprints. The perp wore gloves."

Concho studied the note. At the top were the words, "Deliver to," and beneath were two quick sketches. One showed the head of a wolf with the number "10" written beside it. The other image was of a bull's head with a knife stuck between the eyes and tiny droplets of what Concho assumed was meant to represent blood dripping down.

"Ten-Wolves and Bull Knife," Concho read.

"And the kicker," Solly added.

Below the images were two succinct sentences. Concho studied them, read them.

"No more warnings. Leave town."

***

Samuel "Sammy" Boudreaux was the product of his father's second marriage to a blonde trophy wife and had only just turned thirty. That made him considerably younger than his two brothers, Christoph and Nicholas, and made him feel he had to constantly fight for both independence and his place at the table. Sometimes, he admitted, that made him hard to please. He was not pleased now as he paced back and forth in the combination party and fishing cabin he kept secretly on the South Shore of Lake Pontchartrain.

"You need to let it go, sir," another man in the room said.

Sammy stopped pacing and spun toward the voice. "You don't tell me what I need!" he snapped.

The other voice soothed in response. "I'm not, sir. I'm only letting you know that I have someone dealing with the issue and you can relax and let me handle it."

"The son of a bitch insulted me," Sammy fired back, gesturing wildly. "And now I find he's been to my favorite bar just to mess with me. I want his guts cut out. I'll use 'em for bait!"

"My...colleague is aware of your anger, sir. He is a professional and will take care of everything. You can be sure of it. Much better than Misters Kulick and LeBlanc. May I add that your father is quite wroth concerning those two gentlemen."

Sammy had resumed pacing but stopped again now. He dropped heavily into an easy chair. His voice sounded desperate. "He doesn't know I was involved, does he?"

"Of course not," Piotr Morozov said. "And I'm doing what I can to make sure he never finds out."

Sammy darted a look at Morozov, wondering at the tone in the man's voice. His father's personal assistant was not originally from America. It wasn't always easy to read the emotional meaning behind his words. His last statement could almost have been a threat but Sammy decided that was foolish. Morozov worked for him after all, or at least for his father. Besides, he and Piotr had a very profitable relationship, which neither would want to jeopardize.

Sammy leaned back with a sigh. "I told Kulick to lay low and keep that crazy LeBlanc out of trouble but apparently they're both pretty pissed at being arrested. LeBlanc really wants a piece of this ranger."

"That would be most unwise," Morozov said.

"Right. Well, keep me up on what's happening."

"Of course, sir. I'm on your side here."

Sammy nodded but wasn't really listening. There *was* someone who knew enough of the story to help him figure everything out. And make him feel better at the same time. If only she would.

Cassandra, he murmured silently to himself.

***

Solly Burstein stared across his desk at Concho and Bull Knife. They'd brought trouble into his district and he didn't like trouble. But he couldn't honestly believe they'd had anything to do with Porter House's death, or kidnapping, or whatever. The message the perpetrator had left was a clear threat to both men, meant to convey that they were going to be the next victims unless they took the only path left open to them.

Solly's father had been a doctor, of the once standard general practitioner type, and had often brought his work home with him. Solly had grown up to look at crime as a chronic infection. It was always there in the community's body, mostly at a low grade.

But sometimes things festered and began to come to a head. Then the boil had to be lanced and the pus drained. Maybe now was the time to lance the local infection caused by the Boudreaux family. And maybe the two men across from him were the right tools to use.

"I get a feeling you two aren't going home like the note tells you to," Solly said.

Concho shook his head. "Now we've got another reason to stay. To find out who hurt Porter and make them pay."

"I trust that means pay in court."

Concho's dark eyes met Solly's. "Unless they force it otherwise."

The detective made a face but said nothing else on the subject. "So what's next?"

"I've generally found shaking the trees to be profitable."

"That tactic almost got you killed already."

Concho flashed a quick smile. "But it worked."

Solly nodded. "But which tree to shake is the question."

"When I talked with Roman and Christoph Boudreaux, they denied any involvement in sending Kulick and LeBlanc after us. I believed them. Christoph at least. Porter thought that if anyone in the Boudreaux camp was acting on his own, it would be Sammy. Christoph also mentioned his brothers as possibilities, but his emphasis was on Sammy. I think he's the most likely suspect in both the attack on us and whatever happened to Porter. If he was the one I talked to on the phone and pissed off enough to send killers after us, he can be goaded."

Solly nodded again. "Maybe I've got an idea about how to shake some more trees, then."

"Do tell?"

"Leave it to me."

"We still need to move fast," Concho said.

"I'll set things in motion as soon as you leave here. Just be ready for trouble from the Boudreaux camp. Be ready but don't start any yourself."

"Gotcha!"

CHAPTER 23

Abigail Blackthorne Carmichael woke up alone in the big bed in her house in Covington. Her husband had texted her around 9:00 the previous night that he wouldn't be home and might even be gone for a couple of days. He told her not to worry. She'd wanted to ask for details but dared not.

Pulling on a thick cotton housecoat, she went downstairs and switched on the heater. A cold front must have moved in and seeped through the walls. Or maybe the cold came from within rather than without.

When Nolen was home he usually fixed them breakfast, but Abigail didn't feel hungry this morning. She bypassed the kitchen but stopped in the living room beside Nolen's piano. It birthed memories. The first time she'd seen him had been at an upscale bar in San Francisco. He'd been on stage playing with his blues band, the one founded by Nicholas Boudreaux under the stage name Nick Barron.

Mostly, Nolen had played sax that night, but for one particular number he'd sat at the piano. He'd been so beautiful. She recalled the haunting melody he'd conjured. It wasn't simply a memory but a kind of bodily reexperiencing of the song: *San Francisco Can Be Such a Lonely Town.* One line had compared the city to a beautiful woman who didn't understand how to please a man.

With no exaggeration, she could say that moment changed her life. She'd connived her way backstage to meet the pianist. Three days later she left her father's house forever and moved in with Nolen, or—to be precise—she'd moved *around* with him as he toured from bar to small concert hall up and down California.

Unlike San Francisco in the song, she'd tried to please him. He'd reciprocated. She hadn't even known he came from a wealthy family. Having money herself, she wouldn't have cared. When she did find out, it only made his commitment to beautiful music more impressive.

She lifted the fallboard covering the keys and let her fingers clink across the black and white ivories. It seemed ages since Nolen had played for her. A few tears began to drip down her cheeks.

She thought of the past, of lies told and heard, of things savage and tender. She thought about Concho Ten-Wolves, a nephew who—until recently—she hadn't seen since he was under a year old. She'd never been able to have children of her own and he was her only nephew; she regretted missing his entire childhood.

Much of it was her father's fault—Hamilton Blackthorne. He and Donnell had spent years angry with each other. Not speaking, not forgiving—for things neither of them truly remembered. Hamilton had cut his son out of his life and insisted Abigail do the same. And while she'd fled her father's home as soon as she turned twenty-one, she'd not been able to flee his influence.

Her father's health was failing now. In the past year he'd been trying to remake some lost connections; although, in his typical heavy-handed way, he'd often bungled the attempts. Donnell's murder had much to do with that. She didn't want to wait until she was as old and ill as her father before she tried reaching out.

She wanted to talk openly with Nolen but she'd kept a secret from him too long. She knew he'd lied about identifying Sparrow Woman's body in Las Vegas. She knew who he'd lied for, and why. She couldn't just brace him on it now.

She needed to talk to someone and there was only one person she could think of to call with these thoughts. She wiped her tears and took out her phone. She sat with it on her lap, wondering what kind of hell she might unleash by making this call. She pressed the number and let it ring. She'd just have to weather any storm that came.

"Yes," a voice answered.

"Hello, Nicholas," Abigail said.

***

Solly Burstein hadn't told Ten-Wolves and Bull Knife how he planned to shake the trees in the Boudreaux camp because he wasn't about to air the NOPD's dirty laundry in front of strangers, even another officer of the law. But, he knew Roman Boudreaux had a conduit into the inner workings of the New Orleans Police Department, and he was nearly one hundred percent sure who.

After casually sharing some potentially damaging information about Sammy Boudreaux in front of the conduit, he returned to his desk to await the fireworks. They weren't long in coming.

***

On the way home from the police station, Concho left the I-10 and took a detour down River Road. He was mostly silent, worried about Porter House. He liked the fellow.

Bull Knife, not one for excess talk, finally asked, "Where are we going?"

"Thought we'd swing by the Rivershack Tavern. Check in with Barney the bartender to see if he was able to give my message to Sammy Boudreaux."

"You believe that triggered the attack on Porter?"

The Ranger shrugged. "It's something to do until Solly Burstein's plan unfolds. I can't just sit in the motel and wait."

"You are not to blame for what has happened to the private investigator."

"Are you sure?"

"He is a grown man. I heard you tell him to go away. He *chose* to continue his involvement."

"I know."

Bull Knife said no more. They reached the tavern and pulled into the gravel parking lot. It was only a little after 10:00 in the morning but a few cars and pickups were ahead of them. A cool breeze flowed along River Road. Concho strapped on his shoulder holster and slipped a windbreaker over it.

Three customers sat around one table in the Rivershack when the half brothers entered. Another man leaned on the bar looking seriously drunk. None of them seemed like trouble. Surprisingly, Barney was on duty. He appeared shocked to see them, and far from pleased. Concho slid onto a stool that wore jeans on its wooden legs and ordered a Shiner Bock. Bull Knife asked for water.

After fetching them their drinks, Barney started to move quickly away. Concho stopped him with a question.

"You able to get my message to Sammy Boudreaux?"

Barney stiffened. "Afraid not. He hasn't been in."

"Any blowback from the fight we had with Timbo and his buds?"

"They haven't been in again either. No big loss. They were troublemakers."

"But I bet you're glad to see *us*," Concho said, grinning.

Barney shrugged. "I'd like it better if your friend drank something besides water."

"What can I say," Concho returned. "He's a heathen."

Barney didn't seem to know how to take the joke and started to move away again. Concho had every intention of making the man uncomfortable and didn't plan to let him get away. He grasped Barney's wrist, let the man feel the latent strength in his grip.

"So," the Ranger said softly, "who did you call after we left here the other night?"

Barney's blanched expression belied his quick response. "I didn't call anyone. Was waiting to give your message to Sammy if he came in. Just like you said."

"Pretty sure that's not true, Barn. You don't mind if I call you Barn? I always wanted to be Andy Griffith."

"I…I don't know what you're talking about."

"Andy Griffith! The old TV comedy. Andy was the sheriff of small-town Mayberry."

"No. No, I mean…about you claiming I lied."

"Oh," Concho said. He gave a little tug on Barney's wrist to pull him closer. "I'm talking about hell breaking loose later that night. I have a nagging suspicion the fuse for it was lit right here. By a fellow named Barn."

"You're crazy," Barney said, jerking free of the grip on his arm.

Concho let him pull away. "Now, the friend who was in here with us that night is missing. I'm putting the blame squarely on you."

"You. No. I…."

From the highway out front of the Rivershack came the squeal of brakes and the squall of tires. Instinct shouted a warning in the Ranger's ear.

CHAPTER 24

Concho surged up from his stool, drawing the Colt Double Eagle from his shoulder holster. "Watch Barney," he told Bull Knife as he started for the door.

Everyone in the tavern except the drunk guy at the bar had looked up when the squealing brakes sounded outside. Now they saw Concho with his gun drawn and their eyes got big and round and scared.

Good, Concho thought. Fear might keep them safe.

The Ranger reached the door in a few quick strides and flung it open. He saw what he was afraid he'd see. A midnight black muscle car, still running with a driver inside, had pulled off the highway. Three men had bailed out and were stalking deliberately toward the tavern. All carried weapons and had red ski masks pulled over their faces.

The man to Concho's right held a shotgun; the others carried machine pistols. The men saw Ten-Wolves open the door in front of them only a fraction after he saw them.

"That's him!" one man shouted, his voice familiar.

All three began to swing their weapons to bear. Concho already had his .45 ready. He shouted at the perps to halt but knew as he spoke there was no stopping this short of gunplay. Unsure whether or not the attackers were wearing body armor beneath their clothes, he fired one bullet into the shotgunner's face. The slug struck low, smashing into the chin and tearing open the mouth above it. Blood arced into the air.

The lawman didn't wait to see more. He threw himself back into the tavern, slamming the door as he did so and diving for the floor. His shout of "Everyone get down!" was half-drowned out in the sudden scream of bullets punching into the building from the other side.

Concho twisted over onto his back. A booted foot kicked the door partially open from outside. Concho fired through the gap but the man had already leaped away. He'd underhanded a silver canister into the room, though. It clanked on the floor and rolled. A film of smoke boiled up. The Ranger's eyes began to sting.

Tear gas!

Concho tore off his coat, hurled it over the canister to try and contain the chemical agent. It wouldn't work long but might buy them seconds. He lunged to his feet. A closed interior door stood to the left of the bar. He'd noticed it on his first visit and figured it led to the kitchen and maybe to the outside. He ran toward it. With the front door barred to them, the bad guys would circle around seeking another entrance.

Bull Knife crouched near the bar with Concho's snub-nosed .38 white-knuckled in his hand. Ten-Wolves yelled to him, "Shoot through the front door to let 'em know we're still here."

The boom of the .38 sounded behind him as Concho shoved through the interior door into a narrow hallway with a store-room to one side and a kitchen on the other. Two crouching cooks goggled at him in terror as they clung for faint protection to butcher knives.

He ignored them, rushed down the hall. It hooked to the left and he saw an outside door standing open with a screen across it. He charged it. At the last moment, he noticed the screen was hooked. He didn't stop but bulled through. The frame shattered, tore back.

The Ranger found himself on the top step of three with the screen door in ruins around his boots. He kicked it away. He stood beneath the canopy at the side of the building. Footsteps pounded toward him as one of the attacking gunmen came racing to cover the building's flank.

The man saw Concho looming huge on the steps. He must have been startled; he'd just seen the Ranger out front. He tried to brake but slid in the dirt. That threw his gun off target as he pulled the trigger and a half dozen bullets ripped into the wall beside him.

Concho fired once. The heavy lead slug punched through the bridge of the man's nose and burrowed a lethal hole straight into his brain. He fell back and down. Two of the three attackers were offline now, though there was also the getaway driver to worry about. Concho leaped down from the steps, stalked toward the front of the tavern with his gun in shooter's position.

"TJ!" a voice called from somewhere on the other side of the tavern. "TJ! Answer me, man!"

TJ was beyond any response.

The man calling out sounded like Jason Kulick to Concho's ears. That meant Kage LeBlanc was likely here, too. Kulick must have realized "TJ" was out of the picture. He cursed, then shouted at someone, "Get back in the car, get back in the car."

The driver must have stepped outside to help his buddies but Kulick had decided to cut his losses. Automobile doors slammed; a powerful engine revved. Abandoning caution, Ten-Wolves rushed into the front parking lot.

The getaway car, a 1970s black Dodge Charger, fishtailed out of the lot, spewing gravel. Its tires caught traction on the asphalt of River Road and it rocketed away. Concho fired once at the vehicle, trying for a tire. He missed. The bullet skipped off the highway and smacked into the levee.

Concho ran for the Rivershack's front door, yelling to warn Bull

Knife he was coming. He burst through. Barney and the tavern's patrons had crowded near the bar, many of them kneeling. Some had napkins or handkerchiefs to their mouths as they coughed against the tear gas spreading like a fog in the room.

Concho covered his mouth and nose with a hand as he shouted, "It's clear! Get out the back! Call 911." He beckoned to Bull Knife, who stood over the rest of the crowd with his face wet from the tear gas. "Let's go; they're running."

Bull Knife raced around the smoke toward him. They slammed through the front door into the parking lot and Concho ran for his truck. He threw himself in and had the Ford started as his half brother scrambled in beside him.

"Who?" Bull Knife demanded as he dashed at his tearing eyes.

"Jason Kulick for sure," Concho replied as he wheeled out onto River Road and stomped the pedal to the floor. The 3.5-liter V6 roared as the big truck gathered itself and leaped. "I'm betting LeBlanc is with him."

"Can you catch them?"

"Gonna give it my best."

***

Black as an oil stain against the highway, the Dodge Char-ger fled from the Rivershack Tavern along River Road. The 440 cubic inch engine growled while the two men in the front seat shouted back and forth at each other.

"What happened? What the hell happened?" Kage LeBlanc demanded of the overwrought Jason Kulick.

Kulick twisted back and forth in the passenger seat, throwing wild glances over his shoulder out the rear window of the Charger. His gloved hands held an MP9 machine pistol, the barrel still smoking. He yanked the magazine out of the handle and threw it on the floor, slapped in a fresh one.

"He knew!" Kulick yelled at LeBlanc. "The son of a bitch knew. You saw him. He was waiting for us!"

The Charger wove from lane to lane as LeBlanc pushed the muscle car through the curves of River Road at high speed.

"Stupid!" LeBlanc yelled as he manhandled the steering wheel. "Shoulda let me go in myself. I'd have kill the bastard!"

"I didn't let you go in because I didn't want any *bystanders* killed," Kulick snapped back.

"You want TJ and Casper should be dead instead?" LeBlanc snarled.

"No!" Kulick shouted. "Didn't want that either. Slow down. The cops will have been called. They could be coming along here and they'd flag us for reckless driving."

"Ain't no cop stoppin' me!"

"Slow down, dammit! We're away." Kulick threw another glance out the back window. "No one's following," he continued. "We'll get another chance at 'em. If you don't kill us now!"

LeBlanc growled wordlessly but let up on the gas. The car slowed so the world no longer blurred. Minutes bled away. They made a hard right past a golf course, a quick left again. The road had peeled away from the levee now and was mostly straight. LeBlanc accelerated, though trying not to push it much beyond the speed limit as they began to pass through small communities whose names neither man knew.

"Where at do we get back on a freeway?" LeBlanc demanded.

"Not where we're going," Kulick said. "At least not yet."

"What you say?"

"Don't worry, we're getting close."

LeBlanc glanced over at his colleague, puzzled. "Close to where at?"

"A couple of miles up, the houses thin. You'll see a dirt road on the left called 'Harvest.' Turn down it."

"You tell me why?"

Kulick grinned. "Because I plan ahead. There's a house and a barn down that road. On some land Sammy Boudreaux rents from an old farmer dude. Parked a backup vehicle there yesterday.

We'll hang out a few hours. Maybe the day. Drink a few beers. Let the excitement die down. After, we'll switch the Charger out for the other ride and be home free!"

LeBlanc laughed. "Brains, fer sure, I reckon!"

***

Concho kept the hammer down in the Ford and the big pickup responded like a thoroughbred. The F-150 was fast. He'd tuned the engine himself to get a bit more from under the hood than the standard horsepower. He'd learned the intricacies of motors trying to keep the El Camino he'd owned as a teenager running.

The truck slid smoothly in and out of the curves on River Road, though the light rear end had an uncomfortable tendency to float on those curves. Concho fought that drift, kept them straight as the world flashed by.

"A road made for motorcycles, not pickups," he said to Bull Knife.

"Hmm," Bull Knife grunted.

For a moment, Concho's entire attention had to focus on a set of s-curves they powered through. Then they hit a short, straight stretch and he glanced over at his half brother while punching the accelerator. The truck leaped forward. Bull Knife sat tensely, staring straight ahead. His right hand clenched tight and almost bloodless on the handle of the .38 snub-nose.

"We've gotta get you a bigger gun," Concho said. "Fold down the center of the seat and you should be able to reach into the extended cab. There's a shotgun on the rack there. You might need it."

Bull Knife nodded. He stuffed the revolver into the pocket of his rawhide jacket and did as Concho suggested, pulling a Remington 870 pump-action tactical shotgun into the front with him. This Remington was matte black and had a carrying strap for slinging over a shoulder. Its synthetic stock folded to one side and the gun could be fired in that fashion, though it wasn't ideal. A brutal weapon; it held seven 12-gauge rounds.

Another curve loomed, Concho pushed the pickup through it, straightened again. The world swept past with the levee on one side and homes on the other. He wished he dared use his blue light but the local cops would likely frown on such an act by an out-of-state officer. He had no idea if he was gaining on the fleeing Charger or not.

The Dodge would handle River Road's curves better and probably had a higher top-end than the Ford, but the driver might not know he was being followed. And if he'd slowed down to avoid drawing police attention, Concho might catch him.

Then the Ranger had to slow dramatically himself as they came to a sharp right and another quick left. A golf course popped up on one side, with houses on the other. Soon they reached a straighter stretch of road and Concho upped his speed again, though they were passing through what looked like small towns now and he had to watch for both automobile and foot traffic.

He chafed. There was no sign of the Charger. "Keep an eye out," he told his half brother.

"They could have turned off anywhere," Bull Knife replied. "Or could be miles ahead by now. We've lost them."

"Not yet. I've got a feeling."

CHAPTER 25

"There!" Bull Knife said, abruptly sitting up straight in his seat.

Concho didn't slow the truck, not wanting to give anything away to a potential observer.

"What?"

"Black car. Pretty sure a Charger. On a side road. They turned into a farm."

"You notice the road name?"

"Harvest."

Concho kept driving. They'd largely broken free of populated areas into a more open landscape with fields and few houses. The Ranger continued another half mile before making a U-turn and heading back the way they'd come. "Harvest" was a dirt road headed straight for the banks of the Mississippi River, which wasn't that far away but which remained hidden from view by a long tract of woods.

The side road ran past a weathered gray barn and a small A-Frame farmhouse, a very unusual style around here. No sign of the Charger now, but it could easily have pulled into the barn, which was larger than the house.

"We've got to get a look but we can't just drive down that

road," Concho said.

"There are other roads."

"Right. We find one and hike back to Harvest."

Bull Knife nodded tensely.

Concho studied his half brother. He looked...not exactly scared but apprehensive. The Ranger realized afresh how young Bull Knife was. Twenty-four, twenty-five maybe. Tough. No doubt. Physically strong and so far cool under pressure. But probably not very experienced with lethal conflict.

Bull Knife was still young enough to have illusions about violence. From how he dressed to the bone-handled blade he carried, it seemed the young man fancied himself an Apache warrior from the old days of battle with the bluecoats. But this wasn't the 1800s. No one raised in modern America could know the honed and ruthless mindset of the western Apache. Not even an Indian.

The Ranger knew his half brother could kill; he'd seen him do it to save Concho's life. But he suspected it had been Bull Knife's first time, which always reforges a man. Sometimes it tore them up inside and made the thought of taking another life anathema; sometimes it turned them cold. No way to tell until the moment arose again, and the Ranger had a feeling it was about to arise. He had to make sure that what might be his only living blood relative survived it.

***

Jason Kulick opened the barn door and Kage LeBlanc pulled the Dodge Charger into the big open space inside to park beside a brand-new white Chevy Tahoe SUV. Kage climbed out. He popped the trunk on the Charger to begin transferring weapons and supplies into the back of the Tahoe.

"Don't worry about that now," Kulick said. "Let's go up to the house. I want a beer, and I've got some folks you should meet."

LeBlanc looked up, startled. "Folks?"

Kulick nodded. "I figured even if we made a successful hit on

Ten-Wolves and his brother, the cops would be looking for a group of men together in a vehicle. So, I invited a few ladies over. They'll ride out of here with us and even if we should get stopped it'll just look like we're taking out our chicks. Whatta you think about Applebee's for dinner?"

LeBlanc chuckled and shook his head, not in negation but in approval. "More brain work there."

Kulick grinned as he led LeBlanc out of the barn. He slid the door shut behind them and headed for the small house about fifty yards away.

"There's this one chick you've gotta meet," he chattered on. "But make sure you keep your hands to yourself. She's no hooker. Tell the truth, I'm not quite sure what she is. Except a friend of Sammy's and the Boudreaux family. But dayum! Her name's Cassandra."

***

Three-quarters of a mile down from Harvest Road, Con-cho turned across a cattle grate into a field where a few cows lazed. A dirt road—little more than a set of ruts with grass growing between them—ran through the meadow toward the river. It lay roughly parallel to Harvest and was hidden from the A-Frame farmhouse by a fence line of cedars.

Concho parked several hundred yards into the field beneath the shadows cast by a grove of old river oaks. He climbed out. The wind soughed through the tree limbs, many of which still held on to a few dead leaves. Off in the distance, a red-bellied woodpecker screeched. Otherwise, the afternoon lay silent.

Concho's phone vibrated in his pocket. He pulled it out, checked the caller, then stuffed it back in his jeans without answering. "Solly Burstein," he told Bull Knife, who'd walked around the truck to join him. "Guess he's been told about the incident at the Rivershack. But I'm not going to be called off this trail yet."

Ten-Wolves opened the door of his extended cab and peered in. Pulling the double holster rig he normally wore as a Texas

Ranger out of the back, he buckled it around his waist and made sure both Colt Double Eagles were seated firmly.

Next, he pulled out two bulletproof vests. He'd carried two ever since an incident in which he'd needed one for himself and another for the witness he'd been transporting at the time. He'd given his vest to the witness, and it had been the right decision. But he hadn't wanted to be in the position of making that choice again.

He handed a vest to Bull Knife with a "Put this on."

"I'd prefer not."

"Put it on or you don't go with me," Concho replied.

Bull Knife stiffened but seemed to realize the Ranger was deadly serious. He relented and slipped into the vest, which Concho helped him adjust to fit. Concho turned back to his truck and drew out a colorful blanket he'd recently bought from a Kickapoo woman on the Texas reservation.

Folding the blanket back revealed a bow he'd made from an Osage Orange tree growing on the Rez. It had been strengthened with deer hide and buffalo horn before being etched with symbols of personal meaning to Concho. It came with a deer hide quiver holding twelve ash-wood arrows fletched with wild turkey feathers.

Bull Knife stared at the bow and gave a nod of approval. Concho handed it and the quiver to him. The younger man took them reverently. He hefted the bow, giving another nod at its design and sturdiness.

"Beautiful weapon," he said. "Handmade." His black eyes bored into Concho's lighter brown gaze. "Who?"

"Me," Concho replied. "But I was taught by an elder named Meskwaa."

Bull Knife nodded. "I did not realize you so honored our ancestral traditions."

"When I can."

Ten-Wolves pulled a small yellow tin out of his truck. He twisted the lid off to reveal red ocher. Another tradition he honored when he could was one many native peoples had practiced before going into battle. He expected a fight when they confronted Jason Kulick and whoever hung with him. And right now he had a moment to prepare, both physically and mentally.

Dipping two fingers into the ocher, he swiped a double slash of red beneath his right eye, repeating the act beneath the left. He glanced at his half brother, who nodded again. He offered the tin.

Bull Knife took it, held it. He gently handed the bow and quiver back to Concho. While the Ranger watched, the half-Apache scooped up a fingerful of ocher and drew a V-shaped mark beneath each eye, following with three red dots bleeding from the base of the Vs.

Concho took the tin and resealed it, then put it back in the truck. Both men wiped their fingers on tufts of grass. Concho slung the bow and quiver over his shoulder. He gave Bull Knife a nod.

"Let's smoke the sky."

They moved out. It wasn't even noon. A lot had happened in a short time. The sun beamed down through sparse clouds and it was warm in the light but chilly in the shade of the trees where the two men stalked. They moved swiftly toward the farm where they expected to find Jason Kulick and his partner. Even in the chill they worked up a sweat.

"You think Kulick and LeBlanc are the ones who hurt our little private detective?" Bull Knife asked softly.

"It's a good possibility. I intend to find out before we call in the local cops. Let's try to take one of them alive."

Bull Knife nodded. He'd slung his borrowed shotgun over a shoulder but now drew it down into his arms.

Concho's phone vibrated in his pocket again. He checked. "Text from Burstein," he explained to Bull Knife. He whispered the message out loud. "What's happening? We've got dead bodies. Call me now!"

The Ranger paused to text back. *Closing on the perps. Be in touch.* He turned his cell phone off this time before putting it in his pocket. "Guess Solly's a little old for the angry emojis," he said to his half brother. "But it felt like they were there."

"He's not happy because he told you to stay out of trouble," Bull Knife replied.

"Technically, he told me not to start any. Well, I didn't start this but I'm planning on finishing it."

CHAPTER 26

The two half brothers came to the edge of the woods and looked out on the farm where the black car had turned in. The place was quiet, with no one in sight. If the car were here, it had to be in the barn.

Though it had appeared weathered and gray from a distance, the barn up close looked well-kept and still had faded red paint staining it in places. It was tall enough for two stories. Concho figured it had a loft.

The A-Frame house stood about fifty yards beyond the barn. It wasn't large enough to have more than a few rooms but front and back porches added to its footprint on the land. A pump-house rose close by, with a silver tank outside for watering live-stock. At one point there'd been a garden. Concho could see a fenced off area behind the house that still held the broken brown stalks of old corn.

"First thing to do is check the barn for the car," the Ranger said.

Bull Knife nodded.

The two slipped along the edge of the woods until they were directly behind the barn and hidden from the house. They darted across forty yards of open field to the back of the barn. A rear door to the structure was bolted shut with a chain and rusty lock, but a ladder on the wall led up to a small wooden door opening into the loft.

Before Concho could say anything, Bull Knife slung the 12-gauge over his shoulder by its carrying strap and swarmed up the ladder, moving quickly but silently. The half-Apache carefully opened the door and peered in. He offered Concho a shrug and disappeared inside before Ten-Wolves could respond.

Barely a beat later, Bull Knife reappeared. He grasped the ladder with his hands, slipped his moccasin-style boots free of the steps and slid down to earth, landing easily and with barely a sound.

"It's there," he whispered to Concho. "The Charger and another vehicle. A white SUV."

"Ah. They're playing it smart. Planning to switch getaway cars."

"No one's in the barn. They must have gone into the house."

"Waiting for the heat of their attack on the Rivershack to cool down," Concho said.

"So what now?"

"We add more fuel to the fire."

***

Jason Kulick came out of the bedroom of the A-Frame house zipping up his jeans. The woman he'd gone in with had fallen fast asleep when they were done. But he couldn't relax. His nerves were still frazzled after the events at the Rivershack Tavern. Even sex hadn't taken the edge off.

His partner from the Rivershack, Kage LeBlanc, sat on the couch in the living room drinking whiskey and obviously in a black mood, despite the two girls putting on a show for him. The man looked angry rather than excited. If the girls didn't watch it, they'd get more than they'd bargained for with Kage. The "Skull's" appetites certainly weren't vanilla.

But hey, Kulick thought. The women were pros. They surely knew how to handle men like Kage. Though, come to think of it, there weren't any men like Kage. At least none Kulick could name.

Yawning and scratching at his chest under the purple LSU t-shirt he wore, Kulick gave up thinking about Kage LeBlanc and went into the kitchen to get a beer from the fridge. The last member of their little party stood staring out a back window with a cigarette burning between her fingers. She wore low-rise jeans and a man's white cotton shirt knotted at her midriff.

The woman turned when he entered; he licked his lips with desire before he managed to control himself. Cassandra was strictly no-touch, though every man who saw her wanted nothing more than to do that very thing.

It wasn't even her looks, really. *Beautiful? Oh yeah!* She had paradise blue eyes, long blonde hair, curves in spades on a sweet frame. But those were only adornments. What Kulick wanted— what most men wanted from Cassandra Holmes—was the edge that made her electric. Some combination of danger, sensuality, and controlled chaos.

"Your friend is an animal," Cassandra said.

"What was your first clue?"

"You don't want to know what I'll do to him if he hurts either of those girls."

Kulick shrugged as he pulled a Miller out of the fridge and popped the top. He'd already tried the direct approach with Cassandra and been slapped down. Now he just tried to play it cool and look for opportunities. He took a long sip of his beer and wiped the foam from his lips with a hand before replying.

"What's it to you? They're paid. And you aren't their manager."

"I'm their gender, though. And that's enough reason to put paid to men like Kage LeBlanc."

Kulick shrugged again. "Not my rodeo, not my broncs to saddle. I'm not getting between the two of you."

Cassandra flashed a brief and wicked smile. She sauntered toward him and Kulick felt his backbone tighten. Pulling the beer from his hand, she threw back a few large swallows. Kulick watched her throat work as she drank. He licked his lips again.

She lowered the can and stared at him over it, then dropped her half-smoked cigarette into the can and handed it back. Her gaze taunted as she said,

"Oh? You sure about that?"

Kulick was trying desperately to think of something cool to say when the rattling sound of an approaching vehicle came from outside.

***

The barn off Harvest Road had been used more as a garage than as a storehouse for hay or an animal pen for a long time. The smells were of rust and gasoline and spilled oil rather than cut sweetgrass and manure. While Jason Kulick chatted up Cassandra Holmes in the house, Concho and Bull Knife went to work in the barn.

The Texas Ranger had just used the blade of his Strider folding knife to force open the steering column of the Dodge Charger in preparation for hot-wiring the vehicle. He'd chosen the Charger over the Chevy Tahoe because the Dodge came from an era when automobiles had been much easier to hot-wire than the more recent vintage SUV.

The sound of an approaching vehicle outside stabbed into Concho's awareness. His left hand dipped for the butt of a Colt Double Eagle while he glanced at Bull Knife. His half brother looked startled at the sound, as well, but quickly threw Concho a nod and darted over to a ladder leading into the loft. He swarmed up it. The lower half of the barn had no windows but there were two in the loft, at front and back. The wood floor creaked slightly as Bull Knife made his way to the front window for a look-see.

He returned quickly with a report. "Three men in a Jeep. Guns on them. Kulick met them. Obviously friends. And Kulick had a woman with him too. There could be more in the house."

"That changes things," Concho said. "And not for the better."

CHAPTER 27

Concho's plan *had been* to hot-wire the Dodge Charger and have Bull Knife act like he was taking off in it. That would surely bring both Kulick and LeBlanc out of the house, giving Concho a chance to get the drop on them. Now there were three more men in the house and an unknown number of women. The plan had to be modified. Concho explained his new idea.

Bull Knife frowned as he worked it over in his head. "It puts you at great risk."

"I've been at risk before. And I've got my vest." He thumped the Kevlar body armor he wore.

"The shotgun does not really have the range for me to back you up from the barn. Nor does the small .38 revolver you gave me."

"They don't," Concho agreed. "But this does." He drew the bow and its accompanying quiver of arrows over his shoulder and handed them to Bull Knife.

The half-Apache took the weapon gently, with reverence.

"You know how to use it?" Concho asked.

Bull Knife was not offended at the question. He nodded. "I practiced much with my father. But I never learned how to make one."

"When this is over, I'll teach you."

"And I'll learn."

"Right. Now, get up in the loft and get ready. You'll know when to shoot."

***

With the three newcomers in the house, the party had gotten back into full swing. Music played on the stereo. Kage's black mood seem to have passed and he'd slipped away into the bathroom with one of the hookers and a baggy of cocaine.

Jason Kulick relaxed. He had guns to back him up again if need be, and the incident at the Rivershack Tavern didn't seem to have cost them anything. The two men the Texas Ranger had killed there were hired to be soldiers and could not be specifically linked to him and Kage. The Charger was safely hidden in the barn and the only thing that could make the day complete....

He glanced toward the fireplace and Cassandra Holmes. She'd already slapped down two of the newcomers who'd approached her, but one of them had given her a joint and she toked at it. Maybe the grass would mellow her out; maybe his chance with her was coming. He let himself drift in that direction as a country song he liked came on: *Vice*, by Miranda Lambert

A sound from outside cut through the song and brought his head around. An engine starting up.

***

Concho twisted the ignition wires together and the big 440 magnum engine of the Dodge Charger growled to life. He didn't have much time. Even over their music, everyone in the house would hear the Charger roar as soon as he hit the gas.

He slammed the car into first gear and punched it. The wheels spun up dirt for an instant before catching traction. The muscle car lunged forward like a striking gator. The old wood of the barn couldn't match Detroit iron; the closed door splintered wide as he rammed the vehicle straight through.

The Charger burst into the open, out under the heavy gray sky of the afternoon. Concho twisted the steering wheel. The rear wheels slid, then dug in. Concho floored the pedal as he aimed the car toward the A-Frame farmhouse.

The front door of the farmhouse stood open. A man and a woman leaned close together on the porch, drinking beer and smoking. Both stood agape as the black juggernaut of the Charger suddenly roared toward them. The woman screamed. The man dropped his beer and clawed at a pistol stuck into his belt. An arrow materialized in his throat. He coughed blood.

Fifty yards from barn to house turned to twenty-five, then twenty. Concho had found an old concrete block in the barn and stuck it in the passenger seat of the Charger. He grabbed the block now, thrust it down onto the gas pedal as he removed his foot. He shoved open the car door and threw himself out.

As the Texas Ranger hit the ground and rolled, the front end of the Dodge smashed into the house's low front porch. The left front tire hit the concrete steps and climbed them, twisting the front of the car sideways. The grill shattered through the porch's wooden railing and slammed into the right side of the house with a thunderous bang. The window on that side exploded as the wall itself caved inward.

Concho came to his feet, filling each hand with a .45 semiautomatic. The woman on the porch was down on her belly, screaming with her hands covering her head. The man with her lay dead.

A second man appeared in the doorway of the house. He had a gun in his hand. Concho fired just as he caught a flickering from the corner of his eye and another arrow punched straight into the man's chest.

The man stumbled back into the house, doubly dead as Concho leaped up the steps onto the porch. The Charger's engine still chugged to his right. He ignored it and the smoke funneling up from the busted grill as he darted through the open front door past a fallen body.

The room he entered was in chaos. Loud music jangled. A spinning ceiling fan sucked the smoke from the Charger's engine in through the shattered window. People coughed. A man shouted; a woman cried out. Concho heard slides racking on weapons.

To his right, two people stood next to an unlit fireplace. The woman had blonde hair. The man was Jason Kulick. He had a machine pistol in his hands. He swung it toward Concho but the Ranger moved fast and snapped a shot in Kulick's direction. The bullet struck the mantel, spraying splinters.

Kulick ducked; the woman darted around him and fled for the back of the house. A big white La-Z-Boy stood between Kulick and Concho. The Ranger dove behind it just as Kulick opened fire. Machine pistol bullets whanged into the chair, sending fluff flying. Concho fired around the side of the La-Z-Boy but didn't have a clear target.

Concho's mind worked fast. Where was Kage LeBlanc? And there was a third man somewhere in the house. Even some of the women might be armed. He fired again toward Kulick, who leaped up and ran toward the rear of the house.

Ten-Wolves started to rise to his feet, ducked back down as a thin, dark-haired man stepped through a rear doorway into the room with a pump-action shotgun. He cut the weapon loose; 12-gauge pellets tore into the chair, spanging off the springs and sending stuffing whirling into the air. A wild pellet singed a path across Concho's nylon jacket.

Concho slung lead back at the shotgunner just as the man ducked behind the wall. The bullet missed flesh and plowed into plaster. The Ranger pushed to his feet. A woman to his left crawled on her belly toward the front door. He ignored her as he heard the shotgun man working the pump action of his weapon.

The man stepped back around the corner into the room, swinging his shotgun down toward Concho. Ten-Wolves was ready. He fired first, fired once. The man's head snapped back as the bullet punched him between the eyes. The barrel of his weapon still pointed toward the ceiling and discharged. The buckshot smashed into the ceiling fan and tore it into confetti.

A door to Concho's right swung open. Kage LeBlanc leaped through. He had his shirt off. The tip of his nose glistened white with cocaine residue. He had a pistol in his hand but not pointed at Concho. It pressed against the head of the terrified, half-dressed woman he held in front of him as a shield.

"Drop your weapon, lawman!" LeBlanc shouted. "Or I shoot dis 'ore."

CHAPTER 28

Concho had no intention of dropping his gun on the orders of Kage LeBlanc, who would surely put a bullet in him as soon as he got the chance. But LeBlanc was doing a good job of keeping his body shielded behind the woman he held. The Ranger hesitated as he looked for an opening. Help came from an unexpected direction.

From what must have been the kitchen behind LeBlanc, the blonde woman who'd been talking to Jason Kulick stepped silently into the room. She had a butcher knife in her hand, with at least a six-inch blade. She glided forward, her attention focused on LeBlanc. For a moment, Concho felt confusion over what the woman intended.

Then she made her intentions clear. She slammed the knife into LeBlanc's back just below the right shoulder blade. The tough Cajun gunman screamed as he was taken completely by surprise. He released the prostitute he held—she sprinted screaming past Concho—and spun toward the attack. Instinctively, he lashed out with the pistol, swinging it like a club at whoever was behind him.

The blonde woman ducked under LeBlanc's swing and stuck him again. She punched him with the knife low on the left side of his body, beneath the rib cage. Concho saw the gunman hunch over at the blow, but the outlaw wasn't finished. He brought the barrel of the gun up now, trying to align it with the woman's face. He'd forgotten Concho.

The Ranger hadn't forgotten LeBlanc. He fired twice, once with the hammer back and again by double-actioning the trigger of his Colt. Both bullets struck on target, one beneath the left shoulder blade from behind, the other center of mass.

The first one would have been enough as it cut through muscle and ribs and slammed into the heart. LeBlanc grunted. He stiffened, going almost up on his toes, then crashed forward and down like a tree falling.

Concho shifted his aim toward the blonde with the knife. She met his gaze, straightened, dropped the knife. The white shirt she wore had been spray-painted by LeBlanc's blood. She ignored the gore.

"Where's Kulick?" Concho demanded.

The woman jerked her chin toward the back of the house. "He's running. Probably in the woods by now."

"Anyone else in here with guns? Or knives?"

The woman flicked him a smile with one corner of her mouth. "Only you, officer!"

Concho took a few slow steps forward, not taking his eyes off her, not trusting her.

"Why'd you stab him?" he asked.

"I told him not to hurt any of the girls."

"You their manager?"

"No. But that's not the point."

Concho nodded, took another step forward. His gaze tightened. "You… You were at Lafitte's. That first night. I saw you with another woman. Taller, darker. You tried to keep me from following her."

"I remember. I don't believe I've ever been so soundly ignored."

Concho looked past her shoulder. "I need to catch Kulick. But I have questions. Will you call the police? Then stay here?"

The woman nodded. "Sure. I've got nothing better to do."

She stepped to one side and motioned him past her toward the back of the house. He slipped quickly by and into a small linoleum-floored kitchen. It stank of beer and cigarette smoke, though the back door stood wide open and crisp air slid in.

"I'm Cassandra, by the way," the woman said, throwing the words after him.

Concho did not respond as he ducked out the back with his eyes roving in search of Jason Kulick. He'd considered the possibility of a waiting ambush but didn't think it likely. He was right. The backyard lay empty. Beyond stood an overgrown field full of weeds and mostly brown grass.

Someone had just thrashed through the field. He could see where the wild growth had been flattened by a body's passing. The woods lay about thirty yards off, with no sign of Kulick except his trail.

Concho started along that path, paused again as he heard someone running toward him from around the side of the house. He turned, raising his pistols. It was Bull Knife, still carrying the bow.

"You all right?" Bull Knife asked.

"Yeah. All down except for Kulick." He jerked his chin toward the grass flattened trail in front of him, then started along it again. "He's in the woods."

Bull Knife fell in beside the Ranger, offering him back his bow and unslinging the shotgun from over his back. Concho holstered his pistols and took the bow.

"Good shooting!" he said.

"I tried."

Moving at speed, they reached the edge of the woods, found where Kulick had entered. But now they had to slow. The trail here was harder to follow. Only faint scuffs in the dirt and the dead leaves under the trees led them onward. Five minutes in, Concho paused. He listened but heard nothing except a few distant bird calls and the breeze rattling limbs. He couldn't smell anything but growing things.

"How far ahead of us is he?" Bull Knife asked.

"Don't know. But too far. We can trail him but he'll get wherever he's going long before us. And he'll have his cell phone with him to call for a pickup."

"So what do we do?"

Concho sighed. "Maybe we call in the hounds. Get the police in on it and a manhunt going."

Bull Knife nodded. They turned back toward the farmhouse and were almost to the edge of the woods when they heard it—the sound of a vehicle starting. Concho cursed.

"Could Kulick have circled around?" Bull Knife asked.

The Ranger shook his head. "No. He wouldn't have had time. It has to be the girls running. Can't be the Tahoe. I let the air out of the tires before we started all this. Must be the Jeep the three men came in."

"I took the keys," Bull Knife said. "They were still in it."

"I guess someone had an extra set. Or one of those women can hot-wire." He was thinking of the woman named Cassandra. She seemed like the type to have hidden talents.

***

Sammy Boudreaux sat on the deck of his party cabin on the shore of Lake Pontchartrain and stared gloomily out at the lake. The gray skies and the runoff from a recent rain turned the water an ugly, muddy brown. He hardly noticed. He wasn't really much of a nature guy except to use it as a trash can for his empties.

It was also just too cold by the water. He wore a jacket as he sipped from a glass of whiskey he'd poured himself. It was a little early to start drinking but he'd had a rough day. Piotr Morozov had scared him close to death when he'd mentioned what Sammy's father would do if he found out who'd sicced Kulick and LeBlanc on that Texas Ranger.

And then he'd tried to call Cassandra Holmes for a little emotional support but she wouldn't answer her phone. Nor did she call back, despite the text messages he sent telling her to. He was rich, and good-looking. Women weren't supposed to ignore him.

"At least things can't get any worse," he muttered to himself.

His cell chimed. He grabbed it, thinking Cassandra had called back. The caller ID read "restricted," but he swiped to accept anyway. He tried to keep his voice cool.

"Yeah?"

It wasn't Cassandra; he didn't recognize the caller.

"Consider this a favor," a man's voice said. "A message has gone to your father about your...additional activities. You might want to be prepared for the fallout."

The man hung up. Sammy's heart pounded wildly. He almost threw the phone across the room, then softly placed it down on the wooden table beside his chair. He rose, his hand clenched bloodless on his whiskey glass. With an oath, he hurled the glass toward the lake. It hit and skipped once before throwing off a quick sunbeam of reflected light and sinking from sight.

CHAPTER 29

Concho turned on his phone and saw several new texts from Solly Burstein. He didn't bother to read them but called Solly directly. The detective answered quickly and launched into a blistering series of angry questions followed by orders: "Where are you? What's going on? Why do we have bodies on River Road? Who are you chasing? I told you to stay out of trouble. I want you back here *now!*"

Concho held the phone out from his ear and gave Bull Knife a wink. His half brother grinned. As Solly ran down, the Ranger interrupted.

"We're off River Road. A farmhouse toward the river. On a dirt road called Harvest. You'll want to send in the coroner. You've got more dead bodies here."

"I don't know how they do things in Texas," Solly snarled, "but you are not endearing yourself to me or anyone in Louisiana law enforcement. The Jefferson Parish police have an APB out on your Ford pickup. For all they know, you're a couple of rogue killers they'll have to shoot on sight."

"So tell them we're not!" Concho said, showing his own irritation for the first time. "And whatever you did to stir the pot worked, by the way. We stopped by the Rivershack and four men

came after us. Jason Kulick and Kage LeBlanc among them. I
killed two and we pursued the other two to this location, where
they had backup. We stopped them all except Kulick, who fled
into the woods. We'll need a team to smoke him out."

Solly took a deep breath. "I'm on my way. Don't do anything
but breathe until I get there."

The detective hung up.

***

The sound of sirens reached Concho and Bull Knife be-
fore they saw the blue and red lights flashing on arriving police cars and ambulances. In Louisiana, the term *parish* was the
equivalent of county in other states. The Rivershack Tavern was
officially located in Jefferson Parish rather than Orleans Parish—
where New Orleans stood.

The JP police turned out in force. Four cars whipped into the
farmyard on Harvest Road. Two ambulances followed. Concho
made sure he and Bull Knife were standing in the open when the
cops arrived, with no guns on them, no bulletproof vests, and their
hands in the air. He also pinned on his Texas Ranger badge.

"Follow my lead," Concho said to his half brother, "but one
thing you can't tell them is that *you* killed anyone. All four bodies count to me. They might accept it from a fellow lawman. But
you're a civilian. Otherwise tell the truth."

Bull Knife made an unpleasant face but agreed.

After a tense interval of yelling at them to "turn around and
spread 'em," and a very thorough pat down and subsequent grill-
ing, the JP cops began to relax slightly. They'd gotten background
information on Concho, found out the truth of his employment
as a Texas Ranger. And they'd seen the weapons in the hands of
the dead men, two of whom had already been identified as having
long track records of violence.

By the time Solly Burstein arrived with another NOPD detective in tow, relations between Concho and the police had reached

a comfortable if not exactly cordial point. Solly had calmed down from earlier but made Concho go through it all again, which he did. He understood police procedures and managed to rein in his impatience.

After picking up the gist of what had happened, Burstein ordered a statewide APB on Jason Kulick. The Jefferson Parish police had already sent men to comb the woods for any sign of the outlaw; a helicopter was on the way.

"Tell me about the women," Burstein asked, returning to the Ranger.

Concho repeated their descriptions as best he could. He'd gotten a good look at only one—Cassandra. He didn't mention he'd seen her before but explained that she was the only one who'd engaged in any violence, which had been directed at Kage LeBlanc.

"This Cassandra," Solly said. "You think she gave you her real name?"

"I think maybe she did. But I can't be sure."

"Why would she help you?"

Concho shrugged. "LeBlanc was a nasty piece of work. He might have done something to her before. But she claimed it was because he was hurting one of the other girls."

"Her friend?"

The Ranger shook his head. "Don't know."

Solly sighed. "I doubt the attack at the Rivershack had anything to do with my plan to sow discord in the Boudreaux camp. It happened too quickly. They must have known you'd been there, and were waiting for you to come back."

"Possibly," Concho agreed. "You might want to talk to Barney over there. He was bartending both times. I figured he called Sammy Boudreaux after we left there the first time. Can't prove it, of course."

Solly nodded. His partner, a much younger and nearly silent fellow with thinning hair, wrote it down.

"By the way," Concho said. "Any news on Porter?"

Solly shook his head. "Afraid not. As for the Boudreaux issue, I sowed the seeds I wanted to. There may still be blowback. Watch yourselves."

"Are we free to go?"

Solly considered. He'd examined the scene himself and it told a clear story of the good guys and the bad guys. He nodded his head. "Get your weapons back and get out of here. But don't leave town."

"Not planning on it."

Solly gave an exaggerated wince at Ten-Wolves' words. "And for God's sake try to stay out of trouble."

"I'll do my best."

"That doesn't appear to be good enough," Solly said dryly.

***

Sammy Boudreaux was preparing to run. He held a gym bag in his hand and was stuffing in clothes and money when his cell phone rang. He yanked it out of his pocket, afraid of whose name he might see. It was Jason Kulick.

"What?" Sammy snapped into the phone.

"I need help. Bad."

"Whatta you mean? I told you to lay low. What the hell have you done?"

"It was Kage. He was so mad at the Ranger. He...we tried to hit him again. It all went wrong. Kage is dead."

"I know it went wrong, you son of a bitch!" Sammy yelled into the phone. "Because I'm about to take the heat for it."

"Sorry. Sorry, man! But you gotta help me. Send a car for me. I'm hiding out but Ten-Wolves must be closing in by now."

Sammy was about to tell Kulick what he could do with himself when he realized the man might be the only close ally he had left. Besides, he might need someone to throw to the wolves before this was over. He rewrote the scene with, "Where are you?"

Kulick told him.

"All right! Sit tight. I'll be there myself in half an hour. You better have a bolt hole."

"I do. Thank—"

But Sammy had already swiped off. He missed the days when you could slam down a phone.

CHAPTER 30

As the two half brothers headed back into town, Concho's stomach gave a tremendous growl. Bull Knife jumped in his seat and then glared as the Ranger laughed.

"Are you about to give birth," Bull Knife asked, "or do you have a rabid wolf hidden somewhere in your truck?"

"I don't think I'm pregnant; it must be the wolf. I suppose we better feed him before he gets really mad."

Bull Knife shook his head but said nothing. They soon passed a small diner and Concho pulled off into the parking lot. It was after 3:00 and neither man had eaten today. In all the excitement, Ten-Wolves had forgotten. His body reminded him now as his stomach kept growling and a dull headache throbbed his temples.

The diner resembled a hundred others the Ranger had been in, with a once bright décor now dulled by time and use. The place had booths rather than tables. It smelled of grease and onions. The menu was different than in Texas. No chicken fried steak and no biscuits with white gravy, which were ubiquitous offerings in the Lone Star state.

Concho ordered two hamburgers with fries. When the waitress asked if he wanted the burgers "dressed," he almost told her he "preferred his meals naked," but he figured she'd heard the joke before. Besides, she looked a little harried and might bite his head off. He just said, "yes."

Bull Knife ordered one burger, undressed, but only toyed with it after it arrived. Concho finished his first hamburger in three huge bites, then picked up his second. He held it—it looked like a breakfast sandwich in his large hand—as he stared across the wooden table at his half brother.

"You OK?" he asked.

Without looking up, Bull Knife shook his head slowly from side to side. "I don't know." He took the bread off his patty. Cutting a slice of meat with his fork, he stuck it in his mouth and chewed slowly.

Concho took a small bite himself. "So tell me," he said around his food.

Bull Knife met his gaze. "Porter House for one. Somehow I've grown rather fond of him."

"Yeah, me too."

"Doesn't seem to have affected your *appetite,*" Bull Knife snapped.

The words unexpectedly hurt. Throughout his childhood people had made fun of Concho's big hunger. He would have thought he'd long since toughened beyond such criticism, but it seemed like he was still vulnerable when surprised. He forced himself to take another bite and then put the sandwich down on his plate.

His mind considered a variety of retorts at different levels of acid, but he could see that Bull Knife was miserable, probably from a variety of factors, including having just killed one man and helped kill another.

The Ranger took a deep breath. "I've done it myself but depriving yourself of food or sleep or temporary comfort isn't helping the people you worry about. It's doing the opposite; it's making you less ready and able to respond when your chance to help comes."

Bull Knife's practiced stoicism cracked. His face twisted with even more misery.

"What else?" Concho asked. "Besides Porter? What's clawing at you?"

Bull Knife leaned forward suddenly, his hands gripping tight on the edge of the table. "It doesn't feel like we're making any progress on why we came here. At first it did. Things were happening. I thought we were getting close to a breakthrough." He shrugged. "But now we're spinning our wheels."

"Yeah, I get that."

"Your friend, Solly. It seems he wants us to help bring down the Boudreaux family for their crimes. You seem content to help him. But I don't want to kill for *his* goals. I don't care about any Boudreaux. I care only about our mother. About finding her. Before there's another 'car accident' and she disappears again."

Concho sighed. "All right. You're not completely wrong. I guess I've been going along with Solly because I didn't know what else to do. This isn't my territory. I ran out of ideas after talking to Abigail Carmichael. I've been winging it since then."

"We have to stop 'winging it'! What does a law officer do in this kind of situation? Especially one such as yourself."

Concho took another small bite of burger. He chewed and swallowed while he considered.

"Something that happened today changes things a little," he said. "But, before I tell you about it, it's always a good strategy to recap what you already know."

"All right. Let's."

"From the moment you came into New Orleans they were watching you," Concho started. "Which means someone in Las Vegas told them you were coming. Somehow, they also overhead your phone call to me. So they knew *I* was coming. There have to be two different groups involved. Both want us to stay away. But one is willing to kill to make us. And the other just wants us to leave. That sound about right?"

"Seems so," Bull Knife said, shrugging.

"The ones who are willing to kill are connected to Sammy

Boudreaux. They didn't necessarily want to kill at first. They hired Porter House to follow us and they tried to threaten us away. Until I pissed them off. However, the patriarch and oldest son of the Boudreaux family either didn't know about any of this or they're good liars."

"My bet is on them lying."

"A safe assumption but I'm not convinced. Especially about Christoph, the oldest boy. Anyway, the group that's trying to warn us away…. You think it's our mother. Or connected to her. I think there's another possibility."

"What?"

The night I walked into Lafitte's, there was a woman there with dark hair and red highlights. She had dark skin. Not like mine. More Indian or Spanish type. She also had green eyes. She seemed familiar and she clearly recognized me. Or something about me. I tried to question her but she fled. She had people working for her who slowed me down in pursuing her. One of those people was a blue-eyed blonde. And here's where that 'something' happened to change things. The same blonde was at the farmhouse with Kulick and LeBlanc. She's the one who called herself Cassandra."

Bull Knife straightened in his chair. "You didn't tell me that."

"Sometimes I need to process things before I share them. But seeing Cassandra at the farm makes me think the green-eyed woman from the Quarter is involved in this whole thing. And since Cassandra *helped* me rather than attacking me, I think they're both part of the other faction, those who want us gone but not dead."

Bull Knife nodded steadily as Concho spoke. The lost and suffering look on his face faded. He seemed rejuvenated. At least a little. "Then we are still making progress. It *is* all connected."

"I think so. By the way, the little girl who spoke to me in the French Quarter. The 'Hannah' I mentioned to you."

"Yes."

"Pretty sure she's the green-eyed woman's child. And again, she was giving us a warning. Almost a plea, in fact."

"So, who is this green-eyed woman?"

"The million-dollar question. Cassandra is the key to finding her."

"We don't have Cassandra either."

"No. But I think she gave me her name for a reason. I just have to figure out what it is."

"Only her first name."

"Better than no name."

Bull Knife leaned back on his bench. He chewed at his lower lip. "I think I have hope again."

"Hope can be pretty draining. You better eat. Keep up your strength."

"I am not that hungry."

"Then slide your plate over here," Concho said, as he popped the last bite of his second burger into his mouth. "I'm still growing and I need the fuel."

***

Concho and Bull Knife had finished their meal and were headed for their motel when the Ranger's phone rang. He plucked it from the holder where it was charging and glanced at the caller ID. The name surprised him. Robert Echabarri was head of the tribal police at the reservation in Eagle Pass. He was also a good friend. But to get a call from him here and now felt a little troubling.

"From home," Concho said to Bull Knife, as he swiped receive and lifted the phone to his ear.

"Roberto?" he asked. "Everything OK?"

"It is not Roberto."

"Meskwaa!" he said, surprised. "I didn't think you knew how to use a cell phone."

"Young Roberto loaned me his. And gave me some brief instruction. I am relieved you could recognize me."

"I believe I know your voice."

"Even through this small box?"

"Yes." Concho added teasingly, "It's not like the two cans tied together by a string that you played with as a kid back in the 1800s."

"How nice," Meskwaa said. "Even now at a distance you spew insults like the summer locusts."

Concho chuckled. "You know I love you. But what *is* going on? Everything all right there?"

"Nothing too awful has happened here. The land is generally at peace. But it is part of my burden from your grandmother to check up on you. I'm sure you're eating plenty. As you always do. But how are other things proceeding?"

Concho grinned to himself at the "eating" comment. It was something of a running joke with the two of them and this time it didn't hurt.

"I am eating," he replied. "But I guess you're starving without me there to hunt for you."

"I lived many years without you to *hunt* for me. Perhaps I will survive a few more. But you have not answered my question about your mission."

Before leaving for New Orleans, Concho had spoken to Meskwaa about Bull Knife's call, and that it supposedly had to do with his mother.

"Things aren't going easily," he answered. "But I suppose they could be worse."

Meskwaa didn't reply and Concho could practically see the Kickapoo elder nodding into the phone.

"I appreciate you checking on me, though," the lawman continued. "And I'm all right. Still hoping to be home soon."

"Your lady friend, Maria, will be happy to hear. She has visited your home and made…adjustments."

"Uh oh!"

"Indeed. I visited with her there the other day. I did not say anything about her adjustments except to admire them."

"Wise of you."

"How is it you have entranced such a beautiful young woman?"

"Wouldn't *you* like to be let in on the secret?"

"Ha!" Meskwaa snorted into the phone. "I have many such beautiful women in love with me. I simply do not parade them around."

"Sure," Concho said.

Silence filled the line. Meskwaa finally spoke the reason why he'd really called.

"I have had an experience. I feel it best to tell you about it."

A small chill slipped up Concho's back. "I want to hear," he said.

CHAPTER 31

Cassandra Holmes pulled the Jeep she'd taken into a parking space at the Esplanade Mall in Kenner, one of the suburbs of New Orleans. The other three women from the farm sat quiet and subdued in the vehicle.

"Use whatever cloth you have and wipe down every place you may have touched," Cassandra said. "We don't want any prints."

The women worked for a few minutes with sleeves and the tails of their shirts before Cassandra added. "OK, that should do it. Get going. Separate. Don't tell *anyone* what happened. Don't even talk about it among yourselves."

The women nodded and practically fled. Cassandra climbed out herself. She'd been born and raised in Louisiana; it was cold as far as she was concerned, though the temperature hovered in the low sixties. The perceived chill was an excuse for the heavy coat she wore, which she'd buttoned all the way up to hide the fact that underneath it her white shirt was stained with blood spray.

Cassandra had parked near the rear of the lot and, after looking around to make sure she wasn't observed, took the rag she'd found in the glove box and wiped down all the external door handles to get rid of the last prints. She abandoned the vehicle with the doors unlocked and the keys in the ignition. Her best hope was that someone would take it for a joy ride before the police found it.

She pulled her phone out of her purse. She'd had it silenced but noted several calls and texts from Sammy Boudreaux, each sounding more desperate than the last. She ignored those. She had no intention of talking to him right now. Or maybe ever again. But she did have a Boudreaux to call. She thumbed up the number on her contacts and swiped send.

The man who answered had a voice that could melt frozen butter. He was a singer after all, and though he was in his fifties his tone still rang rich, melodic, and sensual. Cassandra had a thing for voices, like the baritone she'd heard recently from Concho Ten-Wolves. She was fond of the voice on the phone now, though it was no romantic interest.

"I'm calling for Nick Barron," she said. Barron was the musical stage name for Nicholas Boudreaux.

A chuckle came over the airwaves. "Cassandra. That joke's getting old. You know it's me. Were you trying to catch Eve? She took Maggie to a dance class."

"I…uh. Well…."

The tone of the mellow voice changed instantly to register concern. "Cassie! What's wrong? Never heard you hesitant before."

Cassie sighed. "A lot of things. For one, Kage LeBlanc is dead."

A moment of silence held on the other end of the cell. Then, "Tell me."

"We were at the farm. The one off River Road that Sammy rents. Jason Kulick put in a call at the office for some girls. I rode along."

"Why? You know what Kage LeBlanc is like."

"Exactly. I know what Kage LeBlanc is like. I've seen how he treats women. Last time we had a girl with a broken jaw. I wasn't going to let him get away with anything like that again."

"So what happened? Who killed Kage?"

"I didn't realize at the time but they tried to hit that Texas Ranger. Ten-Wolves. Apparently it fell apart and they came to the farm to hide out. But the Ranger found them. He killed Kage and three other men. Jason ran into the woods. They were after him but I don't know if they caught him."

"They?"

"The Ranger had the other one with him. His brother, I guess."

Nicholas Boudreaux blew a long breath into the phone. His voice had a growl this time when he continued, "Sammy is an idiot! So are Kulick and LeBlanc."

"Really?" Cassandra said. "Since when?"

"It's no joke this time!"

"I know. I'm not laughing."

"This guy is really becoming a problem."

"Who? Ten-Wolves? Or Sammy?"

"Both. Though I'm mostly referring to Ten-Wolves, who's now had more than enough warnings to leave well enough alone."

"Have you considered telling him the truth?"

Nick did not respond at first. Then, "He's a lawman, Cassie. A Texas Ranger."

"Which means he doesn't have jurisdiction in Louisiana. Or in Nevada. Or California."

"But he knows people who do. And everything I've read about this guy says he's a straight shooter. He'd be bound to report anything he found out. Even if it's ancient but unburied history."

"You can't be sure of that. I met the guy. Briefly at least. I get a pretty good feeling from him."

"You better stay away from him. If Sammy's in this deep he won't quit until something breaks. You don't want to be around for that."

"And what if it's Sammy who breaks?"

"You know how my father is and what he'll do. Sammy's blood. Ten-Wolves isn't."

Cassandra didn't say anything. She let the silence speak for her. After another moment, Nick continued, his voice higher pitched than usual, as if he were embarrassed.

"Where are you?"

"The Esplanade Mall. Lakeside entrance. Can you send a car?" She felt her own voice go cold as she added, "I'm sitting here with Kage LeBlanc's gore on me. I doubt the Boudreaux family would appreciate me getting arrested because of that kind of blood."

Nick cleared his throat. "I'll send it. Twenty minutes probably. They'll bring you here."

"Good. I need a shower and I'd like to talk to Eve as soon as she gets home. I've also got a few things to tell you in private that I think you ought to hear." She ended the call without waiting for a response.

**

"I want to hear it," Concho repeated to Meskwaa through the phone. "Tell me about your 'experience'."

"I was walking when rain began to fall. Hateful rain. Half frozen water around pellets of ice. The rain was cold. I am an old man. I took shelter beneath a bluff. While I huddled, a whirlwind plowed across the desert before me. There are no whirlwinds here this time of year. I felt the thrum in the air. Like spirit drums. I knew then who the whirlwind had to be. You remember him. The Skinwalker who helped you solve the murder of Agustina Cardenas only weeks ago."

"I remember. Though I'm not so sure he was a Skinwalker."

"Your heart knows differently than your head. But you will learn. After the spirit wind passed, the cold deepened. The sky grew black and colored the world beneath it. We do not see snow here on the reservation. But it began to snow. The snow was white against the darkness. As if each flake were lit from within. It began to spiral around and around, tying itself into knots."

Concho felt himself stiffen. *The knots! The whirlwind!* Like in his dream of last night.

"I began to fear," Meskwaa continued. "I could hear things in the darkness. Approaching things. And I had not brought along any food. Nothing to feed the ghosts."

"A cigarette," Concho whispered softly, vaguely remembering a story his grandfather had told him when he was very young.

He glanced at Bull Knife, who was sitting up straight and listening as if he could also hear Meskwaa. Or perhaps the younger man just sensed the urgency in the exchange between Concho and the Kickapoo Elder.

"Yes. I took one of my cigarettes and broke it," Meskwaa said. "I tossed the tobacco out from my shelter but something rejected it. I began to chant. The dark shredded my voice."

"But at least you are still here," Concho murmured.

He knew Meskwaa had visions, and had trusted them before and been helped. He couldn't be sure how much of what his friend was telling him now had happened in reality or in a vision. But he remained caught in the story. As if he were there, seeing the elements from his own dream drawn in the real world around Meskwaa, an old man squatting alone in the poor shelter of a limestone bluff.

"I *am* still here," the Elder agreed. "Someone heard me despite the efforts of the ghosts. A single boom of thunder pounded a fist against the bluff. It nearly stopped my heart. But after, the darkness went and the rain slowed until it disappeared. The ice and snow melted, as if they had never been. I recognized that Pèthakhuwe, one of the thunder beings, had come to my rescue."

Concho chose his next words carefully. His rational mind told him that Meskwaa had encountered only an unusual storm on his walk. But the elder Kickapoo believed it was more, and sometimes Concho's blood did too—especially after his own eerie adventures over the past few months. For example, what was he to make of the similarities between his dream and Meskwaa's experience? And, he could hear fear in the Elder's voice. It took much to frighten this man.

"I'm happy you're all right," Concho said. "I feel it best to tell you something also. Last night, I dreamt of whirlwinds, and knots, and of angels both cold and hot."

"I am not surprised. The talent lies within you. And in a short time you have become much more aware of the outer world that surrounds the first like a caul."

"So it seems. Though perhaps there are other explanations."

Meskwaa gave a soft "Haa."

"What do you think such things mean?" Concho asked. "I considered the knots in my dream, that they might have something to do with the mystery of Sparrow Woman. Of how convoluted and confusing it is."

"I do not think so. I believe all these things speak of two people, two individuals. One will help you; one will harm. Is there anyone you have met in Louisiana who makes you think of such images?"

"I don't…know. I'll have to consider it."

"It may be you *will* meet them. You must be ready. This is why I came to call you as soon as my experience ended."

"Be ready? For what? And why?"

"Because the cold and the knots had a voice. It whispered to me."

"I'm afraid to ask what it whispered," Concho said. And he *was* afraid.

"Your name. With a hiss like snow."

CHAPTER 32

Porter House snapped awake but had no idea where he was or what had happened to him. He lay on a narrow cot in a dimly lit room. His head throbbed. He sat up, groaning, and memory slapped him in the face. A surge of fear made him gag.

He threw his hand to his mouth as he looked around the room for some place to throw up. An actual toilet stood at one end of the room and he ran for it, dropping to his knees and pushing up the lid just as a wave of puke forced its way free.

For nearly a minute he emptied his guts, then rose shakily to his feet. A sink stood beside the toilet and he washed out his mouth and rinsed his face. The water had a faintly rusty taste but his throat felt sandpaper dry and he cupped his hands beneath the faucet to get a long drink. Finally, he dried off on a ragged maroon towel hanging nearby.

A mirror hung over the sink, of polished metal rather than glass. He studied himself. His eyes and cheeks were sunken. He looked like an invalid; he felt like one. A stinging from his left leg drew his attention and he looked down. He wore only his own gray underwear. Someone had wrapped a white bandage around and around his thigh.

He reached down, touched the bandage. It was clean and not

very old. He remembered this, too. The man who'd invaded his room had made him undress, had gagged him and tied him up. He'd sliced his left leg deeply with one of the scalpels left behind by the doctor who used to rent his apartment. Porter remembered bleeding, and the fear he was going to die. And then a needle went into his arm when he wasn't looking. He'd gone to sleep.

And now?

He examined his prison. No windows. A sink and toilet. The cot, one chair, and a tiny square table. And at the other end…a door. He started toward it, limping now that he knew his leg was injured, though it didn't hurt as much as he thought it should.

The door opened before he reached it. He froze. A man stepped through carrying a plastic food tray. Behind him rose a set of wooden stairs lit by a single bare bulb. He was locked in a cellar somewhere.

His eyes returned to the man, his captor. It had to be the same man, though he'd worn a black balaclava before and now had on a Mardi Gras mask. The mask was full-faced, with a marble white chin and cheeks, lips outlined in green and purple, and a glittering gold from the eyes up.

The tragedy and comedy masks were common symbols for the people of New Orleans during Mardi Gras mania. This mask represented tragedy, with the eye sockets squinted in pain and the mouth shaped into a howl of anguish.

"You should sit down," the man said. "I stitched your leg but if you keep putting weight on it, you'll make it bleed again."

Porter hesitated. His thoughts told him he should rush the fellow now, try to knock him down or get past him. The longer he was held captive here, the weaker he'd get and the less his chances would be.

The man must have read the private investigator's thoughts. He didn't say anything but shifted his stance a little to show the pistol equipped with a silencer hanging in a holster at his right hip.

Porter moved over to his cot and sat down. The man sniffed

the air and made a face. Porter guessed it was the smell of his vomit, though his own nose wasn't that sensitive. Carrying the tray toward him, the man placed it on the small table, which it nearly covered. On the tray sat a sixteen-ounce Coca-Cola and a plastic bowl full of cheerios and milk. A plastic spoon had been provided.

Porter snatched up the Coke and twisted it open. He was about to raise it to his mouth when he hesitated. His gaze sought his captor's but it was impossible to read any emotion behind the mask.

The other man certainly seemed able to read Porter's emotions well enough. "You needn't worry about it being drugged. You're completely in my power here. And you already know I don't need drugs to restrain you."

Porter nodded. He took a swig of the Coke, followed by a bigger swallow. Once he started he could hardly stop and drained nearly half of it.

"Good," his captor said. "You lost quite a bit of blood. You need to replenish. Eat something too."

"After you cut me, I didn't expect to wake up."

"Just for show," the man replied. "I needed to make a point."

"What point?"

"The point that I was serious."

"Look, who are you and what do you want?" Porter asked, but then immediately threw up his hands. "No, wait, I don't want to know. I *don't* know who you are. I'd never be able to identify you. You can let me go and no one will hear anything from me about it."

"Not going to happen. But I wasn't planning to give you my bona fides anyway. Thus, the mask."

"Please," Porter begged. "You sound like a cultured man. Whatever it is, it's not worth killing me over. Just let me go."

"Can't. You're the only leverage I have over your friend Concho Ten-Wolves. Though it doesn't seem like he's too worried about what might be happening to you."

Porter's shoulders slumped. "So it's that again."

"I'm not the one who hired you to follow the Texas Ranger. I'm here to clean up that one's mess."

"So you're gonna kill me?"

"If such were my only intention, why wouldn't I have done it already?"

"What then?"

"I'm going to put in a call to the good Ten-Wolves. Tell him what's at stake if he doesn't do what he's already been told to do."

"And if he doesn't listen?"

The mask's tortured porcelain smile seemed to twist macabrely as the man replied. "I'll start cutting off pieces of you and deliver them to him one by one."

***

Nicholas Boudreaux, better known to the rest of the world as jazz and blues guitarist Nick Barron, sighed after Cassandra Holmes hung up on him. Sometimes she seemed wise beyond her years; at other times she could be so naïve. Like now when she suggested that simply telling a lawman the truth might make everything OK.

He selected and swiped a number at the Treasure Chest Casino and told them where to send a car to pick up Cassandra. After, he lay the cell phone down on the big desk in his home recording studio and stared at the room.

Normally, being in this room brought him peace of mind. Not now. He'd already been disturbed here earlier by a call from Abigail Carmichael. Her husband, Nolen, was one of Nick's oldest and most trusted friends. They'd played music together for ages. But now, Abigail believed that Nolen might have involved himself in dangerous actions, for noble if misguided reasons. So far, Nolen had not answered Nick's calls trying to find out.

Nick picked up one of two framed photos on his desk. This one showed his daughter, Eve, a tall, athletic, lovely young woman, leaning against the blonde litheness of Cassandra Holmes, who he sometimes thought of as his daughter, too.

He put that photo down and picked up the other. Three people stood close together and smiling in this one. He and his wife, with Eve between them. She'd been only four years old at the time—on the beach at Grand Isle with wet sand sticking to her skinny legs.

His gaze shifted to the woman. His wife. She had dark red hair here, cut to shoulder length. It wasn't the same color or length as when he'd met her. But that didn't matter. Nor did the alterations in her facial features. He could focus past those, and she was still the most beautiful woman he'd ever seen.

He wondered sometimes if there was a woman for each man whose appearance perfectly fit their teenaged dreams of a fantasy lover. If so, Maura was his. No matter how much she'd changed over the years, she was still his beautiful one. Even now. After....

CHAPTER 33

Sammy Boudreaux passed the abandoned gas station once and made a U-turn. He pulled his yellow Corvette up to the hole in the cement where the gas pumps used to be. Sitting there quietly, he let the engine run; his right hand clutched the butt of the Ruger Blackhawk .44 Magnum he held down below the seat.

A furtive and disheveled Jason Kulick stepped through one of the old station's broken windows and darted quickly to the side of Sammy's car. He popped open the door and flung himself inside, then promptly ducked down low.

Sammy made a face at Kulick's sweat and dirt slicked features. "You're gonna clean that leather seat off later," he snarled, as he pulled the nickel-plated .44 out of hiding and placed it next to the 'Vette's center console.

"Be happy to," Kulick replied. "Let's just get out of here."

Sammy pulled out on the road and hit the gas. "Sit up in your damn seat," he ordered. "Don't look so suspicious."

Kulick sighed but did as he was told. He rubbed at his mouth with the back of a hand as he stared out the window.

"I can't believe you two tried to hit Ten-Wolves again," Sammy said. "I told you to leave it alone."

"It was Kage, I tell you. You know how he is. The cop handcuffed him to a stair railing. He was furious. He wanted payback."

"*You* were supposed to ride herd on LeBlanc!" Sammy snapped. "Not let him do whatever he damn well pleased."

"You try riding herd on him," Kulick snapped back. "He's like a hungry lion on a bone."

"Humph. Don't reckon he's much like anything anymore."

Kulick nodded. "You're right. That Ten-Wolves is a force of nature. I'll be glad not to have to go up against him again."

"You better rethink."

Kulick twisted his head around. "What?"

"We've got no choice now. We have to take him out. He and his brother both. My father knows about the whole thing. He might, just *might*, let things slide if the Ranger is out of the picture."

"How did your dad find out?"

"Who knows for sure, but he and Chris have spies everywhere."

"Ten-Wolves isn't going to be easy to get. Believe me. It'll take an army."

Sammy offered Kulick a sly smile. "I've got just the guys!"

***

Concho and Bull Knife arrived at their motel around five in the afternoon. Bull Knife went in to have a shower but Concho felt restless. He remained outside and paced around the parking lot. Finally, he jerked out his phone and placed a call to Solly Burstein. The detective answered on the third ring.

"You back at the office?" Concho asked.

"On my way home to eat."

"Any news?"

"A little. Not about Porter House directly. But we had a man watching Sammy Boudreaux and it looks like he may be on the run. He took off in his Corvette an hour ago and hasn't come back yet."

"And you didn't think to call me?"

"It's been an *hour*," Solly said sharply. "Hardly cause to call out the National Guard."

"Sorry," Concho said, taking a breath. "Just...there must be a lot of things going on we don't know about."

"Probably. But that's how it happens. If Sammy *is* going to ground, it could mean the seed I planted is starting to germinate in the Boudreaux camp. That can only be good news for us."

"All right," Concho said. He stopped pacing as his phone buzzed. "Look, I'm getting another call. Keep me in the loop, please. I know you don't have to but I'd appreciate it."

"I'll tell you the same thing you told me, I'll do the best I can." Solly closed the connection.

Concho swiped to take the incoming call without seeing who it was from. A man's voice came over the line—clearly disguised. "Officer Ten-Wolves?"

"Yes. Who is this?"

"I believe we have a mutual acquaintance in Porter House."

Concho's chest tightened. "You're right. How did you get this number?"

"Mister House was good enough to provide it. Or at least his phone did. I believe he's anxious to get everything resolved, though."

"So he's alive?"

"At present."

"How badly is he hurt?"

"The cut that provided the blood was more for show than for effect. He'll be fine. At least in regard to *that* wound."

"And what exactly do we need to do to 'resolve' this issue?"

"You and your brother need to back away. I'd suggest you leave town. The...denouement you're seeking isn't going to happen. There are reasons why. They are personal reasons and don't involve the law. You're both old enough to move on."

"Is Sparrow Woman alive?"

"You're also old enough to understand that life often provides no answers to its mysteries. Sometimes there is no closure. I can assure you there's nothing emotionally, physically, or financially in it for you."

"And if we don't back away?"

"First, Porter will suffer. Believe me, I don't want to do it. I prefer things neat and clean. But," he chuckled, "as I just told you, we can't always get what we want."

"But if you try sometimes, you just might find, you get what you need."

Again came the chuckle. "I'm afraid your knowledge of Rolling Stones' lyrics won't soften my heart."

"Counterpoint," Concho said. "You sound like a careful man. I'm sure you've kept your identity secret from Porter. He'll never be able to point you out. You let him go, and I'll forget you exist. You step back and you're out of it. Free and clear. At least as far as I'm concerned."

"And what will you do if I don't?"

"I'll do to you everything you do to Porter. I may be a Texas Ranger, but I'm also a savage. I don't mind claiming it. And Bull Knife is worse than I am."

"Hmm. You do realize there's no one more savage than a civilized man who decides not to be civilized, don't you? The near genocide against your native tribe illustrates that most abundantly."

"All right," Concho said. "Now we've both shared how tough we are. I have no doubt you mean what you say. So do I. But let me offer a change in narrative. Porter's an innocent man. Before you say it, I know the innocent suffer right along with the guilty. I've seen it a million times. But it doesn't have to be that way. You're the one deciding Porter should suffer. Which means you have the power to stop it from happening."

"Are you appealing to my humanity?"

"I'm appealing to whatever is inside of you that understands right from wrong. You want me to stop doing what I'm doing. Then stop me. Come after *me*. Leave Porter out of it."

The Ranger ended the call. A check on the number showed

"Restricted." Had to be a burner phone. There'd be no way to track it. He paced back and forth in the parking lot again, with his anger growing.

"That's it!" he snapped into the air. He punched up his phone contacts and selected the one for Christoph Boudreaux. He hit send. It began to ring but no one answered. It went to voice mail.

"I just got a call from Porter House's kidnapper," the Ranger snarled into the phone. "I'm on my way to the casino and I'm gonna want some answers!"

He hurried to his truck. The engine seemed to growl along with him as it turned over. He sent one quick text to Bull Knife saying he'd be back soon, then peeled out of the parking lot and laid rubber down the street in the direction of the Treasure Chest.

CHAPTER 34

Porter House slumped on his cot, his head in his hands.
He'd naturally tried the door and, as expected, found it locked.
He'd pushed and pulled on every board in his small cell in hopes
of finding one that gave way. No such luck. His stomach burbled.
His mouth and throat burned with acid reflux. His leg throbbed.
He chewed at his lip.

Only his ears seemed alive as they listened intently for any
sound of his captor returning to "cut off pieces" of him for deliv-
ery to Concho Ten-Wolves. Even so, he didn't hear anyone coming until the door to his prison opened suddenly and the man in
the Mardi Gras masked stepped through.

This time, the man had switched out the tragedy mask for the
comedy one. The porcelain lips curved up in a smile. The eyes
were shaped like teardrops as if with laughter. Porter had always
found the comedy mask more terrifying than the tragic. To him,
the smile looked like a sneer. The curved eyes suggested gleeful
evil rather than joy.

Porter froze where he sat. It had always been his strategy to
talk his way out of trouble. But he had no words now. His captor
leaned against the door frame and stared at him. The gun still
hung on the man's hip but at least he wasn't carrying a knife or

saw or hatchet or machete.

"How's the leg?" the man asked.

Porter jumped at the break in the silence. He took a shallow breath. "Hurts."

"Any bleeding through the bandage?"

He shook his head.

The man nodded, straightened.

"Please," Porter said.

The fellow stuck his hand in a pocket and pulled out an apple. He tossed this to Porter, who fumbled to catch it and finally trapped it with both palms against his stomach. He glanced back toward the man, to say thank you. But he was gone, and the door was shut behind him.

***

Concho whipped into the parking lot of the Treasure Chest Casino and practically slid into a parking space. He stepped out of his Ford and stomped toward the boat. The people going in and out stepped out of his way as they saw his face. All except for two men who were waiting for him right at the opening of the covered walkway leading onto the boat.

These were the same two he'd seen here before, as the muscle standing beside the table of Roman Boudreaux. One man was black, the other white. Both wore black suits with white shirts and black ties. The white bodyguard held up his hand, palm out as Concho stalked toward them.

"You're not welcome here. Turn around and go home."

Concho didn't stop walking. His hands flashed out; he grabbed the man's wrist and twisted it up and out. The fellow cried out in pain as he was forced to bend backward at an awkward angle. His free left hand fumbled at his shoulder holster but it was the wrong hand to reach for his gun beneath his left arm.

Concho slashed the blade of his own hand into the man's throat, pulling the punch at the last second so as not to crush the windpipe. The man gagged; Concho let go of the wrist and let him fall backward as he gasped for oxygen.

While onlookers screamed and scattered, the second bodyguard lunged toward Concho. The Ranger turned into him. The man hooked a right toward Concho's ribs. He blocked with his left forearm, sent a right-hand jab into the fellow's face. Blood sprayed from a smashed lip as the man stepped back and shook his head.

The bodyguard was a big fellow, though, and had obviously been hit before. He came back to get his. His fists were up as he bobbed and weaved like a well-trained boxer. Concho hooked a boot behind the guard's right leg and took it from under him. The man crashed down with a grunt. He wouldn't be down long.

The first bodyguard had regained his feet. Instead of drawing his gun, though, he pulled an expandable nightstick from his belt and whipped it out to its full length—some twenty-four inches. Concho had seen these same batons before—in the parking garage on his first night in town—which meant the men who attacked him then were probably connected to the Boudreaux family.

The baton snapped toward Concho's face. The Ranger leaped backward. The man swung again. And missed. In the time it took the guard to pull the baton back into position, Concho charged him. Once more he grabbed the fellow's wrist, his hand locking down and exerting the crushing grip of which he was capable.

The guard grunted. His hand spasmed, dropping the weapon. Concho hooked his fingers into the fellow's shirt collar, dragged him around and flung him against the wall of the walkway. Everything swayed. He stomped a boot into the back of the guard's left leg, which gave way and sent the fellow collapsing to the floor with a sharp cry of pain. He wouldn't be putting any weight on that leg for a bit.

The second guard had regained his feet and drawn his own expandable baton. Concho didn't give him a chance to use it. He snapped a back-kick into the man's gut. As the fellow doubled over, Concho spun, took the baton out of his hand and popped him with it solidly behind the ear. The guard dropped to his knees, shaking his head to try and clear the bells ringing in his ears.

Still holding the baton, Concho turned back toward the casino entrance. Every onlooker but one had either fled or cowered back against the walls. The one who'd neither fled nor cowered was Roman Boudreaux, who stood heavily in the center of the walkway with his face flushed a bright, sweaty crimson. Concho started toward him.

"You. You. You," Boudreaux said.

"You got it," Concho said. "I'm here for answers."

Roman Boudreaux's fists clenched. He sputtered as his face flushed even more scarlet. His fleshy nose glistened. Abruptly, the scarlet fled and a sickly gray began to spread. Boudreaux threw both hands to his chest.

Concho paused. Boudreaux staggered and nearly fell. The Ranger stepped forward and caught him. He was heavy, a mass of near helpless meat. Against the wall nearby sat a narrow bench. Concho half-dragged Boudreaux over and pushed him down on it. He leaned over him. Roman gasped for oxygen; saliva dribbled from the left side of his mouth. His breath smelled sour.

The casino surely had some kind of paramedic on staff; the Ranger yelled for one of the onlookers to fetch help just as Christoph Boudreaux came running onto the scene.

"Ten-Wolves! No!" Christoph shouted.

Concho straightened. Christoph ran up and dropped to one knee by his father. "It's OK, it's OK," he said. He reached into Roman's shirt pocket and fished out a small glass vial. Quickly twisting it open, he dumped out a tiny white tablet. This, he pushed between his father's lips and under the tongue.

"Just let it dissolve," Christoph said.

Roman nodded, his breathing still heavy. Christoph glared up at Concho.

"Nitroglycerin?" Concho asked.

"Yes. He's got a bad heart. But nitro usually helps."

Several more men arrived, employees of the casino or of the Boudreaux family. Christoph gestured at the two bodyguards, both of whom were trying to get to their feet.

"Get those men out of here," Christoph demanded of the new arrivals. "And someone bring my father a wheelchair."

"No!" Roman Boudreaux said, as he tried to stand. "I can walk!" The gray pallor had receded in his face, though he still didn't look well.

"Dad!" Christoph snapped, pushing his father back down. "Take it easy. I know you can walk but it'll be better to get you in a chair and take you somewhere to lie down."

Roman sighed and nodded. He glared at Concho but quickly looked away in an effort to keep himself calm.

Christoph rose to his feet. A young woman dressed in a casino uniform pushed an extra-large wheelchair into the hallway and positioned it beside Roman Boudreaux. She, Christoph, and Concho got the older man up and into the chair. The woman pushed him away.

Christoph turned toward the lawman. "I need to get my father somewhere he can lie down. But I'll meet you outside the conference room in about ten minutes. We need to talk."

"I'll be there!"

Christoph followed his father's wheelchair. Concho gazed around at the onlookers, who had tripled in numbers now that the violence was over. They didn't understand what was behind the violence, only that he—a stranger—had brought it into their midst. Everyone stared at him, with pupils dilated, as if he might sprout fur and fangs and tear them apart.

For just a moment, he felt like Tony Montana in *Scarface*. He wanted to tell them to, "Say good night to the bad guy." Instead, he gave them his shark smile and felt a tiny perverse glee as they flinched and dropped their gazes.

"Don't be a dick," he murmured at himself, as he headed into the casino and up the stairs.

CHAPTER 35

While he waited outside the casino's conference room,
Concho forced himself to calm down. He wasn't doing anyone any
good, including himself and Porter. His phone buzzed. Another text
message from Bull Knife. He'd gotten several already and had to
respond. His half brother did not deserve to be ignored.

He texted that he was all right and would be back soon. The
phone also told him that over fifteen minutes had passed since his
confrontation with Roman Boudreaux's men. Time might be slipping away for Porter. Where was Christoph?

Even as he thought the question, the oldest Boudreaux son
came walking along the hallway. Alone. He didn't speak but unlocked the door of the conference room and motioned the lawman inside. He closed the door before flipping on the lights.

The brightness made Concho blink. "How's your father?"

Christoph gave him a glare. The Ranger could see an angry
retort forming but Boudreaux got hold of himself and shook his
head. It showed admirable control, followed by a calm response.

"He'll be OK. He has these attacks sometimes. It's not a cor-
onary. The nitro helps. He knows he's not supposed to get upset
but I suppose it's hard to change a lifetime habit."

"I left the phone message for *you*," Concho said. "How did

he find out I was coming?"

"I told him. Stupid, I realize. You've gotta understand. My father's getting old. He used to control everything. Now he can't control his own body. He probably thought he could get a sense of power back by blocking you from meeting with me."

"Why would he want to block it?"

Christoph moved over to a chair and flopped down as if exhausted. "You going to sit this time or hover like a buzzard against the wall like you did before?"

Concho snorted a breath, then sat. "Answer my question."

Christoph considered. He gave a short nod of his head. "Sammy is his youngest son. In some ways his favorite."

"So, Sammy *is* involved?"

"Appears that way. We got a…communique, let's say. The police have connected Sammy to the recent antics of Jason Kulick and Kage LeBlanc. I heard, by the way, that you took care of Kage earlier today."

"Is it gonna be a problem between us?"

Boudreaux's eyelids flashed up and down. "Not for me. I'd say you did us a favor. LeBlanc was a bit of an ass."

"More than a bit."

Boudreaux nodded. "Kulick always seemed smarter but maybe it was just a run of good luck. Anyway, Sammy has disappeared. We don't know where. But he's gotta be aware Dad is mad at him. He'll lay low. I wouldn't doubt he's headed for Mexico."

"He left a loose end I'm worried about."

"What's that?"

"Porter House."

Boudreaux raised an eyebrow but said nothing.

"The PI that Sammy hired to follow Bull Knife and me," the lawman explained.

"Oh, right. What about him?"

"Someone kidnapped him. Left blood behind to show he was hurt. I just got a call from the kidnapper threatening House's life if I didn't back off the search for my mother."

Christoph straightened in his seat. He shook his head. "Doesn't sound like Sammy. Far too subtle. He's more of a bull in a China closet kind of fellow."

"Then someone he hired or works with has more imagination than he does."

"Not Kulick either. He doesn't show that kind of initiative."

"So who?" Concho snapped. "I want Porter out of this alive. It's only your brother's incompetence that got him into it."

"I'll make some inquiries. But with Sammy hiding out I don't know what I'll be able to find."

Concho vented an uncharacteristic curse and pushed to his feet. He began to pace. "Why?" he demanded. "Bull Knife and I come into town to search for our mother, who I was sure had been dead for over twenty years, and we immediately start getting warnings and threats. Your brother hires someone to follow us, then tries to have us killed when that rebounds on him. What's the connection between my mother and your family? It has to be there!"

Christoph tapped his fingers on the table. "You're probably not going to believe me when I tell you I don't know."

"What about your father?"

Boudreaux shrugged. "If he does, he hasn't enlightened me."

"How old are you?" Concho asked.

Christoph blinked. "Why?"

Concho only stared.

"Fifty-seven," Boudreaux answered. "Why?"

"You have a wife? How old is she?"

Now a frown crossed Christoph's face. "I'm afraid you're going to have to explain your curiosity before I start answering personal questions."

"*If* my mother were alive she'd be about fifty-three. The only reason I can think of why Sammy doesn't want me searching in the New Orleans area for her is because she has some connection to *your* family. How old is your wife?"

Christoph looked startled. It didn't seem faked. "That's crazy! You think your mother *married* into my family? She was full-blood Kickapoo, wasn't she?"

"Yes."

Boudreaux shook his head and kept shaking. "There's no one like that connected to us. My wife is fifty-four. But she's red-headed, pale-skinned Irish all the way."

"What about your father's second wife? Sammy's mother?"

"Terry is fifty-nine now. I believe. She's Greek, and blonde."

"Natural blonde?"

"I have no idea."

"Dark or light skin?"

"Uhm…medium."

"Hmm. How about Nicholas's wife."

"She's in her fifties. She's French."

"Her name?"

"Maura."

"She's French? You're sure?"

"Well, of French descent. Nicholas met her in Canada, I think. She certainly doesn't look like a…a Native American."

"We don't all look the same," Concho said.

"For Christ's sake, I was introduced to Maura's *parents*. They're still alive."

"I want to meet the wives. All of them. And any long-term women employees around that age."

"That's—" Christoph started to say.

The lights in the casino blinked; the fire alarm began to blare.

***

Piotr Morozov sat alone in a small, tech-heavy room in the Treasure Chest Casino. A large rack of monitors and controls stood in front of him. Screens mounted on the wall showed the entranceway, the gambling floor, the buffet. He ignored these views as he listened to a single feed coming from the second-floor conference room where Christoph Boudreaux and Concho Ten-Wolves were talking.

There were no cameras in the conference room, and once a week it was swept for bugs. But Piotr was the man responsible for having it swept and had his own hidden ear in place. It had served him many times in dealing with Boudreaux friends and enemies.

His already-focused attention intensified as he heard Ten-Wolves start to ask personal questions about the family. If he kept that up he'd soon reach dangerous ground. And, stupidly, Christoph was *answering*. Of course, Christoph did not know why such a line of questioning was risky. It might have been a mistake not to bring him in on the full story.

Piotr cursed. His hand leaped out, pressed an icon on the computer screen in front of him. The casino's fire alarm system activated. The sound at least. His finger hovered over the sprinkler icon, then pulled back.

"Not yet!" he snapped to himself.

He grabbed the cell phone lying beside him and quickly sent an already written text message. Then he headed for the door to the main part of the casino. He needed to be seen by people. To have an alibi.

CHAPTER 36

As the fire alarm whooped, Christoph Boudreaux went quickly to the conference room door and through. Concho followed, stepping into the hallway. No one was panicking yet, though excited voices came from the main gambling floor beneath them. The Ranger could neither see nor smell any smoke.

Christoph's face paled. "I've got to check on my father."

Concho nodded. "Don't forget Porter House."

"Right," Boudreaux said. "I'll call you." He took off down the corridor, walking swiftly.

Concho headed for the stairs. People who'd been eating in the buffet were crowded at the top. Most were older folks, moving on slow legs. A few heavy-set individuals were being ushered along by waiters. Concho paused and watched to see if anyone needed help. Everything seemed to be going smoothly.

As he glanced over the heads of the crowd, he saw someone in a corridor across the way striding toward the stairs in his jerky style. Their gazes met. The pale eyes of the other glinted like chips of ice before the man looked away.

Piotr Morozov, Concho identified.

Something clicked. Morozov meant "frost" in Russian. Meskwaa had called to tell him about a vision full of cold snow and knots. Those images had matched his own dream of the same day. The Kickapoo Elder had wondered if he'd met anyone in Louisiana who made him think of such things? He'd denied it at the time. But now, Morozov brought just those images to mind—knotted and icy. He should have remembered before.

Concho lifted his hand as a signal to Roman Boudreaux's administrative assistant, but the man turned abruptly away and headed down another corridor. A frown crossed the Ranger's face. Why would Morozov avoid him? Too many people were in the lawman's way for him to get through. He had to wait for the crowd to thin. By that time, Morozov had disappeared.

The fire alarm continued to blare, though still with no sign of flames or smoke. Concho joined the last few people heading down the stairs, even though he had a feeling it was a false alarm—a conveniently timed tactical gambit to interrupt his questions to Christoph Boudreaux. It sounded paranoid but that was part of any cop's life. If it *were* a gambit, though, who had played it? Piotr Morozov?

A woman office worker brushed past him, hurrying on high heels. She stumbled and Concho caught her arm to hold her up. She flashed him a look of thanks as he released her again and she darted onward.

A man paused just behind Concho, crowding close. The fellow had come swiftly down the stairs but stopped suddenly rather than pass. Ten-Wolves smelled cheap cologne and alcohol. And something else. A chemical scent!

He spun toward the man, who drew his right hand from the pocket of his jacket and whipped it downward in a stabbing motion. Concho caught the thrusting wrist. Something glittered in the fellow's grip. It wasn't a knife.

Hypodermic needle, Concho realized. Half full of clear liquid.

Concho twisted the wrist. The hand opened. The syringe dropped onto the carpeted stairs and rolled. A punch from the fellow's left hand popped Concho in the jaw. But this man was no brawler—more of a blade in the back kind of guy. The Ranger shrugged off the punch and hit back.

The blow seemed to cave in the man's chest. He grunted and gasped at the same time, as if his whole body had gone numb. Flailing backward, he toppled over the stair railing. It was barely five feet to the floor; Concho let him go rather than hold onto the wrist and break the man's arm.

A thud sounded as the man hit but Concho had already turned away in search of the fallen syringe. He didn't know what was in it but it couldn't be good. He didn't want anyone in an open-toed shoe giving themselves a surprise injection of the stuff.

A few people still moved past him down the stairs. He glimpsed the syringe just as a foot kicked it down a few more steps. He rushed toward it, using his big body to block anyone else from stepping on it.

The attacker had been holding the syringe in an ungloved hand so the contents had to be injected to be dangerous. He scooped the needle up by the plunger, then leaped down the last few steps and spun toward where his assailant had fallen. No body. The man must have gotten up and run.

Shaking his head, Concho made his way outside, holding the syringe over his head to keep anyone from running into it. The entranceway roiled in chaos. People rushed to and fro, chattering loudly. Others trailed away into the parking area in search of their vehicles. It was after 6:00 in the evening and already dark, though the horizon showed the first hints of a rising moon.

Concho moved along the curb to get away from the crowd. A Treasure Chest limo with its engine running sat parked at the curb about twenty yards ahead of him. The chauffeur held the back door open as a young woman climbed in. She had long brunette hair and an athletic build. Concho had seen her before, at Lafitte's Bar on his first night in New Orleans.

"Hey!" the Ranger yelled.

The woman did not even turn her head. The chauffeur took

one short look and rushed around to the driver's side door. Concho started toward them, calling out again. "Wait!"

But the limo accelerated smoothly away before the Ranger could reach it. He took off running, cutting across the parking lot at an angle to try and head the car off as it swung around the casino's circular drive. The chauffeur must have seen him coming and applied the gas in response. Concho slowed to a frustrated walk. He wasn't going to catch the car.

Perhaps in the Ford, the thought came.

A glance in the direction of his truck quashed that idea. Vehicles were starting to pull out all over the parking lot. Horns began to add their blare to the fire alarm as people got in each other's way. And from down Williams Boulevard came the sound of sirens and the winking of red and blue lights as fire trucks and police responded to the alarm. He wasn't getting out of here anytime soon.

A familiar voice barked his name. "Ten-Wolves!"

He turned. Bull Knife stalked toward him.

"How did you get here?" Concho asked.

"Taxi. What are you doing?"

"How'd you know where I was?"

"It was obvious where you'd go." Bull Knife's gaze traveled along Concho's arm to the syringe. "What's that?"

"Someone just tried to stab it in my back in all the chaos. I don't think it's a 'pick me up.'"

***

Piotr Morozov cursed in Polish as he realized his spur-of-the-moment attempt to have Ten-Wolves murdered during the fake fire alarm had failed. At least the man he'd employed for the attempt had gotten away.

Piotr hurried down an employee-only stairway and out onto the lakeside of the riverboat. The worst part was that Ten-Wolves had seen him just before the attempt was made and, in startlement, he'd quickly turned away to avoid the man. This Texas Ranger seemed a suspicious sort and Piotr's avoidance would likely raise red flags. Still, there should be no way for him to be officially implicated. He'd have to make sure his "assassin" didn't talk.

A combination houseboat/party boat/yacht was tied up to the dock alongside the casino. Piotr watched as Christoph Boudreaux and several assistants pushed his father out to the boat in a wheelchair and transferred the old man aboard. Half a dozen other employees of the family joined them.

Piotr casually mingled with the others and climbed aboard. No one gave him a second look as the craft pulled away from the dock and started across the dark lake toward the Boudreaux compound on the North Shore.

Complaining of the cold wind, everyone except Piotr went below. He'd spent his first fifteen years in Poland with plenty of sub-zero weather. It was maybe thirteen Celsius now. Not even chilly. These soft American southerners didn't understand what cold was.

Lighting a cigarette to calm his nerves, he stared off the back of the boat as the lights of the casino faded into darkness. He considered his options. For the first time since taking this job in the New Orleans area he wasn't sure he could maintain it. Drastic action might soon be called for.

"Ten-Wolves, why will you not die?" he murmured to himself.

The night was an old friend, but this time it didn't have an answer.

CHAPTER 37

Though it was almost 8:00 PM, Concho called Solly Burstein to tell him about the fire alarm at the casino and the attempt to empty a syringe of...something into his veins.

"A poison? Or just something to knock you out?" Solly wondered out loud.

"Guess we can find out. I've got the syringe. Still loaded. You know anyone who can test it for us?"

"Good, good. That's lucky. We've got a chemist who can do it. But not until tomorrow. Can you bring it here in the morning?"

"What time?"

"Eightish."

"Will do."

"What about the perp?" Solly asked.

"Threw him off the stairs. But he got away in all the excitement."

"Too bad. I wouldn't doubt this has something to do with the sudden uproar in the Boudreaux camp. You better stay on your toes."

"I've got my ballet shoes on and I'm pirouetting as fast as I can."

"There's an image I'm going to have trouble getting out of my mind."

Concho chuckled, then said, "You know anything about a man named Piotr Morozov?"

"He works for Roman Boudreaux. Kind of a right-hand man. Seems to keep his nose pretty clean on a personal level. Why?"

"Saw him just before I was attacked. I wanted to get his attention but he deliberately ignored me. Made me suspicious that maybe he had something to do with the attack. Could be he just doesn't like me, of course."

"I imagine you get that a lot."

The Ranger chuckled again but quickly sobered. "Any news on Porter?"

"No. I've got some men running down abandoned places used by the Boudreaux family for illegal activities. So far nothing."

"Gotcha. See you in the morning."

Concho swiped off his phone. Bull Knife stared at him.

"What?" the lawman asked.

"You leave me behind again without any explanation and we're going to tangle. I don't care how big you are."

The Ranger studied his half brother's face, noting the bright shine of the black eyes and the tight knots of muscle along the jawline. He sighed.

"You're right. I handled it wrong. When I was in the army, I knew what it meant to be a team player. But I guess I've been a lone wolf too long. I'll do better."

"Good. See that you do."

***

Porter woke up in his cell and lunged upright on his cot. His terrified gaze leaped around the narrow room. Nothing had changed. There was no one here with him. He sighed, relaxed just a little.

Hard to believe he'd fallen asleep. The combination of constant fear and the fact his captor had peeked in but left without cutting him had over-fried his nervous system, apparently shutting it down.

He pushed to his feet. After taking a pee, he washed his hands and splashed water in his face to cleanse away the cobwebs. It felt late but he had no idea of the actual hour. That bothered him. He was used to checking the time constantly on his phone.

The place was silent. He could almost feel the weight of the house above him, but he couldn't hear any sound of movement. He walked over to the door and leaned his ear against it, listening. Nothing.

His hand found the doorknob, though he didn't expect anything. He'd tried it several times already without success. This time the knob turned. He froze, his heart pounding. Was it some kind of trick?

Using both hands, he eased the door open. The lock clicked; the frame creaked. He froze again, waited. No one came to kill him. He drew the door all the way back and stepped through. The same wooden stairs he'd seen before stretched up and away. The light from a single bulb lit them. A door at the top stood closed.

Porter eased up the steps, his whole body shaking. He started to pray. The door above him would surely be locked. This had to be a trick, a little slice of psychological torture. But the next door opened, too.

The hallway beyond was dark. There were no lights on anywhere, though now he could hear the faint sound of a motor running somewhere. Maybe a generator. The place smelled musty. He wanted to run but forced himself to walk. The wooden floor creaked but the sound stirred no reaction. He reached the front door, his heart beating faster and faster. This door already stood open.

Porter went through, found himself on a porch with pine woods on three sides. It was cold but the sky was clear. Moonlight showed an empty driveway. No vehicle. No sign of anyone. When he turned to look at the house, he made out a dilapidated old one-story cottage badly in need of repairs. He took a deep breath, let it out slowly.

He was free! Had his kidnapper left? Why? He rubbed at his face with his hands and started down the rickety wooden steps to the driveway. A dirt road stretched away through the trees—little more than two ruts really.

He started along it. The moon seemed to watch him hungrily. At every step he expected to hear pursuit behind him, or see his captor step out from the trees ahead with a wicked smile on his porcelain masked face. Porter broke into a mad run in his underwear.

***

Concho dreamed of Maria Morales and woke up to his cell phone ringing. He came instantly wide awake, as he always did. The cell said it was 6:01 AM. The caller ID identified Maria.

Concho snatched up the phone. "What's wrong?"

"Nothing…really. It's…I just thought I'd surprise you. You always get up at six. I didn't wake you, did I? Oh, I hope not."

"No. Not at all." He was only half lying. He'd been on his way up from sleep when the phone call came through. "You just surprised me is all. What are *you* doing up this early?"

She hesitated.

Concho knew his lover. She wasn't usually hesitant to share.

"Maria! Something's wrong. What is it?"

"I'm sure it's nothing to worry about. And you've likely got your hands full."

"Tell me, baby. Please!"

Maria sighed. "It's Mom. She's pretty sick."

"What's wrong?"

"I'm not sure. It might be just the flu. But her breathing is rough. She's coughing hard but nothing is coming up."

"Maybe you better take her to the emergency room."

"I suggested that. She's fighting it. I told her I'd give her a few more hours but if she didn't start feeling better we were going."

"Sooner is better than later, baby."

"I know. I know. She's so…stubborn."

"Guess that's where you get it."

"Probably."

"You have any help?"

"Dad. Though he's not much help. I'll call Henry after a bit."

"Good idea. Get your brother over there. You two double-team her and I bet she'll give in."

"Probably. How are *you* doing?"

"I'm all right. I think we've had a break in the case. But look, if you need me, I can be home in nine hours."

"No, no. Nothing you could do here anyway."

"Your mom likes me."

Maria laughed. "She does. I guess you've just got a way with the Morales women."

"Glad to hear you say that."

"I'll let you go. I just needed to hear your voice."

"Anytime. Even if it's 5:59."

Again, Maria laughed. "I'll remember."

"Call me as soon as you get her to the hospital and get some information."

"I will."

"Love you."

"Love you, too." Maria clicked off.

Concho set the phone down. Another thing to worry about. He glanced over at Bull Knife. The sound of the phone must have awakened him but he seemed to be back to sleep now.

Concho slid out of bed and walked over to the window. He pulled back the curtain just enough to peak out at the motel parking lot. The dark sky glowed beautifully but the streetlights showed the barren harshness of the concrete lot and glinted off the crouching hulks of vehicles. The cars and trucks looked like the fossilized skeletons of alien dinosaurs.

A wave of homesickness swept over him. He felt out of place.

He *was* out of place. He'd not felt at home anywhere since he was fifteen, when his grandmother had been murdered. But now, he realized, the reservation outside Eagle Pass, Texas had become home again.

He had friends there—Meskwaa, Roberto Echabarri, others. And he had a woman close by to love: Maria. These things should have been enough, he realized. But right now he wanted one more thing. He wanted it very badly. He had to know if his mother was still alive.

CHAPTER 38

After dressing in the same jeans and long-sleeved white shirt he'd worn yesterday, Concho went over to the gas station nearby and picked up a microwaveable breakfast. This consisted of two sausage and egg biscuits for himself and one for Bull Knife. He bought his half brother a cup of black coffee while he chose a sixteen-ounce Dr. Pepper.

Bull Knife was stirring when he got back. The "suite" they were staying in was mostly called a suite because it had a microwave. Concho heated their sandwiches while Bull Knife dressed and drank his coffee. By 7:30 AM they were checked out and on their way into the French Quarter to meet Detective Solly Burstein.

They found Solly at his desk in the District 8 police station on Royal Street. Concho handed him the Dr. Pepper bottle, which had been scrubbed clean and which contained the syringe and liquid Concho had been threatened with.

Solly called over a young officer and handed him the bottle with instructions to, "Take it to Doc Ross. Tell him the stuff inside is likely deadly and it's urgent we find out what it is."

"Yes, sir," the officer said, carrying the bottle gingerly away.

Solly motioned his two visitors to sit. Concho did so. Bull Knife remained standing, almost at attention. Solly asked the Ranger to repeat his story of the syringe attack. He did.

"And you think Piotr Morozov might have ordered it?" Solly asked. "Or been there to observe?"

"I'm suspicious."

Solly nodded. "I did some more checking on Morozov. Like I said, he's kept his nose clean on a personal level. However, he appeared suddenly on the scene down here. Right at seventeen years ago. He just moved in and took the job of Roman's second in command. Smooth as a talcum-powdered baby's bottom. I couldn't find anything on him before then."

"Makes me more suspicious."

"Seems like your favorite word lately."

"The right word for the times."

Solly's desk phone rang. The detective frowned. "Excuse me." He picked up the receiver, said "Hello," then listened.

Concho watched the detective's face stiffen in shock and tried to make sense of the next few moments as he heard only one side of a conversation.

"What?

"You're kidding?

"When?

"All right, all right. Good news.

"Where?

"OK. On my way."

Solly hung up and stared at Concho and Bull Knife.

"Tell us!" the Ranger said. His heart thumped.

Solly shook his head, more in surprise than negation. "That was a Saint Tammany Parish police officer named Freedman. Porter House just turned up alive."

***

In the Ford F-150, the Ranger and Bull Knife followed Solly Burstein's New Orleans police cruiser with its lights flashing.

They roared across the Causeway Bridge to the North Shore of Lake Pontchartrain.

Porter House had been brought to the emergency room at the Lakeview Regional hospital in Mandeville, just on the far side of the Causeway. He was still in a room in Emergency when they arrived. A Saint Tammany policewoman watched at his door but passed them through after seeing Solly's badge.

Porter waved from his bed as they came in. A big smile cracked his face. He looked a little wan but otherwise OK. A bag of clear liquid hung beside the bed and dripped steadily into his arm.

"Good to see you guys!" Porter said, looking at Ten-Wolves and Bull Knife.

"Good to see *you*," Concho replied. "How are you?"

The private investigator shrugged. He pointed toward the saline drip. "They say I'm dehydrated. And still needing to rebuild my blood supply. But otherwise, I'm fine. I sure am glad to see you two. I didn't think I ever would again."

"What happened?" Solly Burstein asked.

Concho introduced the police detective. Porter answered his question.

"This big guy. He took me right out of my house. Cut me on the leg so I'd bleed. He told me later that was for show, to get," he nodded toward the half brothers, "their attention. I passed out. Or he gave me something to knock me out. Or both.

"I woke up in a cellar of an old house. He made a few threats. Said he was going to hurt me to make these guys leave town. Then he just…left himself. Left the door unlocked. I couldn't believe it. I followed a dirt road to a highway. Found myself in Abita Springs. Someone saw me limping and stopped to help. They called the police, who brought me here."

"You know where this old house is?" Solly asked.

Porter nodded. "I could probably find it again. If someone could drive me."

"What about your kidnapper?" Concho asked.

Porter shook his head this time. "Never got a good look at him. He wore masks. Pretty sure he was black. From his hair. But couldn't tell you anything more."

"Where's this officer Freedman who called?" Solly asked. "He the one first picked you up?"

Porter frowned. "Who? I don't know any Freedman. It was an officer Hanes who brought me here and took my statement."

"But you must have given this Freedman my number to call," Solly said. "Or my name at least."

"I didn't even know your name until a couple of minutes ago. What are you talking about? Who's Freedman?"

"You didn't have an officer call the New Orleans police station for Solly Burstein?"

Porter looked totally baffled. "I didn't have anyone call anyone. I wanted to." He gestured toward Ten-Wolves. "I would have called you as soon as I got to a phone but I couldn't remember your number. Had it stored in my cell but when he took that he took my memory for phone numbers with him. I borrowed a phone just a bit ago and called my uncle. Benedict Cooper. That was about the only number I knew. He's on his way to pick me up."

Solly glanced around with a confused look on his face. "So who is this Freedman? I remember him giving me his name. My hearing's not that bad."

"It's the kidnapper," Concho said. "He must have followed Porter. I guess to make sure he got somewhere safe."

"The kidnapper!" Porter and Solly exclaimed together.

"Gotta be. The name, 'Freedman,' too. It's a message."

"What does it mean?" Solly asked.

"It means he's out of it. He's 'hauled his freight' as they used to say."

"How can you be sure?" Solly asked.

"I talked to him. When he called to make his threats. I thought he wasn't too enthusiastic about his choice of actions."

"So it's over?" Porter asked, his voice filling with relief.

Concho shook his head. "No. Not even close. Someone hired him. They'll hire others. And keep on bringing them until we find out who's behind it. Or they get us first."

CHAPTER 39

Porter was released with a clean bill of health and was able to guide the law officers to the run-down domicile where he'd been held prisoner. It did no good. The kidnapper had been thorough. No prints were to be found inside or outside the house, nor any other good evidence of who might have committed the crime. They used flashlights to examine the cellar, though Porter claimed there'd been electric lights and running water before.

"A portable generator," Concho said. "And he must have taken it with him."

"I did hear a machine running," Porter said.

Outside, they found automobile tracks and took photos of them. No one expected anything to come of it. This kidnapper was meticulous. If they found the tires, the vehicle would likely be untraceable. If they found the vehicle, the tires would have already been replaced.

Porter rode home with his uncle, with a police escort. Solly returned to New Orleans, as well. Concho hung back with Bull Knife. After the others were gone, the Ranger spoke his thoughts.

"Pretty clear the kidnapper started trailing Porter sometime after he got free. He had to have followed on foot most of the way. The only question is, how soon after Porter left here did the man pick him up? I doubt he followed him *from* the house. The drive-way here leads only to the main dirt road. The main road dead ends past this place, and there are no side roads turning off of it in the other direction for nearly a mile."

"You're thinking he parked his vehicle down the road some-where and waited to pick up Porter when he came past?"

"Yep."

"The first side road would be the obvious choice," Bull Knife said.

"So we'll start there."

"Even if we find the place where he parked, what will that give us?"

"Don't know yet."

***

Sammy Boudreaux checked his phone. His father and both his brothers had been blowing him up with voice and text messages—mostly demands to come home immediately and ex-plain himself. He ignored them all. He couldn't go home weak; he had to show his strength first, his ability to handle problems. One text message wasn't like the others, however. He opened this one and immediately called the number indicated.

"Good," Piotr Morozov answered. "I'm not going to ask where you are. But can I assume you're out of the public eye?"

"Yeah, I'm with Kulick. Somewhere even my family won't think to look for me."

"Stay in place. But I have someone you need to contact."

"The brothers?" Sammy asked.

"The brothers," Morozov agreed. "No one else seems capable of taking down, Ten-Wolves."

"I was already thinking about them. They'll do it. They've never failed before. But they're expensive. I don't have enough cash handy to pay them."

"I do. I'll send a text message after we get off the line on how to access it. There's sufficient to pay them double. If they balk at the initial price, offer it all to them. It'll be worth it to get this thorn removed. I'll tell you the instant I get a line on where Ten-Wolves is so the brothers can set up a surprise for him."

"Hear you," Sammy said.

He hung up and waited. The text came through. He opened it and smiled. He'd pay the brothers well, all right, but maybe keep a little slice of this for himself.

"Mexico money," he murmured. "If I need it."

***

The two men who Piotr Morozov and Sammy Bou-dreaux were plotting to kill cruised slowly down the dirt road away from the cottage where Porter House had been locked up. The windows in the Ford were down as they checked every roadside thicket for possibilities.

At the first place where a road branched off from the main road, they stopped. It proved to be nothing more than an overgrown driveway to the yard of a fallen down farmhouse.

On they went. The next turnoff was more than a driveway. It kept going past five hundred yards but Concho didn't keep following it. He pulled over. To his right sat a cow pasture, empty of any animals. It had a barn, though, which would have provided any observer a good concealed view of the main road. Concho studied it.

"You believe our kidnapper might have waited there to pick up Porter coming along the main road?" Bull Knife asked.

"I figure. This guy…he thinks a little like me. That's where I would have waited."

Bull Knife opened his door. "Let's have a look."

A metal pole fence provided ingress into the field but was chained and locked. Concho examined the lock, noting some silverish scratches around the bottom of it where the weathered patina had been scraped away.

"This lock's been picked," he said.

Without waiting for a response, the Ranger climbed over the gate and dropped to the ground, then loped toward the barn, which sat about thirty yards away. Bull Knife followed.

Sliding back the big front door of the barn revealed an empty interior, dimly lit by sunlight filtering in. The ground was hard but the impression of automobile tracks remained. Not distinct enough to identify but likely their elusive kidnapper. The two men walked back and forth searching for clues. As with the cottage, there didn't appear to be any.

"I do not like this guy," Bull Knife said.

"Maybe not," Concho replied. "But I can respect him." He sighed and scratched his head.

Stepping out of the barn, the lawman glanced toward the main dirt road, about fifty yards away. Despite the moon last night, it would have been dark enough to make it hard to see a man walking along the road.

"He had night vision goggles," Concho said to Bull Knife, who stood nearby.

"Makes sense."

"And," the Ranger added as he moved along the rough outside wall of the barn to a little rise of earth, "he watched from about here. He squatted to make sure Porter wouldn't see him."

Concho went down on his haunches. The ground was packed flat, revealing little. But he could feel the impression of footprints as he ran his hand over the soil. He could still see the road easily but anyone under six feet tall would have had a problem. That was a clue in itself, and there was another to be found here. But where? Looking out over the field, he remembered a very different field, of years gone by.

***

The Hindu Kush, Afghanistan, 2011:

The Hindu Kush Mountains were officially part of the Himalayan range. They extended five hundred miles across Afghanistan and offered many hiding places for Taliban fighters. Concho's Army Ranger team had worked these mountains before. Ten-Wolves had never enjoyed it. He'd grown up in the mostly flatlands of southern Texas. But he'd adapted. Any wild place, he could make his own.

Two hours before, a Boeing Ch-47D transport helicopter, generally called the Chinook, had dropped off Concho's twelve-man Operational Detachment Alpha (ODA). Two other Ranger teams were in the vicinity, along with French and Afghan government forces. Navy Seal teams played backup.

As was too often the case in the army, now they all waited. Another helicopter was bringing in an intelligence expert as some kind of consultant. All Russ Adelaide, Concho's commanding officer, could tell the team was that a Taliban leader known as Tamir was supposedly in the area. He needed to be taken out.

Concho spent his time cleaning his M4A1 carbine, occasionally glancing up to note the incongruity of snow-capped peaks in the distance while here it was a dry and boulder-strewn desert, hell-hot and brutal. Resting the rifle across his legs, he drew the hunting knife from his belt. The butt end of the handle unscrewed. He opened it and dumped a small plastic vial into his hand.

Inside the vial were matches, a needle and surgical thread for sewing up wounds, and a small tube of red ocher pigment. He opened the tube and squeezed out a dollop of ocher onto his index finger. Using the knife blade as a mirror, he smeared two thin streaks of pigment beneath each eye.

Sitting near Concho, engineering sergeant David Lanoue watched his friend put on warpaint. "You know something I don't?" Lanoue asked.

Concho grinned. "A lot of things probably, but one thing for sure is we're not leaving this place without a fight."

Just as Concho replaced everything into the knife handle

and wiped his fingers on a nearby rock, the throb of chopper rotors claimed his attention. He rose to a crouch, along with the rest of the team.

Lanoue tried to spit and cursed instead. "Fresh out of saliva," he complained.

"Just don't run out of bullets," Concho countered.

They saw the oncoming helicopter then—helicopters rather—another Chinook, escorted by two AH-64 Apache twin-turboshaft attack craft. All were flying low.

"Looks like we're after big game," Lanoue said.

Concho frowned. "They're not on target."

"What?" Lanoue asked.

Concho pointed. "They're too far south. They shouldn't be taking that line to us."

Lanoue grunted. "Damn! You're right."

Concho was already moving. Captain Adelaide crouched behind a boulder ten yards ahead. Concho reached him, mouthed his name.

"They're off course!" he said as Adelaide turned toward him.

Adelaide realized it too. He spun toward the communications sergeant next to him. Too late.

A spear of light, like a streak of the sun going home, leaped upward from the ground toward the Chinook. The helicopter staggered in the air, then fireballed as the rocket propelled grenade hit it and ignited.

The Apache helicopters split to the left and right as they went into evasive maneuvers. Another RPG leaped upward. This one missed. The wounded Chinook spun downward, shedding debris and bodies. It disappeared from sight but they all heard the crash and the sharp screams of fellow troopers.

Adelaide straightened tall behind his boulder; he stuck his left arm up, yanked it forward. As one, the ODA raced toward the crash site. The Chinook hadn't exploded on touchdown. There might be survivors.

At a dead run, Ten-Wolves and Lanoue threaded their way close together through boulders. A spiral of black smoke guided them. Gunfire crackled ahead, a mixture of American M16s and the Russian-made AK47s and AKMS commonly used by the Taliban. Most of those had been captured from the Russians during the Soviet-Afghan war in the 1980s, but they were still deadly.

The ODA reached the edge of a valley, little more than a crease in the landscape. The Chinook burned just below them but some American soldiers still lived and huddled with their buttons to the ground as they took cover from heavy fire.

A Taliban soldier in a purple head-wrap spun toward the approaching Army Rangers. He held a Russian-made machine gun. Concho gave a quick pull on the trigger of his M4A1. Half a dozen slugs from the fully automatic rifle struck the enemy fighter, shredded through him and sent him tumbling to earth. Lanoue shot a second foe. He pulled a grenade and hurled it at a nest of boulders where the heaviest fire came from.

The crashed Chinook lay surrounded by the enemy. Lanoue's grenade did little against the grouping of entrenched fighters, but as a unit the ODA was able to punch a hole in one side of the enemy circle. Survivors of the crash began to filter out through the gap while the Rangers laid down suppressing fire.

By this time, the Apache helicopters had swept back into the fight. Their big guns churned up dust and fragments of rock as they pumped lead and rockets into the enemy. Another streak of light leaped from the ground, however. This RPG clipped the tail of one of the Apaches and blew it off. The chopper began to spin as the pilot fought for control. The pilot of the other Apache must have felt like a sitting duck. He pulled back.

"Take out that RPG!" Adelaide yelled.

Nearly every man in the ODA opened fire on the RPG's location, but the site was surrounded by boulders through which no visual conformation of target was possible. The enemy also seemed

*to have an unlimited supply of rocket propelled grenades. He fired
again, this time into the downed Chinook. The resulting explosion
took off most of the craft's nose and nailed a crawling American
soldier to the ground with shrapnel.*

*The damaged Apache helicopter had managed a controlled
crash landing away from the killing ground. The second chopper was nowhere to be seen, though the throb of its rotors
whacked the air. Concho and Lanoue worked their way closer
to the enemy center through sporadic fire that sent boulder
chips spraying.*

*"I can't see him; I can't see him!" Lanoue shouted to Concho.
"You got a look?"*

*Concho made no response. He'd taken a shooter's stance, had
switched his carbine from full to semi-automatic. He wanted only
one shot now, as he stared at the rocky nest of the helicopter killer.*

"Look for the telltale," he murmured to himself.

*He saw it. The RPG man fired. The grenade slammed into the
ground to Concho's right where his commander lay hidden, sending up a gush of flame. The Army Ranger ignored the explosion,
with his gaze glued to the source. Just as the rocket launched, a
flicker of light spurted through a small gap in the fortress of boulders. In the aftermath of the flash, a reflection lingered.*

*Concho pulled the trigger. The 5.56×45mm NATO round
stabbed through the tiny gap in the rocks and into the body behind
it. The RPG shooter cried out; his weapon clattered to the ground.
With the enemy's best weapon offline, the remaining Apache helicopter surged back into the fight. The rest of the Taliban fighters
began to pull back, some of them running.*

"Nice shot," Lanoue said.

"All in the details," Concho replied.

Concho's memories of Afghanistan subsided. He was
back outside the barn looking for clues to tell him who'd kidnapped
Porter House. His gaze dropped to the ground. He let his eyes go

unfocused, looking not for objects but for the "telltale."

A flash of light brown color amid the darker hues of the earth captured his attention. He reached out and picked up a short piece of broken toothpick. He glanced up at Bull Knife.

"I know who our kidnapper is," he said.

CHAPTER 40

Bull Knife arched an eyebrow at Concho's statement. "So, who is that kidnapper?" he asked.

"I'll tell you. But I want to process it first."

"Are we going to confront him?"

"Not yet. Maybe not ever. He's just showed us he's out of the game. He followed Porter to make sure he got help. He's not a danger to us anymore. Besides, I've got something to do across the lake."

"What?"

"Confront Piotr Morozov. He's in this thing up to his long, skinny neck."

"All right. I'm with you."

After returning to the truck, the two men headed for the Causeway Bridge to take them back to the South Shore. They'd barely made it through Abita Springs when a call came in on the Ranger's cell.

"Solly Burstein," Concho said to Bull Knife. He swiped the phone on. "Yeah?"

"Thought you'd like some news. We got a report on that syringe you brought in. You were lucky. The drug would have killed you."

"What was it?"

"I can't pronounce it. I'll have to spell it. S u c c i n y l c h o l i n e. Apparently it's abbreviated "SUX," which I guess makes sense."

"Never heard of it."

"I gather it's used sometimes in surgery. Not as an anesthetic. It paralyzes the muscles. Our chemist said the dose in the syringe would have knocked you down almost instantly and you'd have died within three or four minutes from being unable to breathe."

"Sounds like nasty stuff."

"The worst part is you'd be wide awake while it happened."

Concho huffed a long breath.

"Someone wanted a hard death for you, Ten-Wolves. You don't skimp when it comes to making enemies, do you?"

"I make only the best."

***

Thursday afternoon. Traffic on the Causeway Bridge was sparse. It was nearly 3:00 PM. Rush hour wouldn't start for another hour or so and would mostly be confined to the northbound span, with people leaving work in the New Orleans area for homes in Mandeville, Madisonville, Abita Springs, and Covington.

Concho paid the five-dollar toll and pulled out onto the southbound span of the bridge. The speed limit was sixty-five. The lawman set the cruise control on his pickup. Pontchartrain Lake lay quiescent. Only the faintest breeze trailed gentle fingers on the water. The sun shone brightly, painting a perfect winter's day with the temperature hovering in the high sixties and the placid lake sparkling in the sunlight.

Both the Ford's driver and its passenger remained quiet as they contemplated what might happen when they confronted Piotr Morozov at the Treasure Chest Casino. They each wondered if the case were about to break wide open.

It was.

The highest point of the Causeway came at mile sixteen, where the span had been raised and a drawbridge put in to allow ships to cross from one side of the bridge to the other. On the downslope just past the drawbridge was one of half-a-dozen crossovers, where the two spans were connected so emergency traffic could switch between north- and southbound.

As the Ford F-150 passed the crossover, two cars pulled out behind it. These were wine-red 2006 Dodge Magnums, in mint condition—the SRT-8 models. Concho had always noticed them since they reminded him a little of his first car, an El Camino. They looked like low slung station wagons but were really disguised muscle cars. The 6.1-liter Hemi engines under the hoods could produce 425 horsepower. They were bullet fast.

Concho frowned as he checked out the Magnums in his rearview mirror. He tapped the brakes to release the cruise control on the Ford and accelerated slightly. "What do you make of those cars behind us?" he asked Bull Knife.

The half-Apache glanced out the back window. He followed Concho's frown with his own. "Some kind of car show, maybe?"

The Magnums began to accelerate and close the gap between them.

"Nope!" Concho replied. "Get ready!"

The F-150 had only a 3.5-liter under the hood but had been tuned to generate better than 400 horsepower. The speedometer needle jumped upward as Ten-Wolves punched the gas—from sixty-five to seventy-five, to eighty, ninety.

"They're still gaining," Bull Knife yelled.

"I know," Concho returned grimly. "We can't outrun them."

"Where are the bridge cops?"

"Usually at the crossovers. It's several miles to the next. Call 911!"

Bull Knife grabbed for his phone as Concho swept into the left lane to pass a slower car, then swerved back to straddle the center line of the road. He couldn't let one of the Magnums get ahead of him and cut him off.

Holding the center proved impossible, though. Traffic might

be sparse this time of day but there *were* vehicles. Concho wove around another pickup, jogging left, then right, and back again past another car. The Magnums followed, sliding between the other vehicles like a razor-sharp fillet knife through a trout. They were more aerodynamic than the Ford, and the drivers knew what they were doing.

Bull Knife slammed his phone down on the seat. "I'm not getting through," he yelled. "Could they be jamming cell signals?"

"Don't know. Maybe."

Mile marker 12 flashed by on Concho's right side. Halfway across the bridge. The road was clear ahead. He straddled the center line again and tried to push the gas pedal through the floor. The big truck shattered the 100-mph mark, jumped to 105, to 110. The Magnums bore down anyway, looming in the rearview mirrors.

Fifty yards back.

Twenty-five!

Bull Knife jerked open the Ford's glove box and pulled out the Smith & Wesson snub-nose .38 Concho had loaned him.

Concho nodded but snapped out. "Duck down. They're gonna shoot."

The Dodge Magnum on the right accelerated all the way up to Concho's bumper, threatening to try a pass on that side. The pursuit car on the left edged forward, waiting for room to try its own pass. Concho began to swerve back and forth in front of them to hold them off.

Their speed dropped, though they still covered the ground at better than a 100-mph. A wink of light came from the right-hand Dodge. A window going down; a hand coming out holding the black steel clot of a weapon.

"Here it comes!" Concho shouted. He tapped the brakes and ducked as low as he could behind the wheel. Bull Knife joined him as they heard the squeal of more brakes behind them and a hail of lead pounded into the back of the pickup.

A big metal tool chest sat in the bed of the truck right against the cab. Any shots that whanged into it couldn't penetrate. The rear window was not so protected. Bullets tore through, remodeling the glass into Swiss cheese.

The front window starred as lead burst into the Ford's cab. A wild bullet smashed the radio into junk. Something stung Concho's cheek but was hardly worth worrying about.

Wind curling around the truck began to storm through the cab, sending the long dark hair flying on both Concho and Bull Knife. Bull Knife ignored the raking air and straightened a little. He fired the .38 through a hole in the rear glass.

"Keep down!" Concho shouted.

His half brother didn't listen. He emptied the .38, began to fumble to reload it. More bullets from their pursuers pounded the truck. One of the Magnums nudged in, banged into the right rear as they tried a pit maneuver. Concho had trained in defensive driving; he fought them off. Again their speed dropped. At this point, though, Concho wanted exactly that.

As the Ranger straightened a little in his seat, he saw blue lights flash on ahead, to the left of the main span. At least one of the Causeway cops seemed to have noticed a problem. He had to be sitting at one of the crossovers.

"Crossover coming up!" Ten-Wolves shouted to Bull Knife. "Be ready for anything!"

He eased off the gas a little more. Both the Dodges lunged into the back of his truck. The pickup jarred; the rear end whipped back and forth in a squeal of rubber. Concho fought the wheel savagely to keep the front and back ends from swapping places.

The Dodges dropped back a few feet. More gunfire bellowed. Metal shrieked as bullets tore into the Ford's body. Concho stomped the brakes. Tires squalled as the black smoke of burning rubber tornadoed up from the pickup's rear end. Their speed plummeted as Ten-Wolves kept the brake pedal buried. The nose of the pickup dipped; the rear rose. For an instant, it seemed they were going to flip.

"Hold it together!" the Ranger begged as the Ford screamed like a tortured soul.

He twisted the wheel to the right and the F-150 lunged in that direction. The drivers of the Magnums were riding their own brakes, trying to hold. All the world shrieked. The Dodge in the right lane hit the rail as the driver tried to avoid running up under the Ford and decapitating himself. A front fender tore off, got sucked under the car and spit out to the rear.

They were almost to the crossover now. Concho could see the Causeway police SUV parked there. He could hear the sound of its siren. He swung the Ford back into the center of the road. Their speed had dropped to under fifty now. The rear-end of the Ford settled back onto the highway.

The Dodge on Concho's right surged forward. Its nose eased up past the pickup's tailgate. The window was down on the driver's side. A gun poked through. Concho cut the wheel hard to the left, away from the car. Bullets flew from the Dodge but skittered off the concrete in front of the Ford as the Ranger aimed for the entrance to the crossover.

The driver of the Dodge on the left side instinctively hit his brakes even harder as Concho swung across his front end. The grill of the Magnum punched low into the side of the Ford, adding momentum to Concho's charge for the crossover.

Something broke in the Ford's rear end. The left side of the bed dropped. Metal hit asphalt and sparks sprayed. Brakes and tires screamed like banshees. Concho could smell cooking rubber and the shear of metal.

The Causeway policeman realized what was about to happen. He frantically thrust his SUV into reverse as he tried to back away from the charging pickup. Still moving far too fast, the Ford rocketed into the crossover, just missing the nose of the SUV, and slammed brutally into the rail of the bridge. The air bags opened like they'd exploded. The right rear tire blew out. It didn't matter.

Bull Knife's head banged hard into the window on his side of the truck. It left him woozy. The .38 dropped from his hands. Concho ripped loose both seat belts and grabbed his half brother, yanking him toward him. His honed instincts told him—it wasn't over.

CHAPTER 41

Concho's heart pounded; his mouth felt dry. He wasn't sure how he knew, but the attack wasn't finished. Something more was coming. Through the passenger side window, over the head of the semi-conscious Bull Knife, the Ranger could see the two Dodge Magnums powering away. The tailgate of one swung open. Metal glinted as a fat-headed tube poked free.

Concho's left hand fumbled at the driver's side door latch. He got it open, shoved the door back, threw himself and Bull Knife out. Even as he fell toward the concrete with his half brother on top of him, a wink of fire, like sunlight going home, came streaking.

He recognized it. His memory of Afghanistan. Barely an hour ago. *An RPG!* A rocket propelled grenade!

Ten-Wolves twisted Bull Knife around in his arms and closed his eyes as his back smashed down onto concrete. He didn't quite lose his air but came close. Then his remaining air seemed to suck away as a tremendous whump concussed the bridge.

The day lit up like a nova. Light dazzled even through his closed lids. A sizzling sound cooked up, like all the bacon in the world frying. Heat and the stench of superheated chemicals and metal washed over him in a tsunami. He half rolled, dragging Bull Knife into the protection of his big body.

The whole universe seemed to rock. A shrapnel storm of hot metal and burning plastic whipped through the air, spanging over the concrete. Not a bit of it touched Concho. Nor the half brother he covered with his arms.

Concho opened his eyes on glare. His brain felt numb. His F-150—ever faithful—burned above him. Staying low, he began to crawl away from the fire, using one arm and dragging Bull Knife with the other. Hands grabbed at him. He almost slung a fist before realizing it was the trooper from the police SUV.

The officer was shouting "My God! My God!" like a mantra as he jerked at Concho's arm.

They were far enough from the flames now to stand. Concho pushed the policeman's hand away and climbed to his feet. Bull Knife groaned but started to rise as well. Concho helped him up. He turned to look toward the highway. The two Dodge Magnums had disappeared down the road, heading for the vanishing point.

The Causeway trooper must have realized suddenly that he could be helping the bad guys in this scenario. He stepped back abruptly from the two and drew his service weapon.

Concho lifted a hand. "I'm a Texas Ranger," he croaked. "I can show you ID." If he wasn't wearing his badge, he usually carried it tucked into the right front pocket of his jeans. It was there now. He eased it out slowly and held it face-front toward the trooper.

The man studied it, then nodded. He lowered his gun but didn't holster it yet. "Who's that?" he asked, jerking his chin toward Bull Knife.

"Brother. I think we're OK but we should move farther from the truck. There's ammunition might cook off in the flames."

The officer glanced toward the furiously burning Ford. He nodded again and holstered his pistol. The three moved around behind the SUV. The radio in the police vehicle crackled with voices but the officer must have already called it in. He continued to study the survivors.

"I don't see how you're 'OK'?" he said eventually.

Concho flashed him a lopsided grin. "Living right."

Sirens sounded in the distance as the first responders came rushing. The trooper climbed in his SUV and got on the radio. Concho leaned over Bull Knife, who was coughing up smoke, and checked him for injuries. He found nothing serious, and no problems with the response of the pupils to light.

"Not even a concussion through that hard head," Concho said.

Bull Knife only sighed. He stared at the destroyed F-150. Without fuel, the flames were dying out. Fortunately, the truck had carried less than a quarter tank of gas. Concho had planned to fill up when they reached the South Shore.

"What hit us?" Bull Knife asked.

"An RPG. Basically, a grenade mounted on a rocket. Looks like it struck the bridge railing first, though. If it had hit the truck directly it would have flipped it over on us. We were lucky again."

"Lucky?" Bull Knife protested. "We barely know more than we started with. And now you've lost your truck. Your *bow* was in there!"

"I can make another bow. I can buy another truck. But the two of us lived."

Bull Knife shook his head back and forth. "I am very sorry to have involved you in all this. I am nowhere near as wise as I thought myself a few days ago."

"You learn as you roll," the Ranger replied. "There's a mystery behind all this that needs solving. Maybe it *does* have to do with our mother. Maybe not. But whatever it is, every step that's taken to stop us only makes me more committed. I wouldn't want to be anywhere else."

Bull Knife nodded, though his face had become unreadable. He slid down to sit with his back against the bridge railing. Concho let him have his moment. He looked toward his truck, now a blackened hulk with rivulets of flame gnawing at it.

Not only had his bow been in there, but his body armor, the Texas Ranger Stetson he hardly ever wore, the .30-06 he'd carried through the Neo-Nazi takeover of the Eagle Pass Mall back home, and even the W.E.B Du Bois book he'd bought a few days ago—*In Battle for Peace*. The battle wasn't going smoothly.

Taking a deep breath, he offered a mental salute to his dead F-150. It had served him well and gone out protecting him one last time.

***

Within minutes of the failed attempt on the lives of Ten-Wolves and Bull Knife, Sammy Boudreaux got the call from the men he'd hired. Sammy was already half drunk but talking to the "brothers" sobered him up temporarily.

"We missed this time," the deep voice over the phone said. "But we'll go again. Maybe something smaller this time. We'll earn the money."

"That's…that's good to hear," Sammy replied.

The man hung up. Sammy glanced over at Jason Kulick, who watched apprehensively. Sammy shrugged. "They're still working on it."

Kulick sighed and pushed up from the couch in the single-room fishing camp off the Pearl River. He started toward the fridge.

"Bring me a beer," Sammy called.

Kulick pulled two Abita Turbodogs out of the generator-powered refrigerator. He used the bottle opener on both and carried one over to his boss, who took it as he was placing another call. Piotr Morozov answered; Sammy explained the situation.

"It must be done," Morozov replied.

"Yeah. But no one seems able to handle the job."

"Ten-Wolves is only human."

"I keep telling myself that."

"Be patient."

"Tired a such," Sammy snapped, beginning to slur his words. "I'm thinkin' I jest need to come clean to Dad. Let him take care of it."

After a brief pause, Morozov said, "That's not a good idea."

"I think it is."

"But you are drunk."

"Drinkin', not drunk."

"All right. If the brothers don't succeed on their next attempt, we'll go to your father."

"You'd go with me?"

"Of course."

"Thanksh."

Morozov changed the subject. "Catching any fish out there along the Pearl?"

"No. Jest stayin' inside. Waitin."

"Wait a little longer and it will all be over."

***

The next couple of hours on the Causeway did not pass quickly. An army of police showed up in response to Concho's and Bull Knife's street war. Fire trucks and ambulances joined. The fire trucks sprayed the dead Ford, though most of the flames were already history. Paramedics checked the two half brothers over and gave them clean bills of health, outside of scratches and some small burns.

Traffic on both spans of the bridge remained shut down for over an hour. Concho claimed to feel his ears heating up from all the curses spewed by stalled drivers. Between being grilled by many different officers, he did pick up a few informational tidbits.

The two Dodge Magnums had been found abandoned at another crossover. They'd been wiped clean of prints and emptied of any other evidence. Their drivers and passengers must have switched to a getaway car planted earlier. No one knew what that car might be, and no sign of the attackers had been found.

By six o'clock, after some intervention by Solly Burstein of the New Orleans Police Department, Concho and Bull Knife ended up back on the North Shore where they'd started. It had been easier to move them north than south since the southbound lane was still being checked for debris from the car chase.

A taciturn young officer dropped them off at a car rental place just off the 190 in Mandeville. They picked up a yellow Ford Mustang GT. The low-slung car felt strange to Concho after years of driving pickups.

"I'm getting tired of asking, 'what now,'" Bull Knife said, "but what now?"

"Covington."

"What's in Covington?"

"A kidnapper."

CHAPTER 42

Concho parked his new Ford where he'd parked his old
one before, outside the last house on North Florida Street in Covington. He climbed out. Bull Knife joined him. It was quiet. Night
had found them, though yard lights cast enough glow to reveal the
cypress trees and meadow stretching beyond the house down to the
bank of the Bogue Falaya River.

"Nolen Carmichael the third," Bull Knife said. "I should have
guessed. You said he was dangerous."

Concho didn't reply as he walked over and pressed the button
on the call box attached to the black iron gate. Nolen himself answered. "Yes?"

"Ten-Wolves and Bull Knife. It's time to talk."

A moment passed. The front door opened and Nolen Carmichael came through. He strode purposefully to the gate but
didn't release the lock. "My wife and I are in for the evening.
What do you want?"

"Porter House," Concho said.

Nolen shrugged casually. "Am I supposed to know who that is?"

"You spent the last couple of days holding him in a cellar of an
old cottage outside Abita Springs."

Nolen chuckled. "I assume you have some evidence of this?"

"I found your toothpick," Concho said. "Next to the wall of an old gray barn. Right where you broke it and dropped it while watching Porter walk past."

Carmichael didn't laugh this time. "Since the Texas Rangers have no jurisdiction in Louisiana, if you were here to arrest me for such a thing you would have brought the local police."

"Don't intend to arrest you. I'm only looking for some truth."

Nolen glanced back toward his house. Only a few lights were on. Faintly, Ten-Wolves heard the tinkle of piano music. It didn't sound recorded.

"My wife is practicing," Nolen said. "I'll need to get back to her soon."

"The truth takes less time than a lie," Concho replied.

"You speaking from experience?"

"I am."

Carmichael pressed to unlock the gate but didn't invite his visitors inside. Instead, he stepped through. "Walk with me," he said, as he moved into the meadow and down toward the river.

Floodlights from a big house just across the river cast enough glow to help the men avoid the pitfalls of mudholes and roots. Once they left the shadows of the cypress trees and came to the bank of the Bogue Falaya, the moon showed itself from behind wispy clouds. Its light sheened off the river, mixing with other glows to paint the water a faint purple.

A Chuck-will's-widow called like a lonely child somewhere to the south. Gnats and mosquitoes swirled around the men but mostly didn't bite. Nearly at their feet, a racoon fishing for crawfish splashed away through the shallows. The Ranger smelled the wet and the things growing in it.

"If you think I'm this big, bad kidnapper," Nolen said, "then it doesn't seem very bright of you to walk down to the river with me."

Concho offered a little bit of his shark smile. "You can't take me. Not up close like this."

Nolen studied him. "Once upon a time I'd have accepted that as a challenge. But I'm past it."

"Testosterone is a helluva drug," Ten-Wolves replied.

Nolen nodded. "Used to be. Besides, you're right, I couldn't take you. Not in a fair fight anyway. Now, what truth do you want to know? I'll answer if I can."

"Why'd you let Porter go?"

"You know why. Our talk for one."

"Which part?"

Nolen released a small smile. "Not the threat."

"Freedman," Concho replied.

Bull Knife looked confused. "Huh?"

Concho let his gaze focus on his half brother's face. He explained. "When I spoke to Nolen on the phone. Before he released Porter, I told him he could be 'free and clear.' That's where he got the name of 'Officer Freedman,' which he used when he called Solly to let us know where Porter was."

"Ah," Bull Knife replied.

"That cleverness was a mistake, I see now," Nolen said. "It gave away too much of a hint on my identity. By the way, it doesn't seem like you've kept your bargain. You also said you'd 'forget' I existed."

"Freedman did help," Concho replied. "As for the other, I'll keep my bargain. *No one* will ever get your name from me. Not for Porter. And here and now I'm holding Bull Knife to the same."

Carmichael glanced from Ten-Wolves to Bull Knife, who nodded.

Nolen offered his own nod. "The main point was something else, though. You told me House was 'innocent.' You were right. That bothered me about this from the start. The people I've.... Well, they weren't innocent. Not even close."

"Sounds like you're a good man," Concho said.

"Hardly," Nolen replied.

"Who hired it done?"

Nolen shook his head. "I can't. And you know it. I'm out of it. I told that to the person who hired me. I'll return the money for the contracts but protection of source is not an option. I did suggest it would be better to leave it all alone."

"You think he'll listen?"

"From what I heard on the news a little bit ago about the Causeway being shut down for a shooting, you already know *they* won't. But I think Porter will be safe. If he keeps his head down."

"He's probably learned his lesson," Concho agreed.

Bull Knife had been patient in asking the question most important to him; he couldn't hold it in any longer. "What about our mother?" he blurted. "Wiskenoa! Sparrow Woman. You lied when you said you saw her dead in Las Vegas. We know she survived there. Else I wouldn't have been born. Where is she?"

Nolen studied Bull Knife for a minute, then glanced to Concho. Finally, he let his gaze take them both in. He gave a long sigh.

"Gentlemen, I can assure you...*Sparrow Woman* is dead!"

***

It was dark when Sammy Boudreaux awoke, both in the fishing shack where he'd passed out and outside along the Pearl River. His head felt like it was being worked over by a jackhammer. Beer bottles littered the floor around the recliner where he'd fallen asleep. A nearly empty pint of Jack Daniels sat open on the table next to him, along with cigar butts and a torn open bag of chips. He moaned as he straightened up, his hands going to his forehead, which felt clammy and hot.

"Should never have started on the whiskey," he muttered.

Looking around the small cabin, he saw Jason Kulick passed out face down on the couch. He rubbed his eyes, wondering what had awakened him. Some sound maybe. A splashing in the river?

"Probably a gator."

Stumbling to his feet, he warped his way to the bathroom. After emptying his distended bladder, he came back out wiping his face on a towel. Two men stood in the shadowy room. Both were big, wearing gloves, with ski masks over their faces. The masks bore the Punisher logo, a stylized skull. He recognized the men despite the masks.

"Hey, hey! What's going on?"

One of the men held an extendable baton in his hand. He leaned over Kulick, who was still asleep on the couch, and whacked him brutally behind the ear. Jason gave a grunt and then lay still.

Sammy vented a little shriek and turned to run.

A third man stood behind him, in his way. He was just as big as the other two and wore the same kind of mask. He thrust out his hand and locked it around Sammy's throat. Sammy struggled, clawing at the gloved fingers until the big man punched him solidly in the face.

Sammy's legs went weak, though he didn't lose consciousness as the man pushed him back across the room and shoved him down in his easy chair. Another of the intruders stepped up behind the chair.

Boudreaux heard the ugly stripping sound of duct tape being yanked off a roll. A long piece of gray tape slapped across his mouth and was wrapped around his head. More tape went around his body, and the chair. Soon, his chest and arms were bound up like a mummy.

Trying to babble through his tape gag produced only muffled grunts. He kept shaking his head back and forth as much as he could. He wanted to tell them this was all a mistake. All wrong. He wanted to talk to them about money, all the money he could get for them.

He wanted to beg.

A fourth man came in through the front door. He was just as huge as the others and had a backpack slung over one shoulder. After knocking some empty beer bottles off the kitchen counter and letting them crash on the floor, he opened the pack and started taking things out. Sammy felt his eyes bulging; he couldn't look away.

First out of the pack came a black Colt .45 semi-automatic. The man used the barrel to flip on the kitchen light, then tucked it into his belt where it nestled like a fat snake. Next out of the pack came a plastic baggie holding what looked like an empty shell casing. The man unzipped the baggie and dumped the casing out on the floor. He kicked it under the counter. Finally, an empty Shiner Bock beer bottle was pulled free and mixed in among the various empties scattered around.

All four invaders gathered in front of Sammy's chair then. Only one of them spoke, in a deep voice that Sammy had heard over the phone more than once. The man drew the .45 from his belt and held it in his gloved hand.

"From what we've heard, you skimmed some of our latest pay, Sammy."

Sammy shook his head desperately. His grunts were audible but inarticulate.

"Doesn't matter. We made up the difference elsewhere. Mr. Morozov sends his regards."

He lifted the gun and pulled the trigger.

CHAPTER 43

"You're lying!" Bull Knife snapped at Nolen Carmichael after hearing him claim: "*Sparrow Woman* is dead."

Nolen shrugged. "People believe what they want to believe."

Bull Knife started to say something else.

Concho interrupted, with his gaze focused on Carmichael's eyes. "No! I don't think he's lying."

With his mouth hanging half open, Bull Knife glanced from one to the other of the men. He grunted. His mouth closed with a clash of teeth and he turned away from both and walked to the edge of the river.

Concho continued to study Nolen Carmichael, who did not look away. Dark eyes met dark eyes.

"I have one more question," Concho said.

"If I can answer it."

"Where is this Boudreaux 'compound' I hear mentioned?"

"Not really a compound. Though they do call it that. It's no secret the family owns three houses next to each other in Beau Chêne. It's a community. Sits right on the Tchefuncte River, which feeds into Lake Pontchartrain. Just outside the city limits of Madisonville."

"Three houses? I'm guessing the father, Christoph, and Nicholas. What about Sammy?"

"Officially, Sammy lives in his parents' pool house. But he's hardly ever there. He's got a party shack on the South Shore. Not far from the casino. He won't be there now, of course."

"Tell me about Beau Chêne."

"You said 'one' question."

Concho flashed a brief grin. "It's not a question. It's an expansion."

Nolen shook his head but responded. "It's big houses and condominiums. A gated community. Pretty exclusive." He offered his own small smile. "You're not likely to get invited in."

"I'm pretty resourceful."

"Yes, I noticed."

"Thanks for the information."

"You could have got it elsewhere."

"And…" the Ranger continued, "thanks for Porter."

"Right," Nolen said. He took a deep breath. "One more thing. Nicholas Boudreaux is a close friend of mine. For a very long time."

"I'll remember."

Nolen tipped an imaginary hat to the Texas Ranger and walked away.

Concho strode over to Bull Knife. His half brother's face seemed impassive at first glance but even under the moonlight anyone could see muscles knotted along the jawline.

"I don't believe him," Bull Knife said, still staring at the river.

"I don't think you quite got his meaning."

Bull Knife's head jerked around. "What do *you* mean?" he demanded, clipping his words.

"Consider where he put the emphasis in speaking of *Sparrow Woman*. It's not what he said, it's how he said it."

"Make sense!"

"All right. I believe he was telling us that the woman who gave birth to us, who you lived with for six years, she's gone.

The woman who is still here is not the same. Not Wiskenoa, but someone different."

Bull Knife's eyes glittered as his lids flashed in realization. "So, she *is* alive?"

"For the first time since we came to New Orleans, I truly believe she is."

"But then…what of this…difference?"

"She faked her death twice. That means she had a pretty good reason to disappear. The last time, I'm guessing she made some pretty drastic changes physically. Probably in lifestyle, too. She likely dyed her hair. Maybe changed her eye color with contacts. She probably had plastic surgery. Her nose and lips. Even the shape of her face. They might not be the same."

"But not inside. People cannot so change who they are."

"Most people can't. I've known some who could."

"And you think she is with the Boudreaux family?"

"I think so. Maybe a wife. Maybe a long-time employee. But I'm pretty sure the oldest son, Christoph, doesn't know. He was fed some kind of story and believed it."

"But Sammy does know?"

Concho shrugged. "Still a lot of mystery to solve."

"Then we ride to this Boudreaux complex," Bull Knife said, straightening his shoulders.

"In the morning. I'll call Christoph. I think I can work him around to the idea. After all that's happened today, though, I need a good night's sleep. So do you."

***

Nolen Carmichael watched from a window as his visitors drove away. He went to check on his wife. She still sat at the piano but had stopped playing. Her hands worried at each other in her lap. He kissed her on the forehead.

"It's all going to be all right," he said. "Play for me some more."

She nodded; she began to play *San Francisco Can Be Such*

a Lonely Town.

Nolen stepped into the hallway and pulled out his phone. It was time he returned several calls from Nicholas Boudreaux that he'd deliberately missed.

***

The two half brothers stayed on the North Shore over-night, at a hotel on the 190 outside Covington. Concho woke at his usual 6:00 AM. He managed to get in some exercise and shave with the complimentary razor.

After Bull Knife got up, the two ate breakfast at a café called The Fat Spoon. Concho ordered three eggs, six strips of bacon, and something called a "Big Biscuit and Debris," the debris being thick, juicy scraps of pot roast with gravy.

"This," the Ranger said to Bull Knife as he forked biscuit and debris into his face with relish. "Gotta see if I can find this in Texas."

Bull Knife merely shook his head as he finished his one egg, dry toast, and two bacon strips.

While his brother headed for the bathroom after the meal, Concho stepped outside to call Maria Morales. It was nearly 9:00. She'd surely be up by now, and at work unless she was at the hospital with her mother.

As he pulled out his phone, he noticed he'd somehow managed to turn the sound off overnight. He'd missed half a dozen calls, including three from Solly Burstein and two recent ones from Christoph Boudreaux. He'd deal with those in a moment. He needed to talk to his sweetheart first.

Maria answered with a "Hello, lover."

"Mmm," Concho replied. "I love your voice. How is your mom?"

"Oh! I'm sorry I didn't call like you asked. We got very busy. Henry came over and we took her to the hospital. You'd have thought we were taking her to the gas chamber. They admitted her. She's on oxygen for the breathing issues but the doctors seem to think she's going to be OK."

"What is it?"

"They still haven't told us. I guess they're not sure. She's not out of the woods but I'm feeling better."

"You over there now?"

"No, Henry's on duty. I'm at work. How about you? How are *you* doing?"

"Making tsunamis everywhere I go. But I'm expecting some breaks today."

"That's good."

Bull Knife came out of the café looking impatient. Concho gave him a nod. He finished up with Maria.

"OK, baby, I'll let you go. Give your mom a hug for me. I'll be home soon."

"Call me when you're on your way."

"Will do."

"Love you."

"Love you, too."

After hanging up, Concho considered whether to call Solly or Christoph next. Bull Knife's frowning face persuaded him on which. He tapped the number for Christoph Boudreaux. The man answered on the first ring. His voice was cold, angry. It buzzed like the wings of a hornet.

"Wondered if you'd call," Christoph snapped.

"Sounds like something's happened," Concho said. "What's going on?"

"You tell me! I'd like to know why you murdered my brother Sammy!"

CHAPTER 44

For a long moment Concho had nothing to say, nothing he *could* say through the shock.

"I...didn't," he finally managed. "What are you talking about?"

"Yesterday evening. You beat Jason Kulick's skull in and shot Sammy in the head after duct taping him to a chair. Probably with help from your brother. We got the call from the police an hour ago. It nearly killed Dad. We've taken him to the hospital. His heart!"

"I had nothing to do with it! I've never even met Sammy."

"You'll pay though." The words were bitter. "Run to Texas. Run wherever. We'll find you."

"What's the evidence?" Concho demanded, allowing anger to creep into his own voice.

"Everyone who has seen you knows you use those big .45s. The cops found a shell casing from one of them. A partial print. But yours. And you even drank a beer with him! What kind of man does that? The bottle had your prints all over it."

"It's a frame," Concho snapped. "Use your head."

Christoph didn't appear to be listening. "Go ahead and run!" The phone went dead.

Concho ground out a heavy breath. He studied his surroundings but saw nothing suspicious. Before Bull Knife could ask what was wrong, the Ranger motioned him to the car. They spun out of the parking lot and headed north down 190 toward roads less traveled.

"What's happening?" Bull Knife demanded.

Concho told him.

"Ridiculous! Last evening? It'll never hold up. I can tell them you were with me."

"They think you're part of it too."

Bull Knife grunted. He slammed his hand down on the Mustang's dash.

Concho pulled into a combination gas station/convenience store. He jerked three twenties out of his billfold and tossed them in his half brother's lap. "Fill the tank. Tip top. Get some food inside. Water. Some granola bars. Nothing perishable. I've gotta call Solly Burstein."

Bull Knife scrambled to obey. Concho slid out of the car and yanked his phone free. He pressed the contact for Burstein as he walked around behind the vehicle.

Two rings and Solly answered. "What the hell?" he said.

"It wasn't me," Concho said. "It's a frame job."

"Your run-ins with Kulick are documented," Solly said. "And so is your animosity for everything Boudreaux. Particularly Sammy. They've got half a dozen witnesses to your volatile nature."

"Who's got them?"

"A police detective named Rousselle. Larry Rousselle. And then there's the evidence."

"A shell casing," Concho said. "And a beer bottle. Shiner Bock, of course. With my prints on them."

"It isn't working in your favor to know that."

"Didn't know it until Christoph Boudreaux told me a few minutes ago."

"Boudreaux? He shouldn't have that information!"

"I'd guess your 'conduit' within the department is keeping the

Boudreaux family informed."

"So it seems."

"I tell you…. I *promise* you. It's a frame."

"I believe you actually. You didn't hear it from me, but Rousselle is the conduit. I've known it for a while. He apparently got an 'anonymous' tip last night about the killings. That's why he's lead detective. But how do you explain the shell casing and the beer bottle?"

"Only one place they could have come from. The Rivershack Tavern. I drank a Shiner there. Left the bottle on the bar. As one does. That's also where Kulick and LeBlanc came after me. I shot back. Didn't have time to pick up the empties. I figured the police gathered them."

"We did," Solly said.

"Apparently someone else picked one up first. And the bottle. I'm betting it was the bartender. A guy named Barney. I mentioned him to you before. He knew Sammy. I'd figured they were friends but maybe not."

"Yeah, yeah, I remember Barney. We hadn't had time to check into it. I will now."

"Look," Concho said. "I don't think we dare turn ourselves in."

"Can't believe I'm saying it, but you don't! With Rousselle working for the Boudreaux group, you wouldn't last a day."

"I don't know the area, though."

Solly hesitated, then snapped his fingers. "What about that abandoned cottage where Porter House was held? A good hideaway for a bit. And I can find it if I need you."

"Who else knows about it?"

"Only the junior officer I brought with me. But I'm not going to include him in the loop on this."

"All right," Concho said. "I'm thinking Morozov has got to be the lead behind all this. Get to Barney. He's the weak link. I think he'll crack with the right incentives."

"I'll do my job, Ten-Wolves!"

The Ranger winced at Solly's tone. "I know. Sorry."

"It's OK. I have to go."

The line went dead. Bull Knife came out of the store with two plastic bags full of water and snacks. He stuck these in the Mustang's back seat. Concho tossed him the keys.

"You drive!"

***

Christoph Boudreaux stood alone beside his father's bed in Ochsner Hospital. His stepmother had gone to find the chapel. "To light a candle," she'd said. His brother, Nick, had called to say he was on his way.

Machines around the room beeped. Monitors showed Christoph meaningless scribbles of green light across glass. His father had always seemed a big man. He'd shrunk now. His once strong body lay wasted and waxy. He looked dead.

And Sammy is *dead*, Christoph thought, his mind drifting.

He'd never particularly liked his younger half brother. But Sammy was "blood." Every day of his life, his father had stressed the importance of blood—of kin. Sammy's death had to be avenged, and with his father in a hospital bed, that job fell to Christoph.

But who was responsible? Concho Ten-Wolves? Larry Rousselle said so. He'd told them about the evidence against the Texas lawman. The only problem was, Christoph *knew* Rousselle. The man was neither honorable nor a good detective.

Christoph knew Concho Ten-Wolves as well. At least a little. Their talks had been open, apparently honest. He considered himself a good judge of character. The Ranger did not seem the type for such a thing. But the evidence.... His father certainly believed it.

Something changed in the room, as if the air had gelled. Christoph's gaze darted to his father's bed. Roman Boudreaux was awake, despite the meds his veins were soaking up. The man's eyes glittered like hard little buckeyes in a pasty face.

Christoph reached for his father's hand; that hand clamped down on his wrist like a vice. His father's voice cut through his thoughts, a bandsaw chewing on gravels.

"Ten-Wolves!" Roman said. "See him dead! Make him suffer!"

The old man's hand released Christoph's wrist and dropped onto the sheets. The eyes closed. One of the machine alarms began to shriek. Automatically, Christoph stepped back out of the way as nurses rushed into the room and surrounded the bed. He lifted a hand to his mouth, gnawed at a finger until he realized in shock that he'd drawn blood.

CHAPTER 45

"Where are we going?" Bull Knife asked from behind the wheel of the Mustang as they sped down 190 North.

"Abita Springs first. You know how to get to the place where Porter was held?"

"Ah! I think so. I don't like the idea of hiding, though."

"Nor I. But apparently every law enforcement agency in Louisiana is on the lookout for us as murderers. If we stay in the open, we either get arrested and shot in custody, or we kill law officers to escape. I'm not about to do that. At least Solly Burstein is on our side. We'll have to trust him to get it done."

"I—" Bull Knife started but cut his own thought off.

"What?"

A quick breath. "I don't trust white people."

Concho made a face. "What about black people?"

Bull Knife's cheeks flushed as he glanced at his half brother's dark skin. "Not much either. Usually. But you are not black."

"Black enough," Concho replied. "But none of that matters. You don't trust *people*! Of any shade. You trust motives. Motives determine whether a person does good or bad. Solly's motives here are to find the truth and keep the innocent from paying for the sins of the guilty. I trust those."

Bull Knife turned down a road called Dog Pound toward Abita Springs. He changed the topic. "What about weapons? Your bow and rifle are gone. Your shotgun and the pistol you loaned me." He jerked his chin toward the twin Colt Double Eagles holstered at Concho's hips. "You have any ammunition for those?"

The lawman patted the butts of the guns. "Just what's in 'em. Eight in each magazine, one in each chamber."

"That going to be enough?"

"If we need more weapons we'll make them. No shortage of ways to kill."

Bull Knife nodded. They drove on in silence.

***

Christoph Boudreaux found himself pushed out into the corridor as doctors and nurses worked on his father. He chewed his thumbnail, then looked up as rushing feet came down the hall. He recognized Eve, his brother Nicholas's daughter, and her blonde friend, Cassandra Holmes.

"Is he…." Eve asked as she ran up.

"I don't know," Christoph said. "They're working on him now."

Both women nodded; they hugged him.

"Where's your mom?" Eve asked.

"She went to find the chapel."

"All right," Eve said, taking a deep breath. "I'll go find her."

Christoph nodded. His focus kept shifting to the door of this father's room.

Eve sped off; Cassandra stayed. She patted Christoph's shoulder. "Did he have a heart attack?" she asked.

Christoph nodded. "When he heard about Sammy."

Cassandra winced. "I'm sorry."

Christoph nodded into her blue-eyed gaze. "Those who did it will pay."

"Who?"

"That Texas Ranger. Concho Ten-Wolves."

Cassandra looked surprised. Her patting hand dropped from Christoph's shoulder. "I don't think so," she said.

***

Within an hour of arriving at the abandoned cottage where Porter House had been held prisoner, Concho and Bull Knife had set it up as best they could as a defensive fortress. They'd also explored the woods surrounding them, marking out good cover and trails useful for escape or maneuver.

Concho stepped out on the front porch of the house. Bull Knife sat in a rickety, left-behind rocking chair using his hunting knife to sharpen the tip of a six-foot oaken spear. Two completed spears leaned against the wall near him.

The Ranger unhooked his gun belt and removed one of the filled holsters, which he handed to his half brother. "Use it wisely."

Bull Knife nodded as he took the holster and .45. He slipped it on his own belt, stood and buckled it on his hip. "I have a feeling they're going to come."

"Same here. They've proven to be resourceful. They'll figure it out. The only question is how soon. But this is as good a place as any to make our stand."

***

Piotr Morozov recognized the number and answered the phone. He also recognized the voice, one of the four assassins for hire people generally called "The Brothers."

"Yes," Morozov said.

"We've got a line on them. North Shore. Outside Abita. Right where you suggested we look. Still want 'em dead?"

"Absolutely. Only…if you can take the one named Ten-Wolves alive, let me know. I'd like it. I owe him a few cuts."

"We will if we can."

"Good. I'm on my way in that direction. This needs to get done for all of us. Before too many questions get asked about Sammy's death."

"You're paying enough for it." The man hung up.

Morozov nodded to himself. The timing was nearly perfect. With Roman Boudreaux in the hospital and the rest of the family distracted, he could pin everything on Ten-Wolves and make sure the man was not around to defend himself. The only troubling thing was the two calls this morning from Nicholas Boudreaux. He'd avoided answering them for fear he'd hear something he didn't want to hear. Eventually he'd have to deal with that.

But, first things first. He went to his desk in the Treasure Chest Casino and pulled a mahogany case from a bottom drawer. Opening the lid revealed a gold-plated Heckler & Koch VP9 semiautomatic pistol and two loaded magazines. The pistol was German made, a gift from his true employers. Not the Boudreaux family.

In the box next to the pistol nestled an HK knife with a matte grey aluminum handle and a three-and-a-half-inch blade sharp enough to cut a silk scarf draped across it. Morozov liked the pistol but loved the blade.

Calling his personal driver, Morozov told him to bring up the car. And to come armed. They were taking a little trip. He closed the gun case and carried it with him as he left the office.

**

Concho stared out a cracked front window of the cottage. He was eating a granola bar when he heard a sound he'd been waiting on. Nolen Carmichael had chosen well when he'd picked this place to hide himself and Porter. Something in the local geography funneled sound straight up the old driveway through the woods to the house. No one could approach in a vehicle without being heard. Even if they stopped well back out of sight.

Bull Knife came in from the kitchen. He'd heard the sound, too. His gaze met Concho's. A nod passed between them. Both men had bound their long hair behind them and wore warpaint made from grease and charcoal.

Carrying three homemade spears, Bull Knife headed through the front door and into the woods. Concho went out the back and circled around. He'd set up a combination lookout/sniper post in a nest made of boulders and a fallen tree. There'd been no time to build a bow but he'd used nylon rope and part of an old tarp Carmichael must have left behind to construct a sling.

He pulled the primitive weapon out of his pocket now. Since guns were rare on the reservation when he'd been a kid, slings had often been his weapon of choice for hunting small game for the cookpot. He hadn't used one in years but a little practice brought the knack back to him.

The sound of the approaching vehicle had stopped. The day lay sun-dappled and silent now, though surely their enemies were creeping through the trees toward them. The temperature hovered in the low fifties. Normally, he'd find that a bit chilly, but the adrenaline already coursed through him and he was plenty warm.

A bird called. And quickly called again. Except it wasn't a bird. He and Bull Knife had arranged signals their enemies wouldn't understand. Bull Knife had sighted two foes approaching. There were almost certainly more.

Concho remained very still in his shadowy nest. He had a good view of the cottage's porch and small front yard, and of any approach to it from the front. They'd parked their rent-a-car Mustang out of the way to one side under the shade of an oak.

The dirt driveway leading to the cottage split the yard into two halves with a bordering ditch on either side and a culvert under the driveway itself. Untended, the ditch had started to fill up over time with soil and bushes.

A darkness moved at the edge of the yard and sank into the ditch amid the covering brush. Concho made out a single man, big but trying to hide beneath camouflage clothing over body armor. He also wore a green and brown patterned balaclava and held a scoped rifle in his arms.

One moment later, a second shadow slunk into the same ditch about a dozen yards from the first. This man, also camouflaged and wearing Kevlar, had a rifle slung over his shoulder. In his hands he held an RPG.

Concho had arranged a little deception. He'd found an old coat rack in the cottage with a coat still on it. He'd made a makeshift toupee for the rack from a plastic bag and positioned his creation where it cast the silhouette of a man across the front window. Now, after studying the place, the man with the RPG took aim at the same window. Seconds spilled away. Concho waited for the opening bid and prepared his counter.

CHAPTER 46

The RPG ignited with a hiss. Concho closed his eyes brief-ly but the lance of flame that leaped toward the house still burned itself into his retinas. Big fragments of window glass shattered into pointlets. A whump shook the air.

Concho opened his eyes as the shock of the exploding grenade collapsed the cottage walls inward and flame tunneled upward through the falling roof like a Saturn V rocket igniting. The stench of superheated chemicals broiled in his nostrils.

One brief instant later, a high-pitched, ululating howl stabbed the day. It did not come from the house. It did not come from pain. It was Bull Knife, venting an Apache war cry. The men who hunted the half brothers were not militarily trained, though they had military weapons and wore army style clothing. They'd failed to scout the whole area before opening fire. Now, both the ones Concho could see looked to their right, toward the howl.

Unseen to the men's left, Concho rose from his cover, spun the sling up and whipped a stone flat and hard at the RPG shootist. The rounded gravel struck like a bullet into the man's temple; his shout of pain came reflexively as he dropped his forehead into the dirt and unconsciousness.

The second man must have heard the whirr of the sling. He

twisted back toward Concho, swinging his rifle to bear. Even
through the eye holes of the camouflage mask, the man's pupils
were dilated widely in shock. His gun moved slower than his gaze.

Concho dropped the sling and palmed his .45 Double Eagle. He pulled the trigger once. By the time the butt kicked back
against his palm in recoil, the rifleman was bleeding out from a
bullet through the face.

Rapid gunfire erupted from the ditch on the far side of the
driveway. It wasn't a .45, which meant it wasn't Bull Knife. Nor
was it aimed at Concho as it slashed into trees, snipping limbs
and leaves.

Concho stepped around the boulders protecting him and ran
crouched over toward the sound, knowing Bull Knife was being
fired upon. He stepped over the dead body of one shooter but
heard a moan from the RPG man, whose head must have been
coated in concrete since he was already waking up from the stone
blow to his skull.

The lawman had no choice of actions. He couldn't let this one
get back into the fight but couldn't shoot him in cold blood. Dropping to a knee, Concho yanked the handcuffs from his belt. He
slapped a cuff around one of the man's wrists, then bent the leg on
the other side up at an angle and hooked the ankle. No one was
going anywhere like that.

Rising again into a crouch, Concho heard more shooting
straight ahead. A streak of movement caught his eye but he
couldn't fire without knowing Bull Knife's location. He also didn't
dare straighten to his full height and become a target himself. He
pushed forward through the brush with gun to hand, weaving as
fast as he could through the obstructing growth.

The brush broke away as he found the driveway. His visual field
opened up. Just across the rutted dirt span, two men with AR-15s
blazed away into the trees. Both were big men, like the others, and
wore body armor and balaclavas. Four men total. It felt like the
last of their attackers. Concho swung up his pistol.

One man heard something and turned just as Concho fired. He'd targeted the head but the sudden movement spoiled his aim. The .45 slug punched into a shoulder protected by Kevlar. Bullet shock knocked the man down, his rifle flying. But the shell hadn't penetrated and he wouldn't be down long.

Concho's gaze darted to the second man, who'd also started to turn. That gave the lawman a perfect view as Bull Knife leaped out from behind a bullet-ridden tree and rushed straight at the fellow with a spear in his hands. The half-Apache vented a savage war cry as he ran. The gunman froze between two threats.

Ten-Wolves held his fire for fear of hitting his half brother. Terror of the spear won out for the gunman, who tried to swing back toward Bull Knife. All that did was make his throat a target as the sharpened tip of the weapon rammed into the soft flesh below the mouth and tore upward.

Two screams sounded almost simultaneously, a gurgling one from the stabbed man and a higher pitched one of terror from the fellow Concho had shot. As Bull Knife released the quivering haft of the spear and yanked the Colt .45 from his holster, the remaining assassin ran.

No one could blame him. The fellow had just witnessed the brutality of old-style hand-to-hand combat. And he'd seen Bull Knife's face covered with warpaint and the spatter of his companion's blood. It was enough to cool any warrior's fervor.

But the Ranger didn't want the last foe to get away. He double actioned the Colt, shooting to wound rather than kill. The slug burned just wide of the target and tore up dirt. Bull Knife fired, too, missed too. The fellow moved at a dead sprint but wove back and forth.

"There's a live one handcuffed back in the ditch," Concho yelled to his half brother. "Watch him. I'll get this one."

Bull Knife barely had time to nod before Concho lunged past him into the woods. The access road to the cottage curved back to the main road. That had to be where their enemies had parked. Cutting straight across through the trees might head off the fleeing killer.

Despite the cool temperature, sweat poured off the Ranger as he ran. He shoved his .45 into its holster and hooked the thong to hold it so he could run faster. The woods here was old growth, uncut for years. There wasn't much underbrush. Concho wove swiftly through the broad boles of oak and hickory as he thundered onward.

The access road was partially eroded. The woods where Concho ran made higher ground. He suddenly burst free of the trees onto the top of a small rise some four feet high bordering the main dirt road. Just below him sat a Hummer H2 model in dark grey. The last of the would-be assassins came sprinting out of the cottage's long driveway and turned toward it.

The timing couldn't have been better. Concho barely had to break stride as he flung himself off the short bluff and down. His body struck the assassin and knocked him flat. He grabbed for a hold on the man's arm but missed as he hit and rolled past his target.

Both men bounced to their feet. The killer was almost as tall as Concho and bulkier in his body armor. He charged into the Ranger, chopping with his fists. Concho blocked all but one blow, which slammed hard into his shoulder. He caught the arm, though, twisted it to one side and sent an open-handed punch into the chest.

The fellow staggered back but the blow did little against his vest and he wasn't hurt. He grabbed for the pistol holstered at his hip. Concho lashed out with a kick that caught the arm and sent the semi-automatic flying.

"Kill you!" the other man snarled as he charged again with his head tucked down between his shoulders.

Concho backed up, seeking something to hit besides Kevlar, which might break his hand. The two fenced with their fists. To no effect. The killer tried the chopping maneuver again, swinging his arm like an ax. Again, Concho caught the arm and twisted, but this time he continued the twist and threw the fellow over his hip.

Dust spurted up from the road as the man crashed down. Concho came after him. A desperate kick got lucky as a boot caught the Ranger in the side of his knee. A spasm of pain flashed up that leg like an electric shock. Concho stumbled sideways; the knee gave out and he fell to his other knee.

Another kick from the killer blasted into the Ranger's chest and flung him back. He hit hard on his shoulders and slid in the dirt. The other man was up. He lunged toward Concho, trying to stomp him.

The lawman got his hands high, caught the work-booted foot. He hadn't been truly angry before but the pain brought it out of him. He snarled as he twisted the boot in his hands and shoved with all his strength. The fellow yelped in surprise as he found himself thrown numbingly back against the side of the Hummer.

Concho rose. He ducked a wild swing and sent a right-left combination into the man's chin. The killer groaned and sagged. He flailed a weak punch at the Ranger, catching him on the shoulder. Concho shrugged it off.

Stepping toward the man, Concho threw another right and watched it explode under the chin. The back of the fellow's skull bounced off the Hummer's window. Teeth clacked together. Blood and what looked like a sliver of tongue came spraying out of his mouth.

Concho started to sling a left and pulled it as the killer folded and slid down the side of the vehicle. Instead, the lawman stepped back, breathing hard and wincing as he put weight on his right knee, which was surely sprained.

"No more, no more!" the downed man pleaded, the words distorted by the sliver of missing tongue

"Lie there and don't move!" Concho ordered.

CHAPTER 47

Concho found all kinds of supplies in the Hummer, in- cluding camping gear and some duct tape he used to bind the would-be assassin's hands and ankles. He hauled the fellow to his feet and shoved him in the back seat of the H2 SUV.

Yanking off the man's balaclava revealed a shaved head and heavy, florid features. Part of the flushing was likely due to the mask and the circumstances, but much of it came naturally.

"What's your name?" Concho asked.

A head shake gave his only answer.

Concho shrugged and shut the door, then climbed in the front seat of the Hummer to find the keys in the ignition. Planning for a quick getaway, he imagined. He started the engine and drove up the road into the front yard of the cottage. Or, to what had *once* been the cottage. The fire ignited by the RPG had gutted the place and still fed on the innards.

Concho parked well back from the ruin and climbed out, leaving his prisoner in the vehicle. Bull Knife had dragged the hand-cuffed killer out of the ditch into the front yard. He'd pulled off the man's balaclava, revealing an identical shaved head and features to those of Concho's prisoner.

"Twins!" the lawman exclaimed.

"Quadruplets apparently," Bull Knife replied. "The other two look just like this one."

The Ranger wanted so badly to arch an eyebrow but had to content himself with a "Wow!" He went over and released the man's ankle cuff. Pulling him to the Hummer, he cuffed the fellow's wrists over his head to the luggage rack.

"I have to feel for their mother," Bull Knife said.

"Bastards!" the man cursed.

Concho rubbed his right knee, which had started to feel better but still left him angry. "I don't remember asking you to try and kill us by burning a house down around our ears," he snapped at the man.

The man only cursed again. "You killed my brother."

"You tried to kill mine first."

"Two of your brothers," Bull Knife said to the assassin. He glanced at Concho. "Maybe three."

The Ranger shook his head. "The other one's in the back seat with nothing worse than a headache."

"I'll slaughter you!" the fellow shouted.

"Don't plan to give you another chance," Concho replied. "What's your name and who hired you?"

"Go to Hell!"

Concho glimpsed the outline of a billfold in the man's front pocket. He pulled it out, flipped it open to the driver's license and read the name.

"Gus Billings, it says here. Maybe his real name. Maybe not."

"This ain't over!" Gus growled.

Bull Knife struck like a rattler. He wrapped his arm around Gus's head and grasped the chin, arching the neck up. His hunting knife whipped into his hand and he pressed the business edge to Billings' scalp just above the eyes.

"No, no, no!" Gus yelped. "Don't!"

"Normally," Concho said in a conversational tone, "the Apache prefer scalps with hair on em. But maybe he can make a coaster out of yours."

"Don't!" Gus begged.

"I was thinking the cover for a baseball," Bull Knife added. "'Course, I'll have to tan it nicely and paint it."

"Please!" Gus begged, his body shaking.

Concho stepped closer to Gus and offered one of his shark smiles. "Two of your brothers may be dead but that leaves you and another alive. If you want to keep it that way, you'll answer my questions."

"You're a lawman!" Gus protested. "You can't do this."

"I'm not doing it."

"You can't *allow* it!"

The edge of Bull Knife's blade was sharp enough to shave with. He made a tiny nick in Gus's skin right at the hairline.

"Ow!" the man yelped.

"Things are a little different in Texas," Concho offered.

"OK, OK, you probably already know anyway. Piotr Morozov."

Concho nodded. "Yep, I did know. Why?"

"I...I couldn't tell you. He didn't explain it to me. To any of us."

"And you didn't need it explained as long as you got paid, am I right?"

"Yes. Yes."

"How'd you find us?"

The man had started talking now. He'd keep on talking as long as Concho kept asking the right questions.

"Morozov," Gus said. "He had...information about you renting a yellow Mustang. I guess through your credit card company or something. He knew you still had to be on the North Shore since you would've been picked up by the Causeway cameras if you tried to cross."

Concho's glance met Bull Knife's. The credit card information had probably been pulled by a cop. Most likely by Larry Rousselle, who was in charge of arresting the two and was apparently on the take from someone in the Boudreaux camp.

"Keep going," Concho said to Gus.

"Morozov also had the idea to check this place. Don't know why. We were able to access satellite imagery for the area. When we spotted the yellow Mustang, we knew he was right."

"Smart!" Concho said. "Think of what you could have achieved if you'd gone straight. I'm joking by the way. Don't imagine you've ever done anything straight."

Gus ignored the jape. "Can you…make him stop now?"

Bull Knife released the man's chin and stepped away. He wiped a droplet of blood off the knife on Gus's shirt before sliding it in its scabbard.

"What were your exact orders concerning us?" Concho asked.

"Kill you. Only…" he looked directly at Ten-Wolves, "he said if we could take *you* alive, we should. Said he owed you a few cuts."

"Nice guy," the Ranger replied. "Guess that means you had a way to contact him if you took me alive."

A side pocket on Gus's BDUs held the outline of a cell phone. Concho pulled it out and swiped it on. The command screen came up.

"Not even a password," the Ranger said. "You fellows ain't too good at this."

Gus said nothing as Concho scrolled through the man's contacts. They were all just numbers with either one or two letters behind them. It didn't take long to figure out.

"17PM," the lawman said. "Piotr Morozov. Right?"

Gus had recovered a little from his terror. He mostly looked embarrassed now as he answered, "Yeah."

"How were you supposed to contact him?"

"Just a call saying we had you."

"What about a text?"

"Sometimes. If we don't have good reception."

Concho nodded. There were no texts to Morozov on the phone. Concho glanced at some other text threads to get a feel for

Gus's style. Then he tapped in the number for 17PM, chose text, and typed in: "Got Ten-Wolves. You wanna make those cuts come ahead." He hit send.

A response came back. "On my way. Thirty minutes."

Gus apparently liked simple emojis so Concho sent back a "thumbs up" before sliding the phone into his own pocket.

"Morozov is on the way," the Ranger told Bull Knife. "I doubt he'll be alone. Let's get a welcome party ready."

***

When Piotr Morozov arrived at the burned-out cottage in a Treasure Chest limo, he noted that everything looked pretty much under control. The house was destroyed but Concho Ten-Wolves sat with his hands bound behind him in a folding lawn chair in front of the Hummer H2 the "Brothers" drove.

One of the brothers—Morozov could never tell them apart— stood directly behind Ten-Wolves with a pistol in his hand and the Hummer's hatch open at his back. On the ground nearby lay a body under a tarp. The one called "Bull Knife," Morozov imagined.

Even with the evidence of his eyes, Morozov ordered his driver/bodyguard out first. The man obediently walked toward the bound Ten-Wolves. He stopped when he saw ropes around the Ranger's ankles and empty holsters on his hips. Everything looked normal.

"We good?" the bodyguard asked the "Brother" with the pistol.

"Good," Gus replied.

The bodyguard turned and nodded through the tinted windows of the limo. Morozov climbed out. He wore a dark blue pinstriped suit today, over a starched white shirt with a blue tie and silver stickpin. After adjusting his tie, Piotr leaned back into the car and pulled out a mahogany box about sixteen inches long, polished to a high shine.

Carrying the case, Morozov strolled casually toward Concho with a smug expression filling his face. "Just an average little cop after all," he said as he studied the Ranger with pale gray eyes.

Concho smiled. His teeth were large, even, and white; they looked like they could crush hammers—and had.

"Not so little," the Ranger said. He kicked his feet and the ankle ropes fell away. He rocked forward in the lawn chair and stood up, revealing hands that weren't bound at all but were full of pistols.

The bodyguard grabbed for the gun under his left arm. Concho shot him in the shoulder and he cried out as he stumbled back against the limo and sank down on the hood.

Morozov screamed a curse in Polish and threw open the lid of the case he carried. Before he could even reach inside, however, Concho stepped forward and clubbed him in the face with the butt of a Colt. Piotr folded like a fitted sheet and lay on the ground in a knot, moaning as blood dribbled from a broken nose and split lip.

Concho picked up the case from where it had fallen. A very nice Heckler & Koch VP9 had spilled out, along with a wicked-looking knife from the same manufacturer. He pushed them back in the case and snapped it closed, then walked over and disarmed the bodyguard, who was holding his shoulder with all the fight shot out of him.

Bull Knife climbed out of the back of the Hummer, pushing Gus out of the way and removing the empty pistol they'd given the man to hold. He holstered his own pistol, which he'd taken off a dead assassin, then handcuffed Gus back to the H2's luggage rack. Next, he picked up a roll of duct tape and moved to stand behind the nylon camp chair, which they'd discovered among the equipment in the hired guns' vehicle.

"Morozov's throne awaits," he said.

CHAPTER 48

Piotr Morozov returned to full consciousness sitting in the same lawn chair where Concho Ten-Wolves had been sitting before. Only, his hands and feet were actually bound. With duct tape.

"Piotr," Concho said as the man's eyes finally focused. "The police are on their way. Detective Solly Burstein that is. As I understand it, Larry Rousselle is off the case."

"Don't know what you're talking about," Morozov said, the words slurred in his swollen mouth. "Don't recognize either of those names."

"You do, but we'll let it ride for the moment. I'm afraid your hired gunmen gave you up right quick."

Morozov twisted his head looking for the "Brothers," or for his bodyguard, but all three had been taken out of earshot and tied to trees.

"I know no gunmen. I'm a businessman." He tried to spit out blood but it mostly dribbled down his chin to spackle his shirt and tie.

"Sure. You just happened to show up here at this random time of day. In a place where Bull Knife was supposed to be dead and I was supposed to be ready for you to...cut."

Morozov coughed and cleared his throat. "This is Boudreaux

property," he eventually managed. "I was merely checking on valuable land for the corporation I work for."

Concho leaned down to rest his hands on the arm of the lawn chair, bringing his face close to Morozov's.

"You're not gonna fox your way out of this one. But I would like to know why. Men dead, property destroyed. None of this needed to happen."

Morozov seemed to forget the dignified façade he normally strove to display. He practically spat as he snapped, "Realize what you can do with yourself, pig."

Concho huffed through tightly pursed lips. Frustration raged inside. He was so close to answers to the questions that had brought him to Louisiana but could see that Morozov was not going to break the way Gus had. His hands clenched on the plastic arms of the chair, crushing them.

Morozov flinched but didn't speak.

Concho released the chair and straightened. He pulled out the cell phone he'd taken from Morozov and poked in a number. Someone answered.

"Christoph," the Ranger said into the phone. "Just listen! Don't talk! I've got Piotr Morozov here. He just tried again to have me and my brother killed. According to the lackeys he hired, it seems he's the one ordered the hit on your brother Sammy. I reckon it's his fault your father is where he is. I told him I'd called the police. I lied. We're at your property on the North Shore. Outside Abita Springs. Off a dirt road called Greenwood. You know it?"

Whoever was on the other end of the line must have agreed he did.

"All right," Concho added. "Time to plumb the depths of this. Then you can have Morozov. Come get him. But come without your army. I've got no quarrel with you. You won't have one with me after you realize who's behind your problems."

Concho swiped off the phone and tucked it back in his pocket. "He's on his way," he said to Morozov. "Shouldn't be long."

Morozov cleared his throat. "It doesn't matter. Even if he believes you, he won't dare harm me."

"Why is that?"

"Because I don't work for him. Not really. I don't work for any Boudreaux. And they're afraid of those I do work for. Or they should be."

"I think you're forgetting something," Concho replied.

"Oh?"

"Whatever deal you made with the Boudreaux family, it was with the father. And old Roman just had a heart attack and is knocking on Hell's door. I'm pretty sure Christoph doesn't know anything about that deal. Or the secret it's supposed to protect. Whatever it is. All he cares about is payback for his father, and for Sammy."

For the first time, Piotr Morozov began to sweat.

***

Christoph Boudreaux leaned against the wall in a corridor of the ICU at Ochsner Hospital. Others in his family milled around. Terry, his stepmother; Eve, his brother Nicholas's daughter; and her close friend, Cassandra Holmes. Only Nicholas had not shown up yet and Christoph couldn't figure out why. He had no strength to worry about it.

Even without Nick, the corridor held too many people for the ICU but the Boudreaux name carried weight. *If only the name could save my father's life*, Christoph thought, as he stared at the door to Roman's room.

Medical personnel had been coming and going through that door for what seemed like hours, with no news for the waiting family. The alarm which had brought all the doctors and nurses running had been turned off. Christoph didn't know if that were a good thing or a bad.

A young doctor whose name Christoph couldn't remember came out of the room, stripping off his mask. Christoph pushed away from the wall. Everyone crowded around. The doctor held up a hand, though no one had asked a question yet.

"He's stable at present," the doc said. "We're cautiously optimistic but the next twenty-four hours will tell. There's nothing any of you can do here. He's not conscious right now so you all might as well go home and get some rest. Or get something to eat. Even when he regains consciousness we're going to have to limit his visitors to one at a time. We can't tire him too much and absolutely *no* discussion of any topic that might upset him."

Christoph winced. It had been Sammy's death that initiated his father's crisis. And he'd been the one who'd brought the news to Roman. Guilt chewed at him. The cell phone vibrated in his pocket and he pulled it out to see Piotr Morozov's name on the screen. A flash of irritation swept him. Morozov hadn't helped in any of this and if he were calling with some "business" question now, he was about to get an ear full.

"Yes!" Christoph snapped.

The voice on the other end wasn't Morozov's. He recognized Concho Ten-Wolves as he was told to "listen and not talk." A glance toward the rest of his family showed them all still focused on the doctor. Only Cassandra Holmes was looking toward him, with a speculative light in her eyes.

Christoph moved down the hushed corridor as he listened to Ten-Wolves. "Yes," he said in answer to a question. More words passed before the phone went silent. Christoph lowered it.

"Everything OK?" Cassandra Holmes asked.

Christoph turned toward her. She'd followed him away from the others. The speculative look on her face had been joined by concern.

"Yes. Yeah. Just business."

Cassandra shook her head. "It was that Texas Ranger, wasn't it?"

Christoph winced in surprise. "How did you know?"

Cassandra smiled—a genuine smile, not the half smirk she often used to keep people at arm's length.

"I'm good at reading faces," she said.

"It was…him," Christoph agreed.

"He's got something on Sammy's death."

Boudreaux nodded. "I'm supposed to meet him. I'll go now. It'll take an hour to get there."

"I'll go with you."

He shook his head. "No! It's…I'll take care of it."

"You need me. I've met Ten-Wolves. Besides, as you've seen, I'm very good at reading faces."

"It might be dangerous."

Now, Cassandra offered him the smirk.

Christoph sighed. "All right. But don't tell anyone where we're going. Not even Eve. I don't know what this is all about yet but I have to find out."

"Sure thing."

CHAPTER 49

"Guess it's too late now to ask if this is a good idea," Bull Knife said as a second Treasure Chest limo pulled into the yard of the burned-out cottage and parked next to the first. The door opened and Christoph Boudreaux got out.

"Looks like we'll have to start calling this place Treasure Chest North," Concho said in response.

"Plenty of room to build," Bull Knife replied. "At least since the fire."

Winter shadows grew long in the late afternoon. The fire had burned out but the smell of smoke and embers still hung strong. A fitful breeze did little to fight the odor but had brought on a drop in temperature. It would be the coldest night yet in December.

"In answer to your 'good idea' comment, though," Concho added. "It might not be the best but I'm tired of hacking around the edge of the thicket with an ax. Time for a chainsaw."

"Agreed."

Christoph Boudreaux walked toward them, stopped a few feet away with his gaze taking in everything—Concho, Bull Knife, and Piotr Morozov. Piotr sat gagged and duct taped to a lawn chair. Boudreaux grasped the lapels of the gray linen jacket he wore and slowly pulled them back to show he was unarmed.

"I came in good faith," he said. "With no 'army.' What's going on here?"

"Who's in the car?" Concho asked.

"My driver. And a friend."

"Bring them out!"

Christoph beckoned toward the limo. A dark complected man climbed out of the driver's side. He lifted his jacket to reveal a shoulder holster and sidearm. Keeping his movements slow and deliberate, he opened the back door of the car and the "friend" got out. Concho recognized her.

"Cassandra."

The blonde woman smiled as she walked over to the group and spoke. "Ranger Ten-Wolves. We always seem to meet at scenes of violence."

"I guess we just hang out with the wrong people."

Christoph's voice sounded irritated as he interrupted the exchange. "Cassandra is a little bit your champion and a big reason why I agreed to meet you like this. But you have to convince me. I want to know what's going on."

Concho offered Cassandra a nod, then looked back at the eldest Boudreaux son. The man was obviously distraught—probably about several things—but trying not to show it. The Ranger found himself liking something about this man, despite the family's involvement in crime.

"I hope we're about to find out," he said. "But first, how's your father?"

Christoph's face twisted in quick anger but just as abruptly shifted back to worry. "He's stable. The doctors are 'cautiously optimistic.' Who knows what that means."

Concho nodded. "I hope he'll recover."

Christoph studied him. "I believe you're sincere."

"I am."

"That's not why we're here, though."

"No," Concho agreed. "Morozov claims he doesn't actually

work for your family. What does he mean?"

Christoph frowned. "First I heard of it. He's been my father's assistant for…I don't know how many years."

Concho yanked the tape off Morozov's mouth. "Tell him."

Morozov winced, licked at his raw lips. "I don't know what you are talking about."

"You've been claiming that a lot," the lawman said. "Maybe you ought to get your memory checked. The exact quote was that you didn't 'work for any Boudreaux.' And you made sure to add how they should be afraid of those you 'do work for.'"

Morozov glanced toward Christoph. "The cop is lying. You understand how they are."

Christoph frowned again.

"Morozov came to you from Las Vegas, didn't he?" Concho asked.

Now, Christoph looked startled. "Yes. How did you know?"

"Because he's protecting a secret. And I believe it started in Las Vegas. Bull Knife was in Vegas just before he came here. And someone here *knew* he was coming. Had to be someone from Vegas called ahead. I think that call went to Morozov."

Christoph scoffed. "And because your brother went to Las Vegas, Piotr tried to murder you both?"

"He tried to warn us away first. Tried scaring us. But after that didn't work, he went for the kill."

"That's your story," Christoph said. "I have no way of checking if it's real."

"Some of it is at least," Cassandra said.

Christoph turned toward the woman with his gaze narrowed. "What are you talking about?"

"Cassandra!" Morozov snapped.

The blonde woman glanced toward the bound man. She shook her head before looking back at Christoph. "Eve won't tell me all of it. But there was definitely an attempt to make these guys," she nodded her head toward Bull Knife and Ten-Wolves, "leave town.

I even played a part."

"Absolute nonsense!" Morozov snapped.

Concho rested a big hand on Morozov's shoulder. "Keep your mouth shut or I tape it shut again."

The man's gray eyes glared but he recognized the promise in the words and stopped talking.

Cassandra focused her gaze on Ten-Wolves. He returned it.

"In the French Quarter," she said, "you met a young girl named Hannah."

"I remember."

"She's…like a goddaughter to me. But I put her up to approaching you. I wanted you to leave town, too. Because Eve wanted it. Hannah is Eve's daughter."

"And who is Eve?" Concho asked, though he felt pretty sure he knew.

"Nick and Maura's daughter. Nicholas and Maura Boudreaux. You met *her*, too. Or saw her at least. That night in Lafitte's. With me."

"Why'd she run?"

"Wait," Christoph interrupted. He looked from the woman to the lawman. "What are you two talking about?"

Cassandra sighed. "Eve's not gonna be happy with me. Nick's not gonna be. But I can't let the Ranger and his brother…." She shrugged. Her eyes scanned back and forth between Concho and Christoph before settling on a point halfway between the two.

"The secret," she said. "The secret is…Eve Boudreaux is the half sister of Concho Ten-Wolves and Bull Knife. And," her gaze shifted fully to Concho now, "she ran away that night because you seemed to recognize her. She'd heard. From Nick, I guess, that you were coming to town. She was curious. She wanted to see you. But when you started toward her, she panicked. She couldn't meet you. Couldn't…tell you."

Morozov forgot himself and lunged against his bonds. They held while he struggled and spat curses. He fell back in his chair, groaning. At the same time, Concho became aware of Bull Knife breathing fast, almost panting. His half brother was in shock to see his dreams coming true. Concho grasped his forearm, squeezed it.

Christoph's reaction was different. His look of confusion faded; something close to awe replaced it. "That means Maura is…." He turned to stare at Concho. "She's your mother! What you suspected was true all along. I thought it nonsense."

"At first I did, too," the Ranger agreed.

"Eve knew about her brothers," Cassandra continued. "But they never knew about her. Nick and Maura wanted it that way."

"Why?" Christoph asked.

Cassandra shrugged.

"My God," Boudreaux said. "My God." A thought occurred. He stared hard at Cassandra. "But you! You and Eve! Neither of you had anything to do with trying to hurt these men?"

Cassandra shook her head vigorously. "No! We tried to warn them away. Nothing else. At first I thought it was just Sammy trying to hurt them. But…" she offered Morozov a cold stare, "Sammy had a thing for me. I knew he'd been working for Piotr. He bragged about the money he was making. It made me realize Morozov had to be behind it. I just didn't have any idea why. I thought the order had to be coming from your father."

"I don't think so," Concho interspersed. "That's the other secret here. And Morozov knows it. He was behind things from the beginning. Working at first through Sammy, then cutting him loose when it started to go bad. Maybe just to try and frame me."

Christoph fixed a stare on Morozov. His fists clenched. But the bound man's eyes were closed and his breathing shallow. He seemed to have withdrawn from the world.

Boudreaux sighed. "My father surely knew about this, though." He switched his gaze to Cassandra. "Seems like everyone did but me."

Cassandra shook her head again. "No. Terry doesn't know. Your Shannon doesn't know. I only found out last week. From

Eve. Sammy shouldn't have been told either. Maybe he wasn't. He could have been doing Piotr's bidding for some other reason."

Christoph nodded again. He walked over to stand above Morozov. The bound man twisted his eyes tighter shut. Boudreaux slapped him. Morozov's eyes sprang open, sprang wide as he gasped.

"If you want to save yourself, Piotr," Christoph said. "Now's the time to speak."

Morozov shook his head. "Lies. Delusions."

Boudreaux slapped him again.

The gray in Morozov's face darkened, as did the gray of his eyes. "My real employers aren't going to like that," he snarled. "If the truce is broken, they'll come kill you all."

Christoph's confusion returned. "What truce?"

Morozov lowered his chin and clenched his teeth. He said nothing.

Christoph drew back his fist for a punch, then thought better of it and lowered his hand, only spitting to one side as if to clear his mouth of a bad taste.

"Maybe Nicholas will know," he said. "He's got to. About Maura, of course. Maybe about Piotr. About the other secret." He wiped his mouth with one hand. "We go to our place in Beau Chêne. All of us. I'll call Nick. Have him join us there." He let his gaze return to Concho and Bull Knife. "And, I guess, so you two can meet...your mother."

Bull Knife stepped forward eagerly but the Ranger noticed a quick exchange of glances between Christoph and Cassandra that did not comfort him.

CHAPTER 50

"Wait!" Concho said. "We can't just leave a crime scene. We've got two dead bodies here and the local police are still looking to arrest us."

Christoph was already on the phone to Nicholas. He held up a finger to ask for a minute. In about that time he finished sketching the story out for his brother and turned back to Concho.

"No one knows it's a crime scene but us. We'll take the limo but I'll leave Clark here." He pointed toward his driver. "He'll make sure nothing is touched. But we need Piotr at the house for Nicholas to see. Two hours and you'll be back. Maybe with the evidence to clear your name."

Concho hesitated as he tried to think of some alternative.

"If the police show up now, they'll take Piotr into custody," Cassandra added. "He'll clam up for sure and you'll never find out what it's about."

Concho let out a breath he didn't know he'd been holding. It was possible this was a trap, but he didn't think so. Neither Cassandra nor Christoph were telling everything, but he sensed no violence in them. Of course, he'd been wrong before. Spectacularly so. But the need to solve this mystery was a rapidly intensifying itch he had to scratch. And he had to consider that the local cops weren't on the side of justice here. At least not the lead detective, Larry Rousselle.

"All right," he agreed.

"I'll drive," Cassandra said.

Shortly, they were on their way through the gathering dusk. The drive went silently as they cruised through Abita and down to the I-12. After exiting the freeway, a few more minutes took them into the community of Beau Chêne and to the banks of the Tchefuncte River off Lake Pontchartrain.

Cassandra piloted the limo through a wide black iron gate into a cul-de-sac where three large houses sat in a row with big oaks in front and water and gators at their back. Cassandra parked before the house on the far right and everyone exited. Concho pulled Piotr Morozov out. Morozov still had his hands bound but his feet and mouth were free. He used his feet but kept his mouth mercifully shut.

"My place," Christoph explained as he pushed open the front door and ushered everyone inside.

The lights were on. A lot of them. A lovely woman with red hair and green eyes came out of the kitchen drying her hands on a towel. Her smile disappeared abruptly as she stared at the motley crew traipsing into her home.

"Shannon. My wife," Christoph said. To her, he added, "It's OK, Honey. Just some business. There'll be no violence. We'll be in the den."

Shannon must have been used to dealing with such surprises. "All right. Anyone hungry? I've got some fresh lasagna."

"I'm not right now," Christoph said, "but..." He looked questioningly around at the group.

Bull Knife and Cassandra shook their heads. Concho, who'd eaten only candy bars and granola through most of the day and who sometimes ate to calm his nerves, said, "Ma'am, I'd have a bit if you don't mind."

"Certainly," Shannon said. She hustled off.

Christoph led them along a carpeted hall and through a set of double oak doors into his "den," which was half the size of Concho's entire trailer. A desk and computer, a couple of comfortable chairs, and bookshelves stuffed with volumes filled the space.

"Nicholas won't be here for half an hour," Boudreaux said. "Try to make yourself at home in the meantime. I've got to call the hospital to check on my father."

Concho pushed Piotr Morozov down in one of the chairs, then—as a distraction for his roiling thoughts—wandered over to the bookshelves to study the titles. He was glancing through a book on the history of the Roman Empire when Shannon Boudreaux came in carrying a TV tray upon which sat a heaping plate of lasagna, a cloth napkin, and a tall, sweetly sweating glass of ice tea. She offered Concho a smile as she placed the tray in front of one of the chairs.

"Hope you enjoy," she said.

"Ma'am, it looks delicious. I think it'll help my belly survive the night."

Shannon chuckled, and it was a good chuckle. She waved as she left the room.

"I'd like to see my mother," Bull Knife said to Christoph as the man finished on the phone.

Boudreaux nodded. "You will. I promise. But I don't want her here when we grill Piotr. You'll understand why soon enough."

***

Nicholas Boudreaux arrived. He stood an inch taller than his brother and had darker hair and a darker complexion. His eyes were green. With him came a young woman in her twenties. Cassandra rushed to hug her. It was the woman Concho had seen in Lafitte's on his first night.

So, this was Eve Boudreaux, his half-sister. He realized now why she'd looked familiar. A family resemblance. High cheekbones, aquiline nose, wide chin. Knowing who she was, he clearly saw the Kickapoo in her.

Christoph introduced his brother, who offered his hand to both Concho and Bull Knife. Concho took it. Bull Knife did not. Nicholas drew the hand back and gestured toward Eve.

"My daughter."

Eve made only the briefest eye contact before looking down at her feet. She said nothing, just held tight to Cassandra's hand.

Nick Boudreaux turned to Piotr Morozov. Their glances bruised.

"You should have taken my calls this morning," Nick said. "But I guess it wouldn't have mattered. You'd already crossed a line you shouldn't have crossed."

"I do not know what you are talking about," Morozov said.

"Part of it's my fault, though," Nick said. "At least I'm about to correct that."

"You cannot do this," Morozov replied.

Nick huffed a humorless laugh. "A few days ago, I would have said the same. Now, I realize I have to. The deception's gone on too long. Cost too much."

"It'll cost much more soon," Morozov snarled.

"I don't think so. Twenty years down the line. Half the players are dead. The others hardly remember." He gazed at Concho and Bull Knife, gave each a full measure of attention. "You both look like her. A little."

"Where is she?" Bull Knife demanded.

Nick nodded. He turned to his daughter. "Eve. Will you and Cassandra fetch your mother. Give us about twenty minutes, though."

Eve nodded, without speaking. The two young women left the room.

"Eve knows everything I'm about to reveal," Nick said. "If she chooses to tell Cassandra, that's her decision." He glanced at his brother. "Chris, I'm sorry, but much of this will be new to you as well. I didn't like keeping you in the dark but Dad felt it for the best."

Christoph nodded.

Nicholas glanced once more at Piotr Morozov. "Piotr here works for the Las Vegas mob."

Morozov didn't respond but his lips formed a thin, ugly line.

"I met Maura in 1991," Nick continued. "In Vegas. Her name then was Sparrow Woman. Wiskenoa. She was a dancer. Some of you know that. I was a musician. On tour. I sometimes went to…gentlemen's clubs in those days. I helped Wiskenoa out with a handsy customer. And I fell in love. But she was married. And she wouldn't break those vows. Unlike most others in that place, she was a dancer and nothing else.

"Maybe that started the problem. The club owner, whose name isn't worth mentioning here, wanted her. She refused. Every time. One night he killed a man. Maura— That's how I've known her for so long. Maura witnessed it. Accidentally. The owner was a local mobster's son. Maura told him she wouldn't say anything and he seemed to accept it. At first. But he had second thoughts. He knew Donnell, her husband, was a drug addict. How could he trust someone like that?

"Maura came to me. She and I had become friends by then. Of course, I wanted more. She wouldn't have it. But we'd talked a lot. She knew I had certain…connections. We faked her death. She'd already decided to leave Donnell. He'd accepted it. I begged her to join me on tour. She just said 'no.' She'd gotten into drugs herself and said she had to clean up. She moved to Arizona to start a new and very different life."

Nick glanced at Bull Knife. "That's where she met *your* father," he continued. "I was devastated to find out she'd begun that relationship. I'd been holding onto hope she'd come to me. But I had my own drug issues and she didn't want that kind of world anymore.

"I tried to forget her. For almost six years. Then at one show I had an accident. On stage. A bad burn from misplaced firepots, or from my own drug addled stupidity. I've never known which.

Maura showed up out of the blue to nurse me. I told her I was going to get clean and she could never leave me again." He gave a soft laugh. "She let me know she'd leave as soon as I was better.

"I didn't know she was broke. I'd have given her money if she'd asked. She started dancing again. One night a cop came into the club. He'd been in Vegas when that murder happened. He recognized her. And threatened blackmail.

"She had nothing to give him. So the Vegas mob came after her again. I got out of the hospital around that time. I pulled all the strings I could." He looked at Christoph. "I got Dad involved. We worked out a deal with the mobster father of a killer. She'd come home with me to Louisiana. I was through touring. I never wanted to see another stage. Sparrow Woman would come home with me and become Maura. And she'd never leave again.

"We faked her death a second time. She had surgery. Changed her appearance, changed her life. The mobsters agreed. If she kept quiet and out of the public eye, they'd leave her alone. They'd leave her children alone." He turned to nod at Concho and Bull Knife. "But if she ever talked, or if she was found out.... Well, you know.

"Morozov was the final lock on the door. He came to work with us but his real job was to keep watch on Maura, to make sure she never messed up. Dad knew the whole story. No one else did. I introduced the 'new' Maura to my family as French Canadian. Even hired a couple of actors to play her parents."

Christoph snorted and shook his head.

Nicholas smiled, then continued: "We told Eve the story when she was nineteen. But only because she'd overheard tidbits she shouldn't have. Morozov knew, of course. I don't know what he told Sammy to get his help stopping Ten-Wolves and Bull Knife from investigating."

"Bringing in Sammy was a mistake," Morozov murmured.

"Yes, it was," Nick replied. "By the way," he added, still speaking to Morozov, "both Sammy and Jason Kulick had crushes on

Cassandra. They told her things to impress her. Enough for me to suspect that you and Sammy had been skimming the business."

"A lie," Morozov said.

Nicholas smirked. "Dad depended on you too much. But the evidence is there. After a friendly call I got last night, I checked some things. That's why I was late getting to the hospital to see my father. But I had to know. For his sake, and for Sammy's."

"You speak nonsense," Morozov snapped, though his words barely had any fire.

"Sammy was a problem for you, of course," Nick continued. "He was flighty. We all knew it. I imagine that's why you had him killed. Afraid he'd spill everything to Dad. Your Vegas friends wouldn't have protected you from *him*. And I doubt they'll be happy with your handling of this matter."

Morozov shook his head but made no other response.

"We're here," Cassandra said from the doorway.

CHAPTER 51

Concho's gaze leaped toward Cassandra. She stood by herself.

"Maura is just waiting," the woman explained.

"I'll get her," Nicholas said. He strode out of the room while Cassandra came in. She moved to one side. Everyone's gaze focused on the door, especially Concho's and Bull Knife's. Seconds slowed to a molasses crawl.

Eve stepped into the room and Nicholas came walking in behind her pushing a wheelchair. Concho's chest clenched. He glanced quickly at Bull Knife, whose face was a conflicting agony of emotions.

Nicholas stopped pushing. The woman in the chair had long gray hair. It looked thin but had been cleaned and brushed. Her face held just a little makeup, which couldn't hide the twisting of the features on the right side.

Even through the signs of plastic surgery to the nose, cheekbones, and around the eyes, Concho could see the resemblance to Eve, and to himself and Bull Knife. Here was their mother. *His* mother.

"Maura had a stroke two years ago," Nicholas said. "It was left hemisphere, so she can't really speak much. Her right side is either paralyzed or very weak. She has days when she's pretty clear. Unfortunately, today is not one of them."

Maura/Wiskenoa sat quietly in her chair. Her lips chewed at the air, as if she wanted to speak but could not. Bull Knife approached her; Concho remained still. Her gaze shifted to Bull Knife. She stared. Concho stared at her. Was there any recognition for her youngest son? He couldn't tell.

Bull Knife went to one knee. He reached out his hands and took Wiskenoa's left one in his. Tears began running unabashedly from the half-Apache's eyes. Concho chewed at his lip. Behind Wiskenoa, Eve sobbed quietly. Cassandra rushed to her, tucked an arm around her.

Concho released a long breath and shook his head. He brushed at his own eyes, then moved a little closer to the tableau of Bull Knife and his mother. Wiskenoa's gaze shifted to the Ranger for an instant, then shifted immediately back to Bull Knife and lingered.

Nicholas moved to stand beside Concho. "Her memory isn't good. I don't know if she recognizes either of you. Seems like she senses something about Bull Knife. I tried to explain who you both were. Not sure if I got through. She usually seems to know me. And Eve. But not always."

Concho nodded. He took another deep breath and turned to Christoph, who looked like he was in shock. "I'll need the limo," the Ranger said. "And Morozov. I'm going back to the cottage and call the police. I'll send your man home with the car."

Christoph lifted a hand, let it drop. Cassandra came and handed the Ranger the limousine keys. Nicholas sighed; he spoke softly so only Concho and Cassandra could hear.

"I hope you'll agree the police don't need to know everything you've heard tonight."

"As long as Piotr Morozov goes to jail," Concho said.

"He will," Nicholas said. "Call Solly Burstein. He's waiting for you. I know him for an honest man. I spoke to him on the way over here, gave him the information he'll need to arrest Morozov for murdering my brother."

"And I'll testify if need be," Cassandra said.

"So will Nolen Carmichael if he has to," Nicholas added. "He called me last night. He's the one set me on the right track. Sorry it took so long. I tried to discourage you. I got Eve to help and I think she's ashamed now. That's why she won't look at you. But I never wanted either of you hurt. I couldn't harm anything that was part of Sparrow Woman."

"Thank you both," Concho said. His voice sounded almost normal to his ears. He walked over to Bull Knife. His half brother wasn't crying anymore. His face was…joyous.

"I think she knows me," Bull Knife said, looking up. "I'm sure of it. I'm going to stay a while. If that's OK? Unless you need me?"

"No, man. Hang around. Everything's under control."

"He can stay as long as he wants," Nicholas said. "And you're welcome to come back. After…."

"We'll see," Concho said.

The Ranger reclaimed Piotr Morozov, hauled him outside and pushed him into the limo. He drove through the night, back to the burned-out cottage and the men there—both the dead and the living. He sent Christoph's driver home and called Solly Burstein.

Then he stood in the cold darkness and waited. Alone.

A LOOK AT:
AVENGING ANGELS:
VENGEANCE TRAIL

SADDLE UP FOR A HEART-POUNDING, BULLET-BURN-
ING, BIBLE-THUMPING WESTERN SERIES LIKE NONE
YOU'VE EVER READ BEFORE!

Reno Bass and his sister Sara are young, blond, blue-eyed twins from
western Kansas. Raised right in a good Christian family, they're
pure as the driven snow. But when their family is massacred, they
ride the Vengeance Trail to fulfill their father's dying request—to
purge the earth of the Devil's spawn in the name of God.

In the first book of this shocking new series, Reno and Sara's
farm is burned and their family murdered by a group of ex-Con-
federate soldiers known as the Devil's Horde. These ex-Confeder-
ates—led by Major Eustace The Bad Old Man Montgomery and
Major Black Bob Robert Hobbs—have a chip on their shoulders,
and they're burning a broad swath across the Yankee north, murdering, pillaging, and raping their way to the Colorado Territory.

But when they burn the Bass farm, they find out not every fol-
lower of God is a sheep. Sworn to vengeance, Reno and Sara
become black-winged avenging angels on a mission from God.
Hounding the Confederate devils' every step, these black-winged
angels begin efficiently and bloodily killing them—one by one and
two by two—reading to them from the Good Book while sending
them back to Hell.

AVAILABLE NOW

ABOUT THE AUTHOR

Charles Gramlich lives amid the piney woods of southern Louisiana and is the author of the Talera fantasy series, the SF novel Under the Ember Star, and the thriller Cold in the Light. His work has appeared in magazines such as Star*Line, Beat to a Pulp, Night to Dawn, Pedestal Magazine, and others. Many of his stories have been collected in the anthologies, Bitter Steel, (fantasy), Midnight in Rosary (Vampires/Werewolves), and In the Language of Scorpions (Horror). Charles also writes westerns under the name Tyler Boone. Although he writes in many different genres, all of his fiction work is known for its intense action and strong visuals.

9 781639 770731